The Isaac Project

Sarah Monzon

RADIANT PUBLICATIONS

Published by Radiant Publications
Moses Lake, Washington

Cover photography by Adrienne Scott, photographer

Manuscript edited by Dori Harrell
http://doriharrell.wix.com/breakoutediting

For my wonderful husband.

We have a love to last the ages.

Chapter One

Rebekah

In the fourth grade we made little rockets out of old film canisters, baking soda, and vinegar. Put in the ingredients, snap on the lid, shake it up, and watch out. The pressure built and—*pew*—that small black cylinder shot to the sky. I felt like that outdated film container. My excitement was building by the second, and any moment I was going to explode and gush all over everyone around me.

I glanced at my watch. Four hours until Poppy's surprise birthday party, but about twenty minutes too early to head to Frostings and pick up the cake. Barb had specifically told me it wouldn't be ready until ten.

No matter. This would give me time to pick up my surprise at Hank's shop. I had spent hours figuring out the perfect birthday present for Poppy. I mean, what did one give to the greatest man in the world? A mug with those words might have worked if I were six, but I needed something more. I needed something that told Poppy just how much he meant to me.

He was, in my humble opinion, the finest man to walk the

earth. My parents died in a car accident when I was an infant. Poppy took me in and raised me even though he was already retired and was supposed to be relaxing and enjoying the good life, not changing diapers and waking up for midnight bottle feedings. Growing up, people had always asked me if I felt like something was missing since I never knew my parents. I know it must sound strange, but I never did. Poppy was everything a girl ever needed, and more. I never felt jilted. I only felt loved.

As I walked along Main Street, a chickadee with its telltale black head and bib and white-streaked cheeks crossed my path, hopping across three of the red bricks laid in a herringbone pattern before taking flight and landing on a nearby streetlight. She lifted her tiny beak and sang out—*ti-ti-ti.*

I took a deep breath, relishing the soft breeze that teased my hair and the warm sun that kissed my skin. Yes. Today was going to be a wonderful day.

Ducking under the green-and-white striped awning of Hank's store downtown, I stepped through the entrance. The bell above the door jingled its welcome.

"I'll be right with you." A male voice floated from a back room.

Hands behind my back, I scanned the wares on display behind the glass display at the register. A music box with a posed ballerina stared back at me. I bent down for a better look, drawn to it like I was to anything with tutus and pointed dance shoes.

Men's legs filled my peripheral vision, and I straightened. Hank smiled down at me.

"Would you like me to take it out of the case for you?"

I shook my head. "No, thank you." My fingers itched to turn the key. What music would it play? Would the dancer twirl in a pirouette?

Focus. That's not why you're here. "I'm here to pick up

Poppy's present."

Hank snapped his fingers. "Right. I have it waiting for you." He slid his lanky frame behind the counter and bent to retrieve a folded quilt.

My face smiled back at me, hair in long braided pigtails, my adolescent arms wrapped around Poppy's middle-aged neck. Beside it was another picture—Poppy tall and strong grasping the lead rope of a dapple grey mare, my miniature self sitting proudly on her back. The quilt was filled with pictures of us. Some of my happiest memories he could wrap himself up in.

Emotion clogged my throat as I traced the stitches between the pictures. "Thank you, Hank."

Color brightened the man's cheeks as he looked away. "Aw, it was nothin'. Doris did the stitchin'. I just printed them pictures you gave me."

"It's beautiful. My thanks to you and to Doris." I paid Hank for the work he and his wife had done on the quilt and then pushed open the heavy glass doors, the bell jingling at my exit.

The brightness of the midmorning sun caused me to squint, its intensity quickly warming my face and arms.

Barb should be done with the cake by now. Better drop the quilt off at the truck before heading over to Frostings.

I'd left my old black Dodge parked along the street across from the city park. It took a couple of yanks before the door finally opened. Too bad I didn't have a can of WD-40 lying around on the floorboard. I'd have to scrounge one up before the thing stuck for good.

The blanket found a temporary home in the passenger's seat before I slammed the door shut again. I rubbed my hands together and licked my lips. Now for Frostings. Maybe Barb would let me sample one of her freshly made pastries.

Giggling drifted from across the street. Curious, I looked over. A couple sat close together on a park bench. The man's head was bent to the woman's ear...or was that her neck? She giggled again.

Normally I would have rolled my eyes, but instead I smiled. I knew that feeling. The one you get when you're so in love you can't stop grinning or humming for no reason at all. James made me feel that way.

A deep, contented sigh escaped my lips. James Anthony—the kind of guy every girl dreamed about. Pure man, from the top of his Stetson to the bottom of his leather Ariat cowboy boots. Some might consider his somewhat crooked nose a flaw, but considering he'd held on for more than eight seconds on a raging bull, it only added to his dangerous charm.

Speaking of James, he never did get back to me on if he'd be able to make it to Poppy's party. I pulled out my cell from my pocket and sent him a text. Hopefully he'd respond soon, and we could drive to Grandview together.

The smell of fresh brewed coffee and confectioners' sugar hit me as I stepped in to Frostings. Barb's back was turned toward me, her wiry white hair somehow making it past the black hairnet on her head.

"I don't know how you stay so thin making all these delicious treats all day, Barb. I think I've gained five pounds just breathing in here."

Barb whirled around, her eyes alight. She plopped her hands onto ample hips. "Don't try to butter me up. I already set aside a cherry turnover for you."

"You're an angel."

A napkin was placed on the counter in front of me, quickly followed by a triangle pastry with red gooey filling. The sugar crystals on top glistened in the bakery's fluorescent lighting. I sunk my teeth in, my eyes immediately rolling into the back of my head. Heaven. Tart cherry, puff pastry, sugary heaven.

"Poppy's cake finished?" I asked around a bite of turnover.

She placed a large sheet cake on the counter next to me. Happy birthday in red frosting decorated the top.

Perfect.

"Are you sure I can't change your mind about the candles?" Barb worried her lip, her hands spinning in a wringing motion. "I have an eight and a zero candle you can have."

Eighty tiny flames seemed to worry the woman. But what sort of impact would two measly little candles have? None. I pictured the surprise on Poppy's face when I walked out with eighty lit candles on his cake. That was the look I was going for.

I shook my head. "I'll stick with what I'd originally planned."

"Suit yourself, but don't say I didn't warn you if you end up burning that sweet little nursing home down."

Laughter bubbled inside me. "I'll be sure to have a fire extinguisher with me."

Barb rang up the price of the cake and candles on the register, and I pulled out my phone just enough to check if I'd missed a text. Nope. James still hadn't gotten a hold of me. I'd give him a little while longer, but then I'd have to call him. If he wanted to go to the party together, we'd need to leave early so I could decorate the dining hall.

"See you later, Barb," I said as I used my backside to push open the door. No point in risking accidently dropping the cake by balancing it in one hand.

I glanced through the large storefront windows as I walked along Main Street back to my truck. The flash of a familiar blue denim jacket had me slowing my steps. James. A smile blossomed in my heart and then bloomed on my lips. His back faced me on the other side of a revolving seed rack. Wouldn't he be surprised to see me? I balanced the cake in one hand and raised the other to tap on the glass but stopped as his head dipped and angled. Ten perfectly manicured fingers snaked around his waist.

No!

This couldn't be happening. I shook my head, desperate to make sense of the scene before me and dislodge its searing image.

Maybe it wasn't James. Maybe it was only someone who had the exact same jacket. I mean, surely the manufacturer made more than just one, right? It was possible the man was someone else. Someone completely not James. Someone with the exact same shade of brown hair and the exact same casual air about him. The same muscular build. The same...

But even as I tried to conjure up different scenarios, my stomach churned itself into a tornado, squeezing bile into my throat.

I couldn't move.

I wanted nothing more than to be transported to another place, any place. Too bad my brain stopped sending signals to my feet. I was forced to watch in horror as the man I desperately hoped was not James held another woman in his arms, kissing her with a passion we'd never shared.

Violent spasms gripped my muscles. How much longer would my shaky legs hold me? Before I had a chance to find out, the man disentangled his lips from the woman's. He turned. Our gazes locked. Chocolate-brown eyes peered into mine.

If a heart could literally fall apart into a thousand tiny pieces, mine did at that moment. Shards—that was all that was left.

The tightness in my chest loosened. My lungs expanded as I drew in a breath. I spun on my heel and ran as tears welled in my eyes and blurred my vision. I angrily wiped them away, Poppy's cake clutched to my chest.

"Open. Open. Open." Stupid truck. Stupid, uncooperative truck. The sticking push button and rusty hinges refused to allow me the haven of the cab. I slammed my open palm on the window, the sting a welcome change to the ache in my heart. Finally the lock disengaged, and the door creaked open.

I slid into the driver's seat, deposited the cake on top of the quilt, and then gripped the steering wheel so hard my knuckles turned white. Where were the keys? Shaking hands glided keys along the ring. Slip. They landed with a taunting thump. An animalistic cry tore from my chest. There went my Mario Andretti getaway.

A tapping sound to my left crept its way into my consciousness. Now what? I sniffed and wiped at my burning eyes. I didn't want to see or talk to anyone, but it didn't look like I would get the luxury of a choice. Taking a shaky breath, I turned and peered into the face that would forever haunt me—dark wavy brown hair, milk-chocolate eyes, and the most kissable lips. Well, someone else thought so too. I sighed and turned the crank, lowering the window. My spine straightened, and I pushed my shoulders back with each revolution.

Love at first sight was a myth, and the way my traitorous heart reacted to the man before me, it seemed one couldn't fall out of love in a single moment, either.

Seconds ticked by. Why hadn't he said anything yet? The scene from Ernie's Feed and Seed played over and over in my mind. Love sifted from my heart and hardened like the ground under the hot desert sun.

James ran his fingers through his hair. A sure sign of

discomfort.

Well good. I wasn't exactly enjoying the moment either.

"Becky, darlin'," James drawled.

I cringed at the endearment.

"I'm sorry you had to see that. I didn't plan on it happening. You have to believe me." He moved as if to reach out and touch me but then dropped his hand back to his side.

Wow. Common sense. Who knew he'd have some in that thick skull of his.

"One thing led to another and, well, you know." He shrugged his shoulders.

Even he knew a lame excuse when he heard one.

I refused to spout a how-could-you diatribe. To belittle and embarrass myself further with an ugly public scene. This was a small town. The news of James's betrayal... I shook my head. Wagging tongues would burn ears over this one. Ernie's wife was at the head of the gossip ladder, and I was sure she didn't wait a blink of an eye before sharing this juicy tidbit. I didn't need to add further fuel to the gossiping fires. I had my dignity. What little I could salvage, anyway.

"Good-bye, James," I clipped. As he stepped away from the truck, I rolled up the window and drove off.

Had there been any signs to his duplicity? Was I just a blind and naïve fool? I sucked in a breath. Had he ever loved me?

Lady waited, her tail wagging, as I entered the house. Loyalty personified. I should have stuck with dogs instead of men to begin with.

I sat Poppy's cake on the counter and then sank to my knees and wrapped my arms around Lady's furry neck. Hot breath panted against my ear, and her quick tongue lashed out in a slobbery kiss. My lips wobbled a small smile. Okay, maybe my *entire* life wasn't shattered.

Pushing myself back up to my feet, I beelined it to the freezer. Cake wasn't for another three hours. I needed my favorite ice cream *now*. Ah, Cherry Garcia. Comfort food in all its caloric glory. Large serving spoon and cell phone in hand, I collapsed onto the couch and pulled my knees up close to my chest, hugging them. I swiped the screen and tapped the green icon on the bottom corner. Lisa's name blipped on the screen. Putting the phone to my ear, I counted the rings.

"Hello?"

"Lisa, it's Becky." That was all I managed to get out before I lost it again. Good grief. Just when I thought my eyes were finally dry. I'd better get it pulled together before I had to leave for Grandview. This was Poppy's birthday. He didn't need all this drama.

"Are you okay?" The concern in Lisa's voice was palpable. I sniffed and nodded even though she couldn't see me.

"Yeah," I squeaked.

"I'll be right over."

Mittens jumped on the couch beside me, butting my leg with her head, purring for me to pet her. Picking her up, I buried my face in her silky fur.

Animals were so much easier than men. Unconditional love, zero judgment, and most important, they didn't cheat on me or throw my love back in my face. They were always there for me with a warm lick on my hand or a wag of the tail. Why couldn't men be more like that? Minus the licking and wagging, of course. Lady came and lay by my feet, and I bent to pat her on the head. Ten minutes later Lisa busted through the door, not bothering to knock, as usual.

"What's wrong? What happened?" She dropped onto the couch next to me and took my hand.

"James...I...we..."

She tugged me forward and wrapped her arms around me.

My inability to speak coherently doubtless gave her a vague picture of the day's events, but she didn't push for answers.

With one arm still around my shoulder, she used the other to take away the half-eaten, half-runny ice cream container from my hand and set it on the glass-top coffee table in front of us. Her hand dug in her purse. She brought out a travel-size box of tissues and pressed it into my hand. The Kleenex absorbed the moisture dripping from my eyes and nose.

"Want to talk about it?"

I uncurled from my upright fetal position and flopped back onto the secondhand Goodwill special that, with its plaid design, might have been fashionable in the sixties.

"What's wrong with me?"

Okay, so that wasn't really what I'd planned on saying, but I couldn't keep myself from thinking it. Out loud. There had to be something wrong with me. Wasn't I pretty enough? Nice enough? Good enough? Smart enough?

What did she have that I didn't?

My mind turned traitor, taunting me. Stupid. Pathetic. Ugly. Unlovable. Unwanted. I squeezed my eyes tight and shoved the heels of my palms into my sockets. Circles of light danced in my vision as I refocused.

Lisa's mouth opened and closed like a fish out of water, and she shook her head. "How could you even say that?" The words shot out of her mouth. What happened to my soothing and sympathetic friend? She'd transformed, fire in her eyes.

A long breath puffed out my cheeks. "I don't know." I massaged my temples, too tired to think straight.

"Let me tell you right now, Rebekah Ann Sawyer, you're an amazing woman. You have a kind heart and a giving spirit. You're determined, tenacious, and independent, and I admire you for all that you've done. Her arm swept out. "Just look around you. Look at all the people you're helping. This ranch alone should tell you how wonderful you are. You practically live in a shack because of your generous spirit. And on top of all that, you are beautiful. Both inside and out." She jabbed the air with her finger as if to punctuate her remark. "Don't ever let anyone tell you or make you feel any different."

My head pounded, but I struggled to pay attention to her rant. She was trying to make me feel better, bless her heart. Dutifully, I surveyed my humble dwellings. The kitchen and living room shared the same space without even enough room for a proper dining area. A row of cabinets and outdated olive-green appliances lined one wall of the kitchen, and the sofa and coffee table comprised the living room. A bedroom barely large enough to fit a full-size bed and dresser, and a small bathroom with just enough room to turn around in finished the place off. Lisa was right. It did look more like a shack than a home, but it served its purpose. It gave me a roof over my head, and, really, wasn't that what a house for anyway?

But, like she said, the house was tiny. Fit for one person. Me. Alone. By myself. Maybe that was the way it was supposed to be. My nose started to burn, but I clamped my jaw tight.

I would not cry. Not again. Not over James. Not over any man.

Chapter Two

Luke

The sound of country fried potatoes sizzling in a skillet on the stove battled with the hum of the refrigerator as I stuck my head inside. Now where was it? My face split into a grin as I snagged the cool bottle. This was going to be great. I glanced up at the clock hanging above the sink and quickened my step. Not much time left before the two shifts converged and the feeding frenzy started. Six bubbling pancakes cooked on the electric griddle sitting on the dark granite countertop. Stacks of perfectly round flapjacks were keeping warm in the oven. I twisted the lid on the bottle, my nose instantly tickling from the pungent heat. Just a couple of drops would do. I put the cap back on and shoved the bottle toward the back of the fridge. The spatula twirled in my hand. Slide, lift, flip.

Bang!

Baxtor. Our newest rookie—a bit on the scrawny side and in need of some discipline, but overall a good kid. Needed a new car though. His ancient Pinto was in dire need of a new muffler. It coughed and sputtered more than a chain smoker. I glanced at the golden-brown circles on the griddle. Maybe the kid needed more than a new car. Like some welcome-to-the-team pancakes. I mean, we couldn't let him feel unwelcomed.

The recruit entered, making exaggerated sniffing sounds and rubbing his hands together. "Something sure smells go-od."

"Get it while it's hot." I slid the pancakes onto a plate and handed him the bottle of syrup.

His eyes went wide. "Wow, six?"

I pinched his shoulder. "You need to muscle up." I nodded to the potatoes and scrambled eggs still in skillets on the stove.

"Don't forget those."

Heavy footfalls sounded behind me, and two more guys came in through the door. I spooned eggs onto my plate and grabbed a couple of pancakes before sliding onto the bench seat beside the long roughhewn table. Out of the corner of my eye I looked at Baxtor's plate. Still piled high with pancakes. Dan and Pete dropped onto the bench, and I passed them the ketchup and syrup.

A hand slapped the table, and five heads swiveled. Red-faced and bug-eyed, Baxtor's hand covered his mouth while his jaw still worked. He swallowed, eyes glistening. "Water," he croaked.

Laughter erupted around the table, and my cheeks hurt from smiling. Baxtor received hard smacks on the back. Chuckling, I stood and grabbed a cup from the cabinet and the milk from the fridge. Milk would cut the heat better than water.

"Hot sauce in the pancakes, Luke? Classic. Better than the ashes Dan put in my brownies when I first started," Pete said as I poured the milk.

I walked back to the table.

Baxtor snatched the cup from my hand and gulped it down, white rivulets streaming from the corners of his mouth.

"Welcome to Station Five." I cuffed his shoulder.

He wiped his mouth with the back of his hand. His forehead glistened as he turned toward me, his wide smile showing crooked teeth. He'd do. It was a hard job, but he'd do.

Dishes started to pile in the sink as everyone finished breakfast. Gathering my gear, I followed the crew into the apparatus bay. Instead of staying for roll call and assignment duty, I continued out of the fire station and into my Jeep to head home.

My eyelids grew heavy as I drove along Highway 31. Every blink felt like sandpaper rubbing against my sockets. I pressed the heel of my palm to one of my eyes. Visine would help, but then again, so would a few hours of uninterrupted sleep.

My body would never fully adjust to having its sleep interrupted. And no matter the reason for the call, as soon as the tones dropped, adrenaline punched my veins. Every time. Great for getting me up in a flash, but when it was all over, it left me drained.

I arrived at the complex and trudged up three flights of stairs to the place I called home sweet home. I fished my keys out of my pants pocket and then unlocked the door. Dumping my gear just inside the entrance, I stumbled the fifteen feet to my bed and collapsed. Moments like this made me glad I lived in a studio apartment rather than a large house.

It might be a guy thing, a firefighter thing, or something simply unique to me, but I literally fell asleep as soon as my head hit the pillow. Some people needed to watch TV or read a book to unwind after a shift, but that'd never been the case with me.

Six hours of sleep and a hot shower later, I felt human again. Good thing. I was going to need all the strength I had to get through the next hour if I couldn't avoid Marty's mom.

The image of Joseph in front of Potiphar's wife played out before me whenever I stood in the same room as Colleen Stabler. I could run into a burning building without a second thought, but being in close proximity to that woman made me more nervous than...well...honestly, I didn't know what to compare it to. Let's just say it was as if I was in the Savannah and a hungry lioness was crouched down behind tall grass ready to pounce on some unsuspecting prey. And I was the prey.

It wasn't that she was unattractive. In fact, the exact opposite was true—and she flaunted it. But I wasn't looking for what Ms. Stabler was offering. Unfortunately the *offering* was getting more forceful every time I saw her.

Thankfully Marty was outside shooting hoops when I pulled up to his house.

"Hey, squirt," I said as I shut the Jeep's door. Marty seemed to be alone, and I let out a sigh of relief that his mom wasn't in sight.

"Hi, Mr. Luke."

I signaled the gangly eleven-year-old to pass the ball, and dribbled it a few times against the concrete driveway. The ball soared out of my hands for a nothing-but-net three-point shot.

"Nice one." Marty grinned as he rebounded the ball. I caught him around the neck in the crook of my elbow and rasped my knuckles back and forth on his head. Ah, the classic noogie.

"Hey! What's that for?" He protested while rubbing the top of his head when I released him. He tried to look offended, but the sparkle in his eyes gave him away.

I grinned and braced myself. Three...two...one.

Sure enough, the pipsqueak launched himself at me, and we tumbled to the ground. Squeals of delight and half-hearted protests burst from Marty, interrupting the quietude of the suburban cul-de-sac.

"All right, go get your homework." At least some of his pent-up energy had been spent. "We'll work out here today."

He trotted into the house, and the screen door slapped shut behind him. Moments later he reappeared toting his backpack. He plopped down cross-legged beside me and took out a thick textbook with an abacus on the cover. Opening it to the right page, he handed it to me.

"Mean, median, mode, and range," I read aloud.

Marty chewed his bottom lip and pulled at the grass by his feet.

Boy, did I have my work cut out for me. I searched my brain for a way to explain the challenging math concepts so a sixth grader could understand.

The ball under the hoop snagged my attention. Brilliant.

I pushed the textbook aside and stretched out on the lawn, resting my weight on the palms of my hands behind me and crossing my legs in front of me. "So who won your basketball game last night?"

At the unexpected question, Marty's head snapped to attention. The glazed-over look in his eyes faded away, replaced by an enthusiastic grin. "Mr. Luke, it was such a great game. We won forty-three to twenty-seven, and I scored eight points!"

"Way to go, squirt." We high-fived.

I nodded toward the notebook on the other side of Marty. When the boy handed me a piece of paper, I jotted down the number eight.

"Who else scored?" I asked, pencil poised to write down the numbers.

His face scrunched in concentration. "Matt had a couple of good lay-ups and some free throws so I guess he scored six of the points. Billy made two lay-ups. Pedro had an awesome three pointer. You should have seen it. No one thought it was going to make it in."

Marty continued to give me a play-by-play of the game, and I wrote down the points scored by each player.

"Okay, Marty, you know how all the NBA players have different stats, right? I bet you could even tell me what Kobe Bryant's average points per game are."

He gave me a knowing smile.

"Well, statistics like those are figured out using things like mean, medium, mode, and range."

I glanced at Marty.

His face scrunched up. Still didn't get it.

I took the paper and placed it in front of him. "If we take all the numbers and add them up, then divide that number by how many numbers there are on this list, we get the mean. To find the median, take this list of numbers and then write them in order from smallest to greatest. The median is the middle number. The mode is the number repeated the most, and to find the range you subtract the smallest number from the largest. Get it?"

His mouth formed a silent *O* as he snatched the paper out of my hand and grabbed his textbook. Stretching out on his stomach, he spent the next fifteen minutes figuring out the problems in his book that were assigned for homework.

A feminine voice cut the relaxed air. "Oh, Luke, can I have a word with you for a minute?"

Turning, I lifted my hand over my eyes to shield them from the sun's glare. I cringed.

Marty's mom stood in the doorway dressed a little too scantily for even the warmth of late August. Her miniskirt showed the smooth length of her legs, and the deep V-neck cut to her blouse revealed the soft curves of full cleavage. She must've had Marty at a young age, because she didn't look old enough to have an eleven-year-old son.

Do I have to? "Sure thing, Ms. Stabler."

Her eyes narrowed in dissatisfaction. She insisted I call her Colleen. I insisted on calling her Ms. Stabler. I wanted as much of a professional line between us as I could build. More than a line, really. The Great Wall of China would be better. As I walked up to the house, the lyrics of "Maneater" ran through my head.

"Now, Luke," she purred as I stepped through the door, "I wanted to thank you for all you've done for my Marty."

"It's my pleasure ma'am. He's a good boy. Bright, too." Maybe if I stood right by the door, I could make a quick escape should this conversation take a turn for the worse.

Slender fingers, tipped with hot-pink nails, curled around my forearm and directed me farther into the house. If the talons of an eagle had seen a manicurist, there would probably be a resemblance.

The woman indicated a chair in the living room.

Great. My mother's voice echoed in my head. "Be polite, Luke." Did Mom ever have this scenario in mind? My shoulders drooped, but I sat anyway. The moment my backside hit the cushion of the teal wingback chair, the walls closed in and drew the man-eater closer as the space shrunk.

She stalked toward me, her hips swaying dramatically like the models on a catwalk. Her head tipped down and to the side, and she looked at me through long dark lashes. Placing one polished finger on my shoulder, she pivoted until she stood behind me. Every muscle in my body tensed as she cupped my shoulders and then gently stroked my biceps.

An involuntary shiver swept up my spine. And not the good kind. My knuckles were starting to turn white from the grip I had on the armrest.

"Ms. Stabler—"

She leaned down behind me. Peppermint filled my nostrils as her warm breath caressed my ear.

"Colleen," she breathed as her hands slid around my shoulders and down to my chest.

Whoa. That was enough. I shot out of the chair faster than water out of a fire hose. Mama might have taught me manners, but she also taught me not to get burned, and this woman was pure fire.

Her eyes flashed. I knew I'd insulted her, but what could I do? If I thought I'd done something wrong, I would've apologized. Shoot, if I thought it would make any difference at all, I would've apologized, whether I was at fault or not. But it was her problem. She kept crossing the line. I groaned. I guess it was my problem too. The only reason I'd stayed with the job was because of Marty. The kid didn't have a father figure in his life, and I thought I could make a difference for him. Not to mention, he was finally starting to catch on with his school work.

I'd made it clear in the past where I stood with this woman, but it looked like I needed to say it again.

"Ms. Stabler," I ground out. My voice was firm, but she needed to know I was serious. "I am here for Marty and only for Marty. Got it?"

Her bottom lip pushed out in a well-formed pout. She took a step toward me, the lioness stalking her prey. I stepped back. This woman needed to keep her distance, and if she wouldn't, then I would.

"If not," I continued, "then you can find another tutor for your son."

She crossed her arms, and a scowl contorted her face. Her pouty lips closed to form a tight, thin line, and her once-fluid body became stiff and rigid. A storm was brewing, and I was about to bear the brunt of it.

"How dare you," she seethed, her voice growing louder with each word. "How dare you talk to me that way. How dare you give me an ultimatum. Get. Out. Now. Get out of my house this minute. And don't you dare come near Marty again, you hear me?"

She continued her tirade as I exited the house. Marty was staring at me, his lips pulled down, and his chin trembling.

"So I guess I won't be seeing you anymore, huh?"

"Guess not, squirt." I squatted down so I could be eye level with him. Ripping off a piece of his paper, I took his pencil and jotted down my phone number. "If you ever need anything, call me, okay?"

"Okay."

I tousled his hair before turning and then hopping into my truck. A crank of the ignition fired the engine, and I drove away. *Don't look back.* I was really going to miss that kid. I prayed God would send another man who could make a difference in Marty's life. Kids, boys especially, needed male role models in their lives. Dads preferably, but I understood that couldn't always be the case.

Anger boiled in my veins for the way things had turned out. I needed to blow off some steam before I exploded. Flicking on my blinker, I turned down Bartlett Avenue and headed to the Bunker.

After I parked in the front of the old red brick warehouse-turned-boxing gym, I grabbed my green gym bag from behind the passenger's seat and went inside. The smell of stale air and sweat greeted me as soon as I opened the door. The tense muscles in my shoulders eased. Safer in the ring than in that house.

I snagged a pair of hand wraps from my bag and wound them around my wrists and knuckles. Typically, I used boxing gloves on the punching bag, but today the wraps would do. The look of disappointment on Marty's face ate at me, and if my hands ended up stinging a little, then that was punishment I deserved.

Walking over to one of the available bags, I bent my knees and clenched my fists in front of my face in a boxing stance. Pivoting on my front foot and throwing all my weight behind my punch, I jabbed at the bag.

Left. Right. Left. Right.

A few hooks and uppercuts added variety to the routine. Salty sweat beaded on my forehead and ran down my face, stinging my eyes. Not taking the time to wipe it away, I continued to strike at the stuffed leather cylinder.

"Hey, hey, hey—what is up my friends?"

Rolling my eyes, I glanced over my shoulder. Yep. Angelo Moretti with his long slicked-back black hair and signature wifebeater shirt. I thought he wore them because he didn't want to hide the twin tattoos on his deltoids. He thought they gave him street cred, or some such nonsense. Not that he needed any in the Midwest, except for perhaps Chicago. Maybe someone needed to give him a map, because Niles, Michigan, wasn't Chicago.

I swung my arm wide in a cross and connected with the bag with more force than before. My knuckles throbbed from the impact. Instead of shaking it off, I went into double-time jabs.

The scent of garlic permeated the air. My nose wrinkled, whether from the acrid scent or the man it came from, I couldn't tell. With the amount of hair gel Angelo used he should reek of it, but even those chemicals were no match for Mrs. Moretti's famous bruschetta. And from the smell of Angelo, he'd enjoyed a bit too much of his mama's cooking.

"Masterson." He smacked his gum as he came up beside

me, thumbs hooked in belt loops on a pair of pants a few sizes too big. "How about you and me go a few rounds in the ring?"

"No thanks, Angelo."

"C'mon." He winked and nudged me with his elbow. "I'll go easy on you."

I stopped punching and grabbed the bag so it would stop swinging. I gave him what I hoped was a withering glare before turning my back and walking to a bench, unwinding my wraps as I went.

"What? Afraid I'd whip you, pretty boy?" He taunted as if I were a child. Although this was Angelo, and I guess he figured if such tactics would work on him, they might on me as well.

"Drop it," I snapped.

"What's up with you today, man?" He faked a one-two at my arm. "Some skirt turn you down or somethin'?"

I glared, but he continued heedlessly.

"What'd she do? Throw a beer in your face when you tried to smack her—"

"Enough!"

"What?" He shrugged. "Happened to me once."

"Well, that's not what happened to me. In fact, it was the other way around."

The words no sooner left my tongue than I regretted them. The whole situation was not one I'd been planning on sharing, especially with someone like Angelo. By the gleam in his eye, he'd already taken to it the way a bug was attracted to a bright light.

"Wait, let me get this straight. A woman came on to you, and you said no?" His voice rose an octave on the last word.

I neither affirmed nor denied the accusation, for that was what it was. Not a question or a statement, but an all-out accusation. It seemed I didn't need to respond, however, because Angelo rushed on.

"You must be insane or gay or somethin'." Angelo stopped and stepped back "Wait, you're not gay, are you?"

"No, Angelo, I'm not gay." I put his homophobic fears to rest.

"So who's the broad anyway? I mean, if she wanted to jump your bones, imagine what she'd do if she saw me." He raked his fingers through his gelled hair, his head bobbing and hips dipping in a standing swagger.

"A little respect, Angelo." I fixed a glare on him. My patience, which had been a little thin after the events of the day, was ready to snap. The tension I'd released on the bag was beginning to build between my shoulder blades again.

"I only want to—"

"Enough. Instead of calling women 'broads' and 'skirts,' how about showing them some respect and treating them like ladies. They're human beings, not pieces of meat to ogle and crave. When you can treat a woman right, maybe then you'll be worthy enough to have one. Oh, and one more piece of advice," I said as I lifted the strap of my gym bag onto my shoulder. "Lay off your mama's bruschetta. You reek of garlic."

Rebekah

Lisa and I headed through town toward Grandview. I glanced at my reflection in the review mirror. Ugh. Maybe Lisa had some makeup in her purse. I hardly wore the stuff, but my puffy eyes and red nose were in need of some if I was going to successfully mask the unwanted events of the day from Poppy's discerning eyes and focus on celebrating him and his life.

We pulled up to the one-story ranch-style house that had been converted into a nursing home. The wraparound porch and rocking chairs gave the place an inviting feel. Southern charm way out west. The window boxes overflowing with wave petunias of every color brought life to a place that housed those near the end of their own. If Poppy had to be in a facility, at least we'd been able to find a nice homey-feeling one. Not one that resembled a sterile hospital.

I pulled bags of decorations from the back of the truck, and Lisa carried in the cake and a few balloons. I wish I could say I bounded up the steps with the excitement I had felt at the beginning of the day back in full force, but that would have been a lie. Mechanically my legs moved and carried me up those steps. With sheer will I pushed my lips up in a smile and shoved back any threatening tears. No more waterworks. Period.

"Oh, good afternoon, Rita." I greeted the petite CNA helping Mrs. Peter's into her wheelchair on the other side of the porch. Rita was a shy girl about my age, although with her short height and smooth skin, she looked more like a teenager. Poppy had told me that even though she did the hardest, dirtiest work at Grandview, she never complained. She returned my greeting with a small wave of her hand.

"I'll take the cake in to the kitchen. Why don't you go ahead and start decorating the dining hall." Lisa nodded to a pair of double doors.

It took an hour but the room finally looked festive. Nothing Pinterest worthy. Just some brightly colored tablecloths, some streamers, and some balloons. And, of course, all of the guests. Now, time to get the man of the hour.

I peeked around the corner and into Poppy's room to make sure he wasn't napping. Although if he was, I guess I'd have to wake him. He was sitting in his little chair beside his bed reading a book.

"Reading anything interesting?" I asked, a smile in my voice.

He looked up, and his face broke out in a huge grin. His dentures hung loosely in his mouth instead of hugging his gums. I'd have to bring more Poligrip next time I came.

"How's my favorite girl?" he asked. As I bent down to give him a hug, his arms squeezed tight around me, and tears stung my eyes as I soaked in his embrace. *No crying, remember?*

"Fine." I pasted on a smile I didn't feel.

"Come on now. This is Poppy you're talking to." His

eyebrows, which seemed to grow thicker and more unruly each day, knit together. They resembled hairy caterpillars drawn together that way. "I have been there for every knee scrape, broken bone, slumber party, school play, horse show, and breakup you've gone through." He crossed his hands in his lap and leaned his head to one side, a sympathetic smile gracing his face. "Tell ol' Poppy what's troubling your heart."

Now wasn't the time. Not on his birthday Not with a room full of people waiting to celebrate with him. Besides, I didn't want to relive it. Couldn't I just put the whole dreadful thing behind me? Rehashing it wasn't going to solve anything or make me feel any better. I opened my mouth to deflect, to change the subject to anything else, but paused at the gentleness in his eyes. He hurt because I hurt. My eyes stung, but I blinked back the tears as I told him about James holding another woman in his arms—of his lips on someone else's besides mine.

Poppy reached out and squeezed my hand. I fell to my knees and laid my head in his lap like I used to do as a child, and he stroked my hair with his weathered hand. With each gentle touch, anxiety seeped from my body.

"Thank you, Poppy, for loving me."

He buoyed my spirit like a drowning man being thrown a lifeline.

"Nothing will change that, Rebekah Anne." His voice was so soft I had to lean in to hear him.

Dr. Henshaw walked into the room, his eyes darting back and forth between me and Poppy. As his eyes rested on me, they softened in...pity?

Good grief. How in the world had those gossipers managed to spread my personal business out here already?

"Hello, Rebekah." He stepped more fully into the room, his clipboard dangling by his side. His already telltale droopy eyes, which always reminded me of a hound dog, were even more so from the sympathy emanating from them.

"I see Larry has broken the bad news to you."

Poppy's hand on my head froze. His whole body tensed. I looked up and met his eyes, my brow furrowed. What bad news? What was Dr. Henshaw talking about? If the look on the good doctor's face wasn't from hearing any gossip about me, then why did he appear as if he was going to offer his consolation?

"Poppy?" My voice squeaked, sounding more like a scared little girl than a grown woman.

Casting a quick look of flying daggers in Dr. Henshaw's direction, Poppy returned a gaze so tender upon me it was a caress.

My heart stopped. I waited in agony for what was probably going to be the worst thing I'd heard that day. Yes, much, much worse than anything James Anthony could have said or done. I sensed Dr. Henshaw leave the room, but still I sat at Poppy's feet, my eyes never leaving his face.

If possible, the man before me aged drastically in seconds. He reached out and cupped my cheek in his hand. Had I never noticed it before, or had I lived in denial because Poppy had always been so strong in my mind? There was no denying it now. The hand that cupped my cheek, the hand that had picked me up each time I'd fallen and had even swatted my backside a time or two, was shaking in frailty.

"I'm afraid the leukemia has come back with a vengeance this time, my dear. There's not much strength left in these old bones to fight it anymore."

Words stuck in my throat.

"I've lived my life, and I've lived it well. I have no regrets. The only thing I wish is that I would have been able to see you happily married. I know you're an independent girl and can get along fine on your own. But I want more than just fine for you. I want great. I know God has someone in mind for you, but I wish I could be around to see it."

The tips of my fingers began to tingle. I blinked repeatedly, trying to stave off the burn of tears as much as to stop the room from spinning. My eyes locked on to Poppy's.

Please, God, no. Don't take him from me.

I swallowed the lump in my throat. I wanted to smile, to put on a brave face, but my double-crossing lips refused to cooperate. Poppy needed to focus on getting well, not worrying about me.

His eyes remained steady on me, and I read his unspoken question. *Will you be okay?*

No. I wouldn't be okay. But I couldn't say that. So I said the most important thing as I flung my arms around the man who had been a father to me. "I love you, Poppy."

Chapter Four

Rebekah

Sitting cross-legged on my bed, my chin rested in the palm of one hand while I traced the stitches along the patchwork of my quilt with the other. A dark cloud had hovered over the party after learning of Poppy's diagnosis. Honestly, it made the thing with James both better and worse—if that was even possible. But in the light of losing Poppy, losing James was a walk in the park. I loved him, but Poppy, well, he was my rock. Though if James hadn't cheated on me, we'd still be together and closer to fulfilling Poppy's desire of seeing me happily married.

My shoulders slumped.

Not like I'd be able to make that dream come true. I couldn't call the Make-A-Wish Foundation and tell them my grandfather was dying, and could you please fulfill his last request—find me a husband?

I pulled my Bible onto my lap.

Jesus, please show me something in Your Word that will bring me a blessing. I'm in desperate need of one right now. I could also use some guidance. Lord, I need so many things that

I don't even know what *I need. Give me peace, Father.*

Opening my engraved leather-bound Bible to where I'd left off in Genesis, I began to read in chapter twenty-four. As I scanned the words, hope bubbled inside me. I scooped up the book, clutching it to my chest.

I'd read the story of Rebekah and Isaac numerous times before—it was one of my favorites—but it had never seemed so real or poignant to me as it did right then. It was almost as if a choir of angels sang. Their song consisting of one note, one word—an ethereal "aaaahhh." A supernatural light shone on the page, illuminating the inspired words.

The thought that popped into my head right then was a crazy one. And yet, I couldn't shake it. If an arranged marriage worked for Isaac and biblical Rebekah, why couldn't it work for a modern Rebekah too?

If I'd told anyone my thoughts at that exact moment, they would've thought I was beyond desperate. I mean, who in this day and age would let someone arrange their marriage? A blind date maybe, but nothing with such a commitment attached to it as marriage. I must admit, I thought I was a little crazy too. And yes, I suppose I did feel a little desperation. More than anything I wanted to make Poppy happy.

As outrageous as it seemed, it also made sense. I lived in a small town without a ton of people who believed in Jesus as their personal Savior. There were some who went to church and believed in God or a higher power, but even they were few and far between.

The most populated place in town was the bar on a Friday night. Then again, the population of our town was so small that the word "populated" was all a matter of perspective. You could say it was kind of like I was living in the modern land of Canaan. Like Abraham who didn't want his son to have a wife who didn't worship the one true God. So Abraham sent his trusted servant back to Abraham's homeland to find a wife among his own people. But I was born and raised in Meadowlark, California, and goodness knows I didn't have a trusted servant.

Then, as if an apparition, Lisa's face flashed through my mind. Granted, she wasn't my servant or anything, but she was my best friend. Plus, she was getting ready to head back to Andrews University in Michigan, the Christian college she attended. There were probably a lot more fish in that sea than here in my little pond. Besides, who knew me better than Lisa? Maybe God would lead her to the perfect guy the same way He led Eliezer to Rebekah. I suppose most people wouldn't do anything as extreme as what was developing in my head. They would probably enroll and go to the school themselves. Although attending school only to get married seemed equally insane to me. Either way, I couldn't pack up and leave. My work at the ranch meant too much to me. In a way, it was my own sort of ministry.

Glancing quickly at the bedside alarm clock, I realized I had better hurry and skedaddle out to the barn to get Dakota groomed and saddled for Jessica. I only had fifteen minutes before she and her parents arrived.

I grabbed two apples as I passed through the kitchen on my way to the barn. Lady, ever faithful, followed by my side. Biting into the crispy fruit, little rivulets of juice formed at the corners of my lips and, since no one was around to see, I sucked it back into my mouth.

The sun was high and hot. The dried, dead grass crunched under my boots as I walked the fifty or so yards from the house to the barn. The building, a little on the smaller side by most ranch standards, filled me with pride. So the lodge pole hay mow was leaning slightly to the left. So what? It still kept my hay dry and from growing mold. What if some of the stall boards were starting to rot or were half chewed in some places by bad-mannered equines. It was still mine. My own dream come true.

I blinked hard as I entered the barn, my eyes adjusting to the lack of light. Dakota nickered from the first stall, and I greeted her with a scratch to her wide forehead. She nosed my stomach.

"Looking for this?" I held the remaining apple flat in the palm of my hand. I placed the halter over Dakota's head and fastened it securely at her jaw. "Ready for a good day, girl?" Walking her around to the hitching post, I picked up a curry comb from the grooming bucket and vigorously swiped the rubber brush along the mare's coat in small circles. Dust plumed from her body, and chestnut hair pooled in the center of the comb. Dakota, like all the horses on the ranch, loved being groomed. It was like scratching dogs behind their ears. The horses didn't wag their tails or thump their hooves, but they did lean in toward me to show their pleasure. After picking the dirt clods from Dakota's hooves, I swung the lightweight children's saddle onto the mare's back. Just in time, too, because the Burnett's van door slid shut with a bang. A radiant smile spread across Jessica's face as she slowly made her way to the hitching post.

Most of us take little things like walking for granted. We put one foot in front of the other and away we go. After meeting Jessica, I realized what a blessing being able to take a stroll or a hike or a run really was. Jessica had cerebral palsy and had never walked without the aid of leg braces and forearm crutches. Even so, her gait was slow and choppy as her knee came in and crossed the other like a pair of scissors. I thought that was one of the reasons why she loved Dakota so much. She told me once that riding Dakota was the only time she felt graceful.

"How's it going, Jess?" I asked as she greeted her equine pal with some long strokes on Dakota's neck while balancing her weight on one crutch.

"Ready to get in the saddle," she replied with eagerness.

I glanced at my watch and then down the long driveway. "We still have to wait for Mrs. Steinbeck."

Mrs. Steinbeck was Jessica's physical therapist. We collaborated together in Jessica's hippotherapy sessions, and I couldn't start a session without her. Technically, she was the professional, and I was only the horse handler, but she treated me with respect, and we worked together as a team.

I really liked Mrs. Steinbeck. She and Jessica were the only legitimate hippotherapy sessions that took place on my ranch. I say legitimate because for it to be true hippotherapy a professional therapist must be present. There were other children and adults who came to the ranch with varying degrees of physical or behavioral problems, which I tried to help using therapeutic riding strategies.

Jessica didn't seem to mind the delay, and really, I'm not even sure she'd heard me to begin with. She was too busy loving all over Dakota. I leaned against the hitching post and watched her. Her parents had already taken a seat on the few plastic chairs I'd set up over by the arena fence. One day I hoped to be able to build some bleachers or something a little nicer for the parents to sit on, but for now this was about the best I could offer. Jessica's parents used to come over to the horse with their daughter and make small talk, but I think they realized this was a special time Jessica needed with her equine companion. Anyway, it gave me a chance to think as I watched her and waited for Mrs. Steinbeck to arrive.

Even with all of that inner chaos twisting my stomach, somehow—and I couldn't explain how exactly—watching Jessica with Dakota, seeing her eyes sparkle and hearing her tinkling laugh ring out as she shared secrets with the horse—brought me a measure of peace. Hope even.

The crunch of tires on the loose gravel drive announced Mrs. Steinbeck's arrival.

"I'm so sorry I'm late," she said as she stepped out of her cherry-red Prius. Mrs. Steinbeck was a woman of style. Her hair was always perfectly in place, her make-up always perfectly applied, her designer clothes always...well...perfect. I felt frumpy in comparison.

More often than not, my dirty-blond shoulder-length hair was pulled back in a ponytail or braid. I usually wore jeans, a tank top, and some boots, and I hardly ever took the time to put on make-up, since my day usually consisted of tossing bales of hay, mucking out stalls, and working the horses.

Mrs. Steinbeck first made her way to Jessica's parents and shook their hands, then joined us by the hitching post.

"Well, are we ready, Jessica?" she asked, although we all knew the answer to the question.

"Yes, ma'am!"

One of the things I encouraged at the ranch was a sense of independence. Too often children with some sort of disability have too many things done for them that, with just a little reinforcement and direction, they could very well do for themselves. Independence breeds confidence as well. This being the case, Jessica knew no one was going to lead Dakota over and through the gate into the arena for her.

Jessica untied the lead rope from the hitching post and gave it some slack as she gripped both the rope and the handle on her crutches. The extra slack on the rope was so that she didn't pull or jerk on Dakota's head every time she moved the crutch forward. The gate had been a challenge the first time she had tried to maneuver around it, but the girl and horse team had it down pat by now. She led the horse to a ramp and mounted Dakota with as much poise as she could muster.

"Very nicely done, Jessica," Mrs. Steinbeck praised, mimicking my thoughts.

I grabbed the lead rope as Jessica placed her feet firmly in the stirrups. Her back straightened and her shoulders pushed back as she worked on the posture Mrs. Steinbeck would expect.

Mrs. Steinbeck nodded in my direction, and I led Dakota out in a slow, smooth walk. I watched as the rocking motion of the horse's hips swayed Jessica's hips as well. Her once too-tight muscles loosened with the rhythm. We worked using different gaits and motions to reinforce Jessica's muscle tension, balance, and posture.

"All right, I think that's enough for today," Mrs. Steinbeck declared after the thirty-minute session.

As Mrs. Steinbeck walked to where Mr. and Mrs. Burnett were sitting to discuss Jessica's therapy, I made my way with Jess and Dakota back to the hitching post. I lifted the saddle off the horse but allowed Jessica the responsibility of rubbing down Dakota and leading her back to her stall.

After the Burnetts left, Mrs. Steinbeck stayed behind a bit to discuss some long-term goals for the sessions, and then she departed as well. While there were people around me and a task which occupied my focus, I was given a break from the thousands of thoughts warring in my head. But left alone once more, my mind was swamped in all directions. I was drowning in my thoughts as I struggled to sort them out.

Sighing heavily, I picked up the pitchfork that leaned against the barn and threw it into the old, rusted wheelbarrow. I pushed it down the barn aisle to the first stall. No matter what else was going on in my life, there were still daily chores requiring my attention. Whatever else that needed to be sorted or planned would have to wait till the stalls were mucked and the animals fed and watered.

Father, I prayed in my heart as I scooped, lifted, and sifted a fresh steamy pile of manure. *I don't know what to do. Just a few days ago I thought my life was almost perfect.*

I dumped the pile and went back for another.

I thought James and I would get married. That Poppy would walk me down the aisle. That he would be there and hold his great-grandchildren. Those were my plans, God.

I sensed my own frustration mounting at how my plans, my life, had shattered.

For I know the plans that I have for you...

The pitchfork stilled in my hand midscoop. My heart, my mind, my soul, I didn't know where it came from, but I heard the whispering impression from deep within me.

What plans, Father? Please. Tell me.

Plans to prosper you and not to harm you...

Harm me?

I was incredulous. I was talking with the creator of the universe, and He deserved more than an interruption of doubt from a nobody like me, but how else was I to respond?

What am I to think, God? First my heart is broken to pieces when the man I love chooses to be with someone else. Then, on top of all that, You're going to take Poppy away from me too. What do you consider harmful, if not that?

Plans to give you hope and a future...

What future, Father?

I screamed within myself. My whole being shouted my confusion, my hurt, and my annoyance. *The only future I see is one where the people I love either leave or are taken from me. Where is my hope? So far it looks like my future is one of being* alone, by myself.

I will never leave you.

A warm, tingling sensation started at the core of my being and spread throughout my limbs, enveloping me in a supernatural embrace. It calmed my fears and gave me a sense of peace. And I knew. Even without James and even without Poppy, I wouldn't be alone. I would always be loved.

Chapter Five

Rebekah

Three days had passed since my experience with God in the barn. My life continued on as normal, my body going through the motions of my daily routines while my mind continuously turned like the cogs in the big clock on Main Street. It flitted back and forth, resting on one thought for mere seconds and then flying off to the next. Needless to say, I was mentally and emotionally exhausted.

Every morning during my devotions I turned to the book of Genesis and Rebekah's story. I hadn't done it consciously, because the message God had given me in the barn was not to worry or take matters into my own hands but to trust in the plan He had for me. Even so, every morning I found myself turning back to that ancient love story. A sense of urgency rose in my gut and threatened to strangle me with its intensity.

I needed to tell someone my thoughts, if for no other reason than to voice them out loud—maybe work them all out. Normally I would talk to Poppy, but for the first time I didn't feel comfortable with that idea. So who did a girl turn to when she needed to talk things out? Her best friend, of course.

I met Lisa at the diner downtown and ordered a chocolate milkshake and a basket of fries from our server, Wendy. The tangy scent of the night's special—pulled BBQ pork sandwiches—battled with the heavy aroma of cooking oil, the diner being famous for its beer-battered onion rings. As this was the only eating establishment in our small town, the little diner was packed. That was if you call nine out of the ten tables occupied "packed." Since it was the beginning of August, the temperature outside was well into the nineties. I licked my lips in anticipation of my cold chocolaty treat.

Lisa sat opposite me on the red vinyl-covered booth. "So what's up? I haven't seen you in almost a week. You doing okay?"

Lisa and I spent every moment possible together during her breaks from school. After everything that had happened, she knew I'd need time alone to sort things out. Except I hadn't been able to.

"Am I doing okay?" A false laugh forced its way past my lips. "No, not really. In fact, I think I've gone insane."

Lisa's head tilted to the side, and she crossed her arms over her chest. One eyebrow rose over hazel eyes.

"I'm serious! You better have me committed before I ask you to do something crazy."

"Something crazy like..."

"Like arranging my marriage."

I hadn't noticed Wendy approach with our milkshakes until the words had already left my mouth. I prayed she hadn't heard me, but by the way her eyebrows nearly jumped to her hairline like an Olympic pole vault gold medalist, I could tell she had. Great. New fuel for the gossip fires.

Lisa stuck a straw in her milkshake and sucked hard, her cheeks concaving and giving her a fish face. She pushed aside the tall glass and leaned forward on her elbows. "You're serious?"

I nodded. "Afraid so." I put my finger over the opening of my straw and lifted it out of the glass. Sticking out my tongue, I removed my finger and let the delectable sweet treat drip onto my taste buds. Closing my eyes, I savored the explosion of icy goodness.

Lisa scooted back against her seat, the vinyl squeaking with her movement. "Well."

"I know. But the only thing Poppy wants is to see me happily married, and I haven't exactly had the best luck with men of late."

"That's not your fault."

I raised my hand to stop her defense on my behalf. "Look, I know it sounds ridiculous, but I read Isaac and Rebekah's story the other day, and I can't seem to get it out of my head. I've thought about it so much that Abraham and Poppy are starting to morph into the same person in my mind."

"Okaaay."

"Poppy's getting worse, Lisa." I snagged her hand and squeezed. Probably too tight. "I don't know what else to do. Besides, people in India have arranged marriages every day. And what about online dating websites? That's sort of like a western-culture arranged marriage. They say they use an algorithm to match compatibility, but you know me better than any algorithm."

I glared at Wendy, who was taking an order from the booth next to ours. She'd asked the customer what he wanted to drink but kept casting furtive glances in my direction. I looked back at Lisa and let out a long breath.

"Who am I kidding? Even if you agreed to this crazy idea, that would mean there would still have to be a guy out there somewhere—no, not somewhere, specifically at your school—

who would come all the way out here to this dinky little town, all for the purpose of marrying someone he has never met. It's insane. I'm scared to think what kind of person would even consider it."

Lisa spoke once I stopped my pathetic monologue long enough for her to interject. "You asked for my opinion, right?"

I nodded and closed my eyes, almost afraid of what I was about to hear. Even after several moments, all I heard was the humming of conversations from other tables and the clanging of pots in the kitchen. I peeked from behind one eyelid. Lisa was grinning.

"Well?" I asked.

She shrugged, still grinning. "You're right. It's a very...uh...*unusual* idea. Dating websites are a sort of contemporary setup, but I wouldn't go so far as to say they arrange marriages. More like they set people up on blind dates. But let me make sure I understand what you're asking. You want a man to make a commitment of marriage without even meeting you first, right?"

Heat raced up my neck and traveled to my cheeks. When she said it like that, it was even more ludicrous than when I'd said it.

"That's how it worked out for Isaac," I offered weakly. "Eliezer asked God to show him the woman who was supposed to marry Isaac, and He did. When Eliezer asked Rebekah to go back with him to marry his master's son, she did. If we were to do this, and the guy came here, met me, and then decided he'd made a mistake, then of course he'd be free to leave. It's not like I'd turn it into a shotgun wedding or anything."

Lisa fiddled with her straw. What must she be thinking?

"Have you talked about it with Poppy?"

I shook my head as I dredged the last fry through a puddle of ketchup and popped it in my mouth. "He's going to know

I'm doing it for him, and he'll try to talk me out of it."

Wendy laid the check face down on the table, lingering a moment longer than was necessary.

"All right." Lisa dipped one decisive nod. "I'll do it."

Did Wendy's step just falter on the way back to the kitchen?

"I'll be your Eliezer, and with God's help, I'll find you your Rebekah, or, well, in your case, your Isaac. We'll call it The Isaac Project."

"Stop sucking in air, you big lout." I patted Samson's bulging belly before yanking the nylon strap and securing the cinch.

Man, it was a hot one. Sweat trickled down my spine as the full day's sun beat down. It would've been nice if there were even a remote breeze, but the air was as still as a stone. At least it wasn't humid.

I glanced at Lisa, who was slipping Daisy's bridal behind her ears. "We'd better walk them around the arena before hitting the trail. I need to check the cinch again after Samson stops holding his breath. I don't really feel like having the saddle slip from under me because this big galoot was being a stinker."

Lisa grinned. "Yeah, but it would be funny."

I placed my foot in the stirrup and hoisted myself into the saddle, the leather creaking under my weight. Ah, no better place to be than a horse's back, and no better view than the one between a horse's ears. I clicked my tongue, and Samson walked on.

After a few laps around the arena, we dismounted and tightened our cinches.

Lady whined by the fence gate.

"Sorry, girl, but you have to stay." I gave her a good scratch behind her ears. It was hard to say no to those sad puppy-dog eyes.

Samson and I took the lead, and Lisa followed on Daisy as we plodded down the well-worn trail. The trees spread their branches over us like a canopy, and the forest serenaded us with a beautiful melody—the twittering of birds, the rustling of leaves, the snapping of the twigs beneath the horses' hooves.

We reached the part of the trail where the woods ended and the meadow began. I reined in Samson and waited for Lisa to ride up beside us.

"Race you to the old oak tree," I challenged. Without waiting for a reply, I nudged Samson's ribs with my heels and leaned low and forward in the saddle. Samson's legs ate up the distance in giant gulps. This horse wasn't named Samson without a reason. He was tall and strong. With the speed we were going, the wind didn't so much kiss my face as slap it.

"C'mon boy, faster." Maybe I could outrun the impending doom chasing me and leave it in the billows of dust Samson's hooves created.

We reached the weathered old tree, and I pulled back on the reins to slow Samson and wait for Lisa to catch up. I stroked the horse's shoulder and whispered to him. He had let me fly, if only for a moment.

Lisa cantered up on Daisy, a scowl on her face. It was a bit unfair of me to challenge her to a race when she was riding the Morgan mare.

"Of course you win when you're riding Secretariat and I'm riding...well...Little Miss Muffet!" Lisa huffed.

I grinned and dismounted. Tossing the reins over Samson's head, I gave him some slack and walked him to the water's edge.

It was a beautiful day, if a bit hot. The lake looked cool

and inviting, shimmering like glitter in the sunlight. Dropping down on the grassy bank, I plunked off my boots and stripped off my socks. Ah, already that felt better. I rolled my pant legs up over my calves and stood.

The water was cool and refreshing as I slipped my feet beneath the surface. The silt at the bottom of the lake squished between my toes as I wiggled them, burying them deeper.

"So how am I supposed to go about finding you a husband?" Lisa asked as she came up beside me, her own feet bare as well.

My mind went blank. Okay, so I hadn't worked out all the logistics yet, but it would work out. It had to.

She turned to me, eyes bright. "I know! I'll put an ad in the school paper for a mail-order husband. That seemed to work well in the eighteen hundreds. Maybe some flyers hanging on the bulletin boards around campus. Oh!" She slapped her thigh, startling the horses. "A big life-sized cardboard cut-out of you, a dozen red, long-stemmed roses, and my very own version of *The Bachelorette*."

"Yeah. I'm sure that'll work great."

"Seriously though, what do you want in a guy? If you could somehow create the perfect man, what would he look like?"

"I don't know." I shrugged. "I'd thought James was pretty perfect, and look how that turned out."

"No cheating scumballs." Lisa checked an imaginary list on her palm. "Got it."

Samson lost interest in the water and tried to get to a patch of grass. He strained against the bit in his mouth and the reins in my hand. Not wanting my arm to get ripped out of its socket, I stepped out of the lake and sat crossed-legged in the middle of his intended smorgasbord.

I picked a blade of grass and stared off into the distance. "I want a man like Poppy. Someone who puts God first in his life. Who is dependable and can make me laugh. It would be nice if he liked horses and could help me out on the ranch. No stuffy city boy for me, please."

I flicked the blade of grass at Lisa.

"Of course, it wouldn't hurt if he were drop-dead gorgeous and a '49ers fan," I added with a waggle of my eyebrows.

"Oh no. That wouldn't be the least bit painful."

Enough about me. Lisa had a life, too. A way more interesting one, actually. "So how is Sam?"

A telltale blush bloomed on her cheeks.

"Things getting serious?" I pressed.

She nodded, her eyes shining. "He's so wonderful, Becky. I think I'm in love with him. He might...I think he might be *the* one, you know?"

I reached out and squeezed her hand. "I'm so happy for you."

And I was. Truly. Except for some reason I couldn't stop the stinging sensation that suddenly came to my eyes. Or the selfish questions echoing in the dark corners of my mind. What about me? Would someone ever love me? Would there ever be *the one* for me?

Because if I knew one thing, I knew this—the arrangement I'd made with Lisa might produce a husband, but I held out little hope for a happily ever after.

Luke

Late summer sun shone through the open bay doors. Everyone in the North knows to hoard time in the sun in the summer months because it's a rare treat come winter. Clipboard in hand, I checked over the equipment in the storage compartment of the pumper.

A long shadow moved across the concrete floor as a tall man entered through one of the bay doors. He strolled over to me with his hands in his pockets, his face darkened by the sun beating down behind him. As soon as he came fully beneath the cover of the fire station, I grinned.

Sam and I were cousins, our mothers being sisters. Both of us, however, resembled our fathers. Sam had the coloring of the all-American boy next door. Sandy hair and eyes the shade of Lake Michigan in July. He was tall and lean—redwood in height and the girth of an Aspen.

I, on the other hand, took after the Irish ancestry on my dad's side. Dark hair—so dark, in fact, that it seemed almost black, except when the sun hit it at just the right angle so that it shone through with lighter-brown strands woven through. Or so an old high school girlfriend told me once. And where Sam had the smooth face of a newborn baby, my own jawline always sported a shadow. It didn't matter that I shaved every morning—a couple of hours later I couldn't tell a razor had touched my face.

We greeted each other with a man hug. The kind where two hands met to make a sort of fist but then got caught in the middle of a manly chest bump with a couple slaps on the back for good measure. I don't know which guy came up with it, but it sure did stick around. Unlike the secret handshakes my friends and I came up with when we were boys.

"What brings you here?" I asked.

"An invitation. Mom wanted me to come by and invite you over for supper tomorrow at seven."

I rubbed my chin, pretending to ponder the offer. A man would have to be a fool not to accept an invitation to eat Aunt Margaret's cooking. It didn't matter what that woman made, it was always delicious.

"She told me not to leave until you said yes. Said to tempt you by telling you she'd be making arepas and flan for dinner."

My mouth salivated as I imagined biting into one of Aunt Margaret's arepas. Before she had Sam, and even before she'd married Uncle David, she'd spent a year as a missionary in Argentina. It was there she learned how to make the tasty little round cakes made out of very fine corn flour, or *mesa*.

I licked my lips. "You couldn't keep me away now."

"Good." Sam gave me one of his boyish grins that always made the ladies swoon. "I want you there, too. Lisa is going to be there."

"Wait. *The* Lisa? The love of your life, I-don't- know-how-I-ever-lived-without-you Lisa?"

"Yep." If it was possible, his grin spread even wider. "You tease, but just wait 'till you meet the girl who makes your heart stop and race at the same time."

"That's not physically possible," I replied dryly.

Sam opened his mouth to respond but was interrupted by the tones of the station indicating a full set.

"Response needed for a structure fire at 1252 Ferry Street."

Leaving Sam to scramble out of the way as the rest of the Engine One team poured into the bay, I sprinted to my turnouts. Kicking off my shoes, I jumped into my boots and jerked the suspenders attached to my protective trousers over my shoulders. Swinging on my jacket, I continued to prepare for the flaming battle ahead.

"See you tomorrow," I called over my shoulder to Sam as I scrambled onto the bright-red pumper and took the rear-facing seat behind the driver.

Sirens blared and lights flashed as the truck pulled out of the bay and onto the quiet city streets.

God, please let everyone be out of the building. Let no harm or danger befall any of your children today. And if possible, please help us save this house.

People were devastated to see their homes and businesses go up in flames and smoke. Or, sometimes even, to the massive water damage from our hoses as we fought to put out the consuming fires.

But it was always worse if someone was trapped inside. When most people ran out of a burning building, it was our job to run in—even at the risk of personal peril. But if there was someone inside, then the stakes were raised. No one wanted the death of another person on his or her hands. When the worst happened, questions haunted our minds. Did I do my best? Was there anything else I could have done?

Please, God.

The engine stopped. We spilled out of the truck, the reflective strips on our trousers and tunics glaring back at the sun in a staring contest. Quickly, I took in the scene before me. Thick, angry black billows of smoke spewed out the windows of the small house, signaling that this fire had plenty of fuel to feed its enraged temper.

By the look of the older-styled home, I imagined wood paneling, synthetic wallpaper, and polyester furniture. All tasty treats for a fire to gorge on. Not to mention the wooden structure of the building itself.

We all worked as a team, knowing our duty and the part we were to play. The truck we came on was a pumper and held one thousand gallons of water within its belly. That allowed us to be aggressive in our attack against the blaze while we tapped into backup water supplies, such as a hydrant. But before a single drop was sprayed, the situation had to be assessed. Our captain was busy acquiring needed information from concerned neighbors and reading the signs of the fire. He turned and raced to the crew, barking out orders.

"Neighbor reports that a single lady and her teenaged autistic son live here. The neighbor saw the woman leave about half an hour ago, but he didn't see her son with her in the car, so we may have a rescue situation on our hands." He turned to me. "Masterson and Lopez, I want you two inside on recovery as fast as you can. In and out and no heroics, you hear? Josh, grab the chainsaw and get on the roof for ventilation. We need to get a hole open for smoke and gasses to find a way out. Baxtor will work on busting out these windows. Chambers and Richard, man the hoses."

Lopez and I both strapped on our self-contained breathing apparatus, known simply as SCBA to firefighters. The air tanks now fastened to our backs added an extra twenty-three pounds to our gear but allowed freedom of breathing once we entered the smoke-filled house. Shoving the clear plastic shield of the apparatus over my head, I tugged on the nylon straps to make it snug on my face and took a few test breaths. Next came our Nomex hoods and helmets.

By this time, the adrenaline pulsed through my veins the way it always did. We firefighters were known to be adrenaline junkies. There was nothing like the excitement that bubbled in the pit of my stomach whenever I heard the tones of a full set. My body was antsy with it, but I reined it in and channeled it to the challenge before me—finding one scared teen in one dangerous situation.

I twisted the handle and shoved the door with my shoulder. Locked.

"Masterson!" Lopez shouted.

I jumped out of the way as Pedro Lopez lifted the handle of an ax behind him and swung it in a high arch above his head. He brought the razor-sharp blade into the wood, splitting it into shreds by the jam. The door loosened, and I kicked it wide open.

The heat whooshed out like water rushing from a broken dam and slapped me square in the face. If not for the SCBA mask covering my face, the sheer force of the temperature would have reached down my throat and stolen the breath right out of my lungs.

I bolted into the house, Lopez quick on my heels. Family portraits hung, slightly warped, on once-white walls now blackened by smoke and soot. The fire, the heart of which burned in the back of the house, roared and hissed. Flames shot out and licked the ceiling in the corner.

My breathing echoed in my ears with a *koosh* that overshadowed the crackling of the fire around us. We often told kids that Darth Vader was really their friend because that was exactly what we sound like while breathing through a SCBA.

"This is the Niles Fire Department," I called out. "Can

anyone hear me?"

No one answered.

There were no bodies in the main living area, so we headed away from the flames and cautiously made our way down a narrow hallway. The first bedroom proved empty, and I shook my head at Lopez and signaled him to continue. Mario and Luigi posters were push-pinned to the walls of the second bedroom. On the other side of the bed, my attention snagged on a head full of curly brown hair barely visible behind the twin mattress.

"Lopez, over here!"

The boy was crouched down on the ground with his back to the corner where the bed and wall met. His head was bowed, his attention riveted on the screen of a hand held device. Looking more closely, it appeared to be an old Game Boy system. The sounds of game music lightly filled the air around the stooped young man, interrupted with a *boing, boing* every time the character jumped.

I squatted in front of him. "My name is Luke, and I'm with the fire department. I'm going to get you out of here, okay?"

The boy never flicked a glance my way but continued to stare at his game, his thumbs racing on the buttons as he played. I reached out to take both the game and player, but he snatched his hand away.

"No, no, no, no!" He cradled his precious game protectively with one hand while swinging his arm wildly to fight me off with the other.

I glanced back at my partner and the orange glow emanating from the other side of the house. Suddenly the boy was in my line of vision, darting out of the room and in the direction of the heart of the fire. Pedro Lopez might have been the smallest man employed at the station, but he was also one of the quickest. Before the boy could make it two feet down the hall, Lopez snaked an arm around his waist and halted what the boy thought to be his escape but would truly have been his demise.

The neighbor had described the boy as a teenager, and while his face still held the look of a juvenile, he had to be closer to twenty. He was taller than Pedro's five-foot-four-inch frame and right then his eyes were crazed with fear. His arms and legs thrashed wildly, his screams piercing the roar of the fire. Suddenly both the boy and firefighter fell to the ground.

Before I could round the bed to help, Lopez propped himself up from the ground, brought his now clenched fist behind him, and punched the boy square in the jaw, rendering him unconscious. As Lopez scrambled off the floor, I grabbed the limp body and hefted him over my shoulder, pinning his legs to my chest.

Good. Now we can get out of here.

I took the first step toward exiting and—*crack*!

"Look out!" The yell tore from my throat as a rafter in the ceiling came crashing down, raining drywall and burning embers in our path.

Chapter Seven

Rebekah

Poppy and I sat hand in hand on the tufted Victorian style sofa in the front room at Grandview. The sun shone through the large picture window behind us, casting a horrible glare on the television as we watched the 49ers game. I couldn't remember how many Sundays I'd spent this way, just Poppy, me, and eleven men in gold spandex leggings and red jerseys running across 120 yards of green turf, throwing spirals and tackling the other team.

Sometimes after the game, especially the ones we lost, Poppy would get a faraway look in his eye and reminisce about the '49er dynasty when the team won five Super Bowl championships in only fourteen years. He would go on and on about the prowess and athleticism of Joe Montana and Jerry Rice. We even went to a few games when I was younger. He would splurge and buy me nachos and one of those ridiculously obnoxious foam fingers. I loved every minute of it.

Although I wished I'd had one of those fingers right then to poke Mrs. Turlock along. She shuffled at a tortoise pace across the space between us and the television, pushing her walker with the two bright-green tennis balls on the bottom. If she didn't hurry I was going to miss a crucial play of the game.

"Can I help you, Mrs. Turlock?"

She stopped—actually stopped—right in front of the TV! She looked at me, her head wobbling back and forth. I knew it was disrespectful, but I couldn't help thinking she reminded me of a bobble-head doll.

"Oh, no, dear. I can manage just fine."

Oh good. Manage faster, please. A strained smile stretched my lips. I leaned to the right and tried to get a glimpse of the game around Mrs. Turlock. The good thing was the volume had been turned up, so Mr. Peddlemyer could hear the game. If I missed a play while Mrs. Turlock toddled out of the way, then at least I'd be able to hear the announcer's commentaries.

Pphhtt.

I looked at Mr. Peddlemyer.

Please tell me that wasn't what I think it was.

My nose wrinkled against the stench assailing it. I wanted to gag, to bury the bottom half of my face in my shirt and take in filtered oxygen. What was the kitchen staff feeding these people?

Poppy tapped my leg and pointed to the television. Mrs. Turlock had finally made it far enough that she was no longer blocking our view. Just in time for commercials. At least I hadn't missed a game-changing play by my beloved Niners.

Poppy had instilled a lot in me growing up—a love for the game, and the Niners especially, was one of them. Anyone could see I was just as much of a fan as he was. Every Sunday during football season, whether the Niners were playing or not, I would tug on my number seven Colin Kaepernick jersey, pull my hair up in a ponytail, and tie it with a red-and-gold Niners ribbon. Lisa used to tease me about it, but I thought she was coming to accept this side of me.

Embedded in sports, or the fans at least, is a hint of superstition. Now I didn't *really* think that if I didn't wear my Kaepernick jersey and tie my hair with this specific ribbon that the 49ers would lose. But, then again, I didn't want to take that chance.

Eyes glued to the television screen, I scooted all the way to the edge of the couch and leaned forward in anticipation. Colin Kaepernick had just released a perfect spiral, throwing it deep down the field in a Hail Mary attempt to take over and win the game in the last few minutes. My heart pounded against my ribs, and I resisted the urge to bite my nails as my eyes followed the ball on the screen. Whispering "go, go, go" under my breath, willing the intended receiver, Randy Moss, to catch it in-bounds for the touchdown. As the ball descended from its final arch, Moss caught the ball and cradled it safely in his arms as if it were his firstborn child just handed to him in the delivery room.

I jumped to my feet, hands raised over my head to signal a touchdown, mimicking the two referees on the screen. Spinning around, I grinned in triumph.

"Did you see that—" The words died on my lips. Poppy's head slumped forward, slightly angled. His chin rested on his chest. A rivulet of drool pooled in the corner of his mouth.

My heart plummeted. The victory I'd felt moments earlier vanished. Randy Moss could've fumbled the ball, and it still wouldn't have felt worse. Poppy was slipping away from me, and there wasn't anything I could do to stop it.

Swallowing a lump the size of California in my throat, I leaned over my grandfather and pressed a light kiss on his forehead. I tried not to notice the new bruises scattered across his paper-thin skin as I tucked an afghan around his legs.

I turned off the TV and meandered down the wallpapered

halls in search of Dr. Henshaw. Maybe he could give me an update on Poppy's condition. Goodness knows I wasn't getting straight answers from Poppy.

Rita pushed a cart with dirty dishes down the hall toward me. One wheel of the cart squeaked. The plates and cups rattled together even over the smooth carpeted floor. As I came closer, I noticed some of the food had barely been touched.

Aha!

Rita spent more time with the patients of Grandview than anyone, even more than Dr. Henshaw. She probably would know as much about the particulars with Poppy than the good doctor. Oh, he might have known Poppy's latest white blood cell count, but Rita knew the important things. At least what I considered important. Like how he was eating or how he was sleeping or how well he was maintaining his mobility.

"Hi, Rita, how's it going?"

She gave me one of her shy smiles, managed a "fine, thank you," and looked straight ahead again, all the while pushing her cart.

"How's your family?" I tried again to engage her in conversation.

She stopped pushing her cart and looked at me, a question in her eyes. We'd never really conversed more than a casual greeting. She seemed a bit curious, if not suspicious, as to why this moment was any different than the dozens that had come before.

"They are fine too," she answered with a slight accent.

"Rita, I was wondering..."

"Yes, Miss Sawyer?" she prompted.

"I was wondering if you could tell me how my grandfather is doing."

"Me, Miss Sawyer?" Her voice raised at least an octave in her surprise, and her accent grew a tad thicker.

"Yes, Rita, of course you." I smiled and gestured toward her cart. "Who else gives as much time and attention to the patients as you? Who else knows all the details of their everyday lives?"

I let that sink in a moment and continued, touching her arm lightly to try and calm her. She seemed as skittish as a young colt ever since I'd stopped her to have this little chat.

"I know we haven't talked much, you and me, but I've seen you work, and you are diligent and caring. My grandfather speaks very highly of you as well."

"Thank you, Miss Sawyer," she whispered, eyes averted.

I opened my mouth but closed it as my gaze caught sight of the portrait of Susana Beachworth hanging behind Rita. The founder of Grandview, with her beehive hairstyle and cat-eye glasses, stared at me with contempt. As if the picture could talk, I could hear her shrill words in my head. *Way to go, Becky. Of all the times you've come to Grandview, you've never once even said thank you to this poor sweet girl. You should be ashamed of yourself.*

Great. I shook my head. Maybe I really was going crazy, and not just because I was letting Lisa find me a husband. Now pictures were talking to me.

I swallowed my humiliation. Somehow I'd make it up to Rita. She deserved better than how I'd treated her

Rita's gaze darted between me and some unknown location down the corridor.

Right. Back to why I was standing here in the first place.

"Now," I continued, letting my lips form a smile to try and ease Rita's obvious discomfort, "how is Mr. Sawyer doing? Is he eating well? Drinking enough? Sleeping more than usual? How are his spirits? Is he cheerful or depressed?"

"Mr. Sawyer, he a very nice man," she began. "He always smiling, and he say nice thing to me."

She hesitated, and I urged her to continue.

"He no finish his food no more. Say not hungry. He sleep lot more too."

I nodded but continued to pry her with questions. With each answer, my heart fell a bit more. It seemed the leukemia wasn't satisfied with taking Poppy from me slowly. It was moving faster than a Triple Crown winner on race day. Nausea rolled in my stomach. I might as well lay down on the track and let the thoroughbreds stampede over me. A hoof to the heart couldn't possibly hurt any worse. I shouldn't have been so dazed by Rita's news, but being tackled by a three-hundred-pound linebacker couldn't have shocked me more. The squeak of the cart's wheels snapped me out of my stupor, and I managed to thank Rita for her help.

"Yes, Miss Sawyer." Rita ducked her head, her response a mere whisper.

She was halfway down the corridor before I'd worked up enough saliva to moisten my dry mouth and call out to her once more. The clatter of dishes stopped as she turned back toward me.

"You can call me Becky, and...maybe we could be friends?"

A faint blush tinged her olive skin, and she smiled. The first real smile I'd seen on her lips. Not a shy, quiet smile, but one that lit her whole face.

"*Clara que si.*"

Did that mean yes?

Chapter Eight

Luke

Pivoting, we rushed back into the bedroom where we'd found the young man. There was a window, but Baxtor hadn't made it to this side of the house yet to break it for ventilation. A halligan tool would've been handy right about then.

I readjusted the body on my shoulder and got a better grip on his legs. Lopez eased around me and grabbed the lamp on the nightstand. With a throw rivaling a Detroit Tigers pitcher, he heaved the wrought iron light toward the single pane of glass. A small hole appeared in its wake, fissures spreading out from its nucleus.

Thwack! Lopez's elbow clubbed away the jagged shards.

Lopez climbed out the window and reached back to grab the boy's shoulders. We navigated the teen's body through the glass-toothed gap. Once his legs were clear, Lopez hoisted the boy onto his shoulders and jogged toward the horde of emergency vehicles. I planted my palms on the frame of the window, thankful for the gloves protecting my hands, and heaved myself through the opening.

By the time I ran to the ambulance, the boy already lay on a stretcher. An oxygen mask covered his nose and mouth. A paramedic pointed a latex-gloved finger toward the bruise already purpling across the teen's jaw. "What happened here?"

"Look, we had two options. A little bump, or he left that house in a body bag. The bump seemed like the better option, okay?" Lopez ground out before trotting over to the chief.

By this time, we had a fairly large audience, as families who called this neighborhood home stood outside their doors, their bodies and their houses alternately turning red and blue with the rotation of the lights from the fire trucks, police cars, and ambulance. The members of our team were at their appointed stations, each soldier doing his or her part in this war against the destruction and danger of the all-consuming flames.

Feet were spread and braced by those manning the hoses, the pressure of the water threatening to beat them back. The water arched and fell, the blaze sizzling, and the smoke rising. We continued to fight the fire until all that was left were the black, charred remains of what used to be a home.

I coiled one of the hoses when a shrill voice pierced the air.

"My son! Where's my son? Adam! Adam!"

Looking in the direction of the voice, I noted a middle-aged, heavyset woman was being restrained by a uniformed police officer. She screamed and struggled, clearly going into hysterics.

I dropped the hose and rushed over to the crying woman.

"Ma'am," I said, trying to get her to focus on me instead of her overbaked home now in ruins. "Your son is okay."

She looked at me and vaulted herself past the officer's detaining arm. She grabbed my jacket in fistfuls, clinging to me.

"Where is he?" With each word, she pounded my chest, taking my jacket still clutched in her hands back and forth with each strike. She must've put her weight behind her rocking motion because I nearly lost my balance with the movement.

I placed a hand on each of her shoulders to steady her as well as myself. "Ma'am, your son is fine. He was taken to Lakeland Hospital so a doctor could take a look at him."

Without a word she pushed off my chest and waddled quickly back to her minivan. Returning to the truck, I picked the hose back up and finished packing.

Thank you, Jesus, I prayed as I slammed the door to the storage compartment. Praise and gratitude weighed heavily on my heart as I thanked God that everything had worked. The fire hadn't spread to any other buildings, and no lives were lost. There was considerable property damage, but when faced with what could have been, that seemed a small price to pay.

I opened the front door enough to peep my head through. "Hello? Aunt Margaret?"

"In the kitchen." Her familiar low alto voice drifted from around the corner. Uncle David called Aunt Margaret's voice sultry. To me it always sounded like honey on a warm piece of toast. Sweet, inviting, and earthy.

I bent down and planted a kiss on her upturned cheek, depositing a bouquet of carnations next to the cutting board where an onion and a knife sat.

"You're going to make some lady really happy one day." She buried her nose in the soft petals before retrieving a vase from the cupboard and placing the flowers in water.

"You mean I didn't make a lady happy today?"

"Oh, you big tease." She swatted my arm and then turned back to food preparations.

Knowing my duty, I picked up the onion and turned it on its side, sliding the knife through its juicy layers and feeling the sting of its pungent scent in my eyes. I repeated the process until the entire vegetable had been chopped into fine pieces.

Aunt Margaret took the cutting board to the stove, sliding the knife along its surface. The onions landed in the skillet of hot oil with a satisfying sizzle.

"So where is everyone?" I asked as I took a seat on one of the stools pushed under the counter of the peninsula.

"Running late, but so am I, so it's okay." She looked over at me from the stove and shook her head. "Oh no, you're not done yet. See that metal bowl over there? I need you to mix the Maseca and water."

"How much of each?"

"Until it's the right consistency." Like a seasoned chef, she added black beans, cilantro, and some special seasonings to the now translucent onions.

How am I supposed to know the right consistency?

The finely ground cornmeal tinkled into the metal bowl. Reaching around Aunt Margaret, I took a wooden spoon from the pewter utensil holder by the stove. Or at least I tried to. Before I could lift the spoon an inch, Aunt Margaret smacked my hand.

"Mix with your hands. That way you'll know when it's just right."

Adding water in a little at a time, I dove into the yellow contents of the bowl. The water sloshed at first, as it sat above the denser material beneath, but as I mixed and mashed it was absorbed, becoming a compact, grainy dough.

Aunt Margaret inspected my work, poking at the dough with her finger.

"More water. And try to break up all those little grain balls."

I added more water and smooshed the mixture through my fingers. It felt a lot like the sand you would use to make a sandcastle with at the beach, a bit gritty and course. I caught grainy balls between my index finger and thumb and smashed until they were smooth.

"This better?"

Aunt Margaret poked the Maseca mixture again. This time her finger slid through.

"Good." She pulled the bowl a few inches across the counter until it was in front of her. Reaching into the bowl, she pinched off a small portion of dough.

"Now," she said. "You take some dough and roll it into a ball like this. Then you press it flat with your palms and use your fingers to push the ends out while rotating the dough in a circle until you have a little round cake."

She handed me the half-inch-thick circular golden arepa, ready to be cooked on the griddle.

The bowl was almost empty, four arepas were cooking on the griddle, and a plateful was keeping warm in the oven, when the door opened and in walked Sam with a lady I could only assume was Lisa.

A tiny slip of a woman, her head barely reached the middle of Sam's ribcage. She was cute though, with bobbed light-brown hair that reached her jawline and wide almond-shaped eyes. I thought the two of them looked a little out of place together because of the height difference, but I wasn't about to say that out loud.

Aunt Margaret received hugs from the latecomers, and Sam guided his girlfriend over to me with a hand on the small of her back.

"Luke, I'd like you to meet Lisa."

"Nice to meet you, Lisa." We shook hands, and I nodded toward Sam with a wicked grin. "So how did you meet this buffoon here?"

She smiled up at Sam with adoration shining from her

eyes, and my stomach caught for a moment.

That's funny. Must be hungrier than I thought.

"We met on campus. I was studying in the gazebo, and he came up to me and asked me how many times he would have to march around me before I'd fall for him." She laughed, and Sam shifted his weight, obviously uncomfortable with the direction of the conversation. For good reason too. I couldn't believe he'd say something that corny.

"Really?" I hiked an eyebrow. "And that worked for you?"

She shrugged, but there was no way I was going to let it drop.

"I'm surprised he didn't say 'You know why Solomon had so many wives? Because he never met you,' or 'Is your name Faith? Because you are the substance of things I've hoped for,' or, and this is my personal favorite, 'Last night I was reading in the book of Numbers and I realized I didn't have yours.'"

"Ha-ha very funny," Sam replied. "But joke all you want. I got the girl, and you're still single." If we were kids, I'm sure he would have ended that remark by sticking his tongue out at me.

Ouch. I smiled, but man, that was a sucker punch. I mean, Ms. Stabler threw herself at me, but that wasn't the type of woman I wanted. There was no depth of character there. I'd just met Lisa, but already she seemed like a nice girl. She had a real soccer-mom vibe going on. Caring. And, judging by the googly eyes passing between the two of them, she was in love with my cousin.

"Hey, I'm happy for you, man," I said, play punching his arm.

Uncle David came in and laid his briefcase down by the door. He strolled into the kitchen and came behind Aunt Margaret, wrapping his arms around her middle and nuzzling her neck. "Dinner ready? I'm starved."

Aunt Margaret shooed him away. "Almost ready." She finished placing the food on the table, and we all took our seats. Bowing our heads, we held hands as Uncle David said a blessing over the food.

"So where are you from, Lisa?" I asked as I passed her the plate of arepas.

"A little town called Meadowlark in California."

"California, huh? I bet that was a big change when you came out here to Michigan."

"Oh, Michigan has its perks." She grinned across the table at Sam.

I resisted the urge to roll my eyes.

"So how's your search coming?" Aunt Margaret asked as she cut into her arepa, making a pocket, steam rising out.

"Still looking."

"What are you looking for?" I asked as I added the beans and a few avocado slices into my slit arepa.

"Well..." She flicked another look at Sam and I followed her gaze. Did my cousin have something to do with what she was looking for?

"This might sound wild, but hear us out." Sam took the avocado plate and slid a few slices onto his. "You know the story of Isaac and Rebekah?"

"Yes..." What did a Bible story have to do with whatever Lisa was searching for?

"Well, let's just say that Lisa is Eliezer."

"Eliezer?" My face scrunched as I tried to follow the conversation. None of it made any sense.

Lisa nodded but didn't look up from her plate.

"As in the man who was sent to find Isaac a wife?" I asked for clarification.

She nodded again.

"Only I'm looking for a husband," she said when she at last looked up.

I looked at Sam, then back at Lisa, then Sam again. Clearly I didn't hear right. I could tell things between my cousin and Lisa were serious, but I hadn't realized he'd proposed.

No, wait. She'd said she was still looking. Then...why...?

Sam laughed at my obvious confusion. "Not a husband for her. For her friend, Becky."

I leaned forward on my elbows and tried to process what I'd heard. Someone had really asked a friend to find her a husband?

"Why does your friend need you to find her a husband? This isn't 700 BC."

What kind of woman would do that? An image of a socially awkward nerdy type with stringy hair, glasses, and a serious overbite flashed through my mind. Maybe the girl didn't think she could ever get a guy on her own, so she begged her friend for help out of lonely desperation. I vacillated between shock from the sheer ridiculousness of the plan to pity for the outcast lady in question.

Lisa regarded me, searching for something. A test maybe? She gave an almost imperceptive nod of her head. I guess I passed. Or maybe not, because she got up from her chair and went into the living room. I hoped I hadn't offended her with my incredulity.

The sound of small items being pushed around filled the silence of the dining room as the rest of the occupants around the table stared in the direction Lisa had gone. The noise sounded like someone rummaging through a purse. I guess she found what she was looking for, because she came back to the table and extended a cell phone to me. I took it and peered at the screen. Smiling back at me was a beautiful woman standing beside a large black horse.

This couldn't be the woman in search for an arranged marriage. Where I'd been picturing stringy hair and an overbite laid thick, dark-blond hair and straight, pearly white teeth. There wasn't any bookishness or nerdiness about her. This was a woman who wouldn't have had a problem turning heads and receiving offers of marriage based on her looks.

So if she hadn't asked Lisa to find her a husband because she had problems acquiring male attention on her own, then it must be something else. Did her inner beauty not match her outer beauty? Maybe she had a quick temper and a sharp tongue. Was she painfully shy and socially awkward? There wasn't any other explanation.

"Becky is my best friend," Lisa explained. "She was raised by her grandfather, but he's dying of leukemia. He said the only thing he wished he could have been able to do before he died was walk her down the aisle and see her happily married to a man who would take care of her."

Sam stretched out his arm across the table, and Lisa took his hand for support.

"Becky was dating this guy, a real jerk. She caught him cheating on her the same day she found out her grandfather was dying. She was really shaken up about the whole thing. More about Poppy, that's what she calls her grandpa, than about the sleaze-bag boyfriend. Anyway, the next day she read the story of Isaac and Rebekah and got it into her head that if it could work for them, maybe it could work for her, and she could give Poppy his last dying wish."

"So you're looking for a guy who will move to California and marry her?" I tried to soften my voice and remove any trace of skepticism. It was obvious Lisa cared for her friend. It wasn't her fault her friend was a few sandwiches short of a picnic to think anyone would participate in a plan that outrageous. I looked at the picture on the cell phone once more. Her devotion to her grandfather spoke of a tender heart, but that didn't mean I'd changed my mind. The whole idea was ludicrous.

Lisa nodded.

"Well, I think it's sweet," Aunt Margaret said.

She would. Women always thought ridiculous equaled romantic.

Uncle David rubbed his chin. "It could work."

"What?" I whipped my head in his direction. That man sitting at the head of the table was assuredly not my practical, logical uncle. Everyone at the table had lost their minds.

"In this day and age, people are always falling in and out of love like it's some kind of rock to be stumbled over. Love is a choice. Yes, you can feel love for someone. Just look at these two here."

Sam and Lisa smiled at each other, and I suppressed my immature urge to make gagging noises at them.

"Some days the feeling is strong. So strong you think you might burst. Other days the feeling is so insignificant you might believe it isn't even there anymore. Margaret and I have been married for thirty-two years, and not all of them were rainbows and roses, let me tell you. Some days I think we were ready to strangle each other. But we made a commitment to one another in our vows, and we choose each day to love each other. I wouldn't trade this woman for anything in the world." He reached over and brought the back of Aunt Margaret's hand to his lips. "She is the light of my life." After mouthing "I love you" to his still-blushing bride, Uncle David returned his attention to the rest of us around the table. "But the truth is, whether you feel it or not, you still have to choose to love. If someone went down there and chose to love this girl no matter what, then I think it could work."

I thought about what happened to my parents. Dad

claimed he and mom had grown apart over the years until he didn't recognize the woman who shared his bed. He said the love between them was lost. As if love was like a pair of keys that a person could misplace. Uncle David's logic sounded much more, well, logical to me. But this whole conversation was so bizarre. It was hard to wrap my mind around.

Looking back at Lisa, I asked again, still overwhelmed, "Eliezer?"

This time her nod was accompanied with a smile that lit her face, and she laughed. She was enjoying my befuddlement.

"So, Eliezer," I said. "Have you asked God to show you a sign so you know who this husband is supposed to be? I mean, that is what your biblical predecessor did, right?"

Her eyes twinkled as she stared at me with an odd look.

"What?" I looked at Sam but found he was eyeing me with the same bemused expression on his face that Lisa had.

"Was it something I said?"

Rebekah

Tchaikovsky's "The Nutcracker Suite" pierced the silence in my truck as I drove along the pothole-ridden dirt road. I leaned over and picked up the ringing phone, which had previously been tossed on the passenger side of the bench seat.

"Hello?" I tucked the phone between my ear and shoulder and returned both hands to the steering wheel. Just in time too, because I had to swerve left in order to miss a crater-sized pit in the road. The truck bounced along the washboard divots, the springs in the seat of my '85 Dodge vaulting my backside into the air.

"Hello, Becky, this is Dr.—"

Please God. Not Dr. Henshaw. Not Poppy. Not now.

"Smuthers."

I released the breath I'd been holding, my hands loosening the death grip on the steering wheel. No reason to get upset. Yet. Dr. Smuthers was a vet and had nothing to do with my grandfather's care.

"What can I do for you, Dr. Smuthers?"

"Animal control has picked up another horse from the Bronson place."

She didn't have to supply any other information. Anyone who drove by the Bronson residence would weep at the sight of their horses. This was the third horse in the last two months that had been confiscated due to animal cruelty from malnutrition. The other two horses' hips had protruded in such a sickening way. They were so skinny I could've literally counted every rib and every vertebra without the need of an X-ray. Being the closest rescue facility in a fifty-mile radius, the two horses had come to reside with me at the ranch.

My cheeks puffed out like a chipmunk in autumn as I exhaled a long, deep breath. It looked as if I was about to inherit one more horse. It wasn't that I didn't love the pitiful creatures—I did. It just broke my heart to see them so abused and mistreated.

"Okay, I'll swing by my place, pick up the horse trailer, and meet you there." I tried to make my voice sound normal without the resigned, depressed quality I was actually feeling. I didn't want Dr. Smuthers to think my less-than-excited tone was due in some way to not wanting to take the horse or to feeling put out that I'd been asked to help.

Thirty minutes later I pulled up to the paddocks at Dr. Smuther's clinic. The only good thing about these situations was that I could pick up the horses here instead of being in the middle of the drama and witnessing irate owners fly off the wall at animal control. Well, that and the fact the horses would finally be treated like they deserved. Besides, this also let the vet check the horses out first to make sure there wasn't any other medical emergency to attend to other than the issue of the animals' weight. We didn't want any communicable diseases such as strangles or West Nile Virus to spread to the rest of the herd once I got them home.

Surveying the paddocks, they all appeared to be empty. Hadn't the horse arrived yet?

An annoying buzzing sounded in my ear, and I waved my hand, shooing the pesky mosquito away. Just standing there was going to get me eaten alive. It would be smarter to wait inside where there was air-conditioning and no disease-carrying, blood-sucking pests.

With my hand wrapped around the doorknob, I thought I saw movement in the shadows of one of the shelters. Might as well check it out for myself instead of disturbing Dr. Smuthers if she was with a patient.

Puckering my lips, I made kissing sounds in the direction of the paddock as I walked.

Oh, sweet Jesus.

My hand flew to my mouth as bile rose in my throat, and breakfast threatened to make a reappearance. One would've thought I'd have gotten used to it all by now, but I hadn't. How could someone get used to seeing something so heartbreaking?

The animal standing before me could've been a beautiful dapple gray mare. But instead of a sleek and shining coat, her body was a dull and dusty mess. The poor girl's hair was coming out in fistfuls all over her body. She wasn't close enough to touch without entering the enclosure, but even from that distance I would've sworn I'd be able to slide my hand in the deep grooves between her ribs. Her hips rounded and protruded like giant saucers—she was barely more than a skeleton with skin attached. Large brown eyes stared at me from a hollow face.

"Poor sweet girl," I crooned to her.

How could people treat animals this way? Mr. Bronson ought to rot in jail. Maybe the warden could even forget his meals for a few days and see how he liked it.

The mare's nose, mere inches from the ground, drooped between her front legs. She was so depleted she didn't even have the energy to lift her head any longer.

Indignation washed over me. If I could get my hands on Mr. Bronson, I'd have a thing or two to say to that man. Do to him, too. My fist balled, and I imagined a riding crop firmly in my grasp. No one should get away with something like this.

I made my way back to the truck, my angry strides eating the hot pavement. My movements were forceful, fueled by the seething ire boiling in my belly. I jerked open the door to the tack room attached to the front of the horse trailer, ripped off the tin lid to the can of oats, and angrily scooped out a few cups full into a plastic bucket. Slamming the tack door with more force than necessary, I proceeded back to the bay mare.

Dr. Smuthers met me at the corral gate as I was unlatching the handle.

"Kind of breaks your heart, doesn't she?"

There wasn't any point in answering. Anyone with eyes in her head would be sobbing them out at the injustice of it all.

The mare's nostrils flared as she sniffed the food. Dipping her head into the bucket, she scarfed down the food like she was afraid someone would take the oats away any second.

"There's more where that came from," I assured her.

Dr. Smuthers and I went into her office and completed the paperwork required by animal control. Once all the i's were dotted and t's crossed, I headed back out to the mare. Slipping a halter over the horse's head, I snapped the lead rope on under her chin. She plodded along behind me as I led her from the paddock to the trailer, her hooves skimming a line in the dirt.

Once the horse was loaded, I pulled the truck and trailer back out onto the street, but some quick mental calculations confirmed I'd need to pick up more feed before I headed home. I'd been avoiding town, and especially Ernie's feed store, since catching James cheating on me behind the seed rack. Tractor Supply would have what I needed, but it was twenty-five miles in the opposite direction. I went about convincing myself that I had to face people in town sooner or later, and since I wasn't the one who did anything wrong, I shouldn't be hiding and acting so ashamed. Given that Ernie's was just down the road, I didn't have much time to work up my courage.

I put the truck in park and took a deep breath.

You can do this, Becky. It's just a feed store. There isn't a snake that's going to bite you the minute you walk in. I squeezed my eyes shut. Then again, maybe there was. Ernie was the crassest man in Meadowlark, and his wife, Josephine, spearheaded the local rumor mill.

Squaring my shoulders, I opened the squeaky door of my truck—man, I needed to get some WD-40 on that thing—and hopped down. My steps slowed as I entered the store. Hopefully, the action gave me an appearance of nonchalance. Ernie and Josephine didn't need to be privy to my inner turmoil. They didn't need to know that stepping foot into this desecrated area had my palms sweating. My Stetson would have been nice to hide behind, too.

Ernie stood at the counter, red-and-white checkered Purina banners hanging from the wall behind him. The store smelled of dust, oats, and a hint of molasses from sweet feed. I fought the urge to sneeze as I approached the counter and gave Ernie what I hoped was a confident and casual smile.

"Hey, Becky." The proprietor's eyes gleamed as much as his bald head. "Haven't seen you around here lately. Listen, I just heard this great joke. Wanna hear it? You're going to love it."

Ernie didn't wait for a reply but bulldozed his way forward.

"Why does Bill Clinton cheat on Hilary?" He looked at me expectantly, the corners of his lips twitching with restraint as he waited to share the punch line.

My own lips, however, faltered in their imitation of a smile. Ernie was known for his boorish humor and almost bullying ways, but I'd never been on the receiving end before. I opened my mouth to respond but was spared that discomfort.

"Ernie, you leave that poor girl alone." Josephine entered from a back office and swatted at her husband's arm.

She placed her hands over mine on the counter, shaking her head and tsking with her tongue.

"You poor, poor dear," she crooned, her southern accent dripping with false sweetness. "Why, I bet your heart is nigh unto a thousand pieces after what James done to you. ""Yes, well..." I pulled my hands out from under hers. Weren't there any other customers in this place?

"And right out in public too, for the whole town to see. I am so sorry it had to happen here." Her words said one thing, but her eyes said another.

I just bet you are.

"But time heals all wounds, they say," she continued. "Sooner or later you will be finding yourself another young man. According to Wendy over at the diner, maybe even sooner, with Lisa's help. Isn't that right, dear?"

Fishing, fishing, fishing. This bass wasn't that dumb.

"Why, to hear Wendy tell it, Lisa is going to bring you back a husband. But I told Wendy that couldn't be right."

Ernie smirked as he leaned his hip on the counter and crossed his arms. I'd had about all I could take from both of them. I wanted nothing more than to turn around and march right out the door, but I still needed the feed, and I'd already endured their ill treatment. I squelched the urge to give them a good dressing-down and to tell them to mind their own business. Instead I addressed Ernie with as much poise as I could muster.

"I need two bags of beet pulp, two of sweet feed, and one bag of rice bran. Please." I forced myself to tack the word on between clenched teeth.

He rang up my order and loaded it for me in the bed of the truck.

That was the last time I'd step foot in Ernie's Feed and Seed. From then on I'd be driving the extra distance to Tractor Supply.

Chapter Ten

Luke

I licked my lips as I set the square cardboard box down on the small bistro table in my apartment. Lifting the lid, the smell of tangy pizza sauce set my mouth to watering. Dark grease stains dotted the top of the box, along with gooey blotches of cheese. I slid out a triangle of the savory pie and dropped it on a paper plate. I shook my hand and popped my thumb in my mouth. They weren't kidding when they said it was *hot* and ready.

Picking up the remote, I flipped through the channels and stopped on ESPN. Cubs versus Cardinals. Not the most riveting match-up, but it beat reality TV any day. I sunk my teeth into the slice of pizza. Cheese stretched from my lips until I pinched the middle and shoved it into my mouth. The commentators droned on, and I found my mind wandering.

Not every guy on the planet will admit it, but the male sex does think about the future. And not just career-wise, but our romantic future as well. Although we may not actually use the word *romantic*. It's easy for people to picture a group of girls sitting around, eating ice cream and getting dreamy eyed as they talk about the perfect guy they'd love to marry and what kind of dress they'd want to wear and blah, blah, blah. But the truth is, guys think about that stuff too. Well, sort of, anyway. Not the dress part.

We don't sit around with other guys and talk about it, and we definitely don't dream about what we'll wear as we wait for our bride to walk down the aisle. The closest most of us guys get to talking about our feelings for a girl is admitting we think she's cute and that we'd like to ask her out. But we do think about the qualities we'd like in a girl if we were to get serious with her.

And this was where I found myself. I'd considered these things before, but not with any real seriousness. Usually my ponderings and wishes were general, with no specific person in mind. Now, however, I was thinking more and more about a young woman in California. A woman I'd never met.

I admit that when I heard Lisa's story, I was astonished, to say the least. And not in a good way. How could anyone even come up with such a harebrained idea? Who in their right mind would marry a complete stranger? A shudder coursed through my body as I thought about the danger that could befall Becky if her plan turned south. There were too many sick people out there ready to prey on helpless women. Lisa seemed like a woman of integrity, but how was she supposed to sift through the men who would take advantage of a desperate situation?

I shook my head. My initial disbelief had worn off, and I found myself oddly curious. Going back over everything Lisa said the other night at Aunt Margaret's, I had to admit, even though the whole thing was bizarre, it was driven by love—and naiveté. But the depth of love someone must have to potentially sacrifice her own future happiness for that of a dying man's touched a chord with me. The incredulous question of "who would do something like *that?*" that had entered my head last night transformed into the question of "*who* would do something like that?"

Sacrifice—I knew that one. I'm a firefighter. My life goes on the line with every call. But in the mirror of Becky's sacrifice, mine paled in comparison. Any burns I may suffer would heal over time. But time would never give Becky back her girlish dreams of marrying the love of her life.

I wished her well. Lisa seemed determined to follow through on her promise. Even so, the odds for success were definitely not in Becky's favor.

The young woman knelt in front of the marble headstone, her forehead resting on its cold, unforgiving surface. Silent tears streamed down her face, but her hands didn't move to wipe them away. She looked small and forlorn, alone amid a meadow of stone structures attesting to lives lived and generations past. No one should have to shoulder that type of grief alone. I tried to take a step toward the woman but found my feet incapable of movement. I was powerless to do anything but observe her heartbreak and sorrow.

A burly man stalked into the cemetery from the entrance to my right. His face dark and his eyes narrow slits of smoldering fire. By his side, large hands curled into fists, and his unwavering gaze burned a hole in the back of the kneeling woman's head.

"What are you doing here?" he demanded as he clutched the woman's arm and slung her about to face him.

The woman trembled as she looked up at the man, her arm still held firmly in his grasp. The skin where his fingers dug into her flesh was turning a pasty shade of white.

"Answer me!" he yelled, shaking her with enough force to

make her head snap back.

Her mouth opened, but before she could utter a sound, one of the man's cantaloupe-sized fists connected with her jaw, and she fell, her side slamming into the marble headstone in her descent.

I struggled to be free of the invisible hold on me, to run to the aid of the fallen woman, to stop the man as he again raised his fist and brought it down on her head. I opened my mouth to shout, but no sound escaped.

The beating lasted for what seemed liked hours. The woman lay curled in a ball, her knees to her chest and her hands over her head in a futile effort of defense.

"I hope you've learned your lesson, Becky dear." The man sneered and spat on the woman before turning and walking away.

Jolting up in bed, I rubbed the horror from my eyes and looked at the alarm clock on my nightstand. The illuminated numbers shone brightly in the darkness of the room—3:35 in the morning. What a strange and horrible dream. Flinging back the covers, I swung my legs around and searched the floor with my toe for my slippers. Finding them, I slid my feet in and staggered toward the kitchen for some water.

No more pizza before bed. I'd heard certain foods could give a person unusual dreams.

Quenching my thirst, I headed back to bed.

Four hours later, I awoke feeling anything but refreshed. The dream of the night before left me in a foul mood, the images clinging to the recesses of my mind, seeping into my consciousness. Nothing I did shook them loose.

I showered and dressed for church. I'd told Sam and Lisa I'd meet them there for first service. If anything could erase my unease from the previous night's disturbed rest, church would.

Finding a parking spot proved more difficult than I'd

thought. The church I ordinarily went to was smaller and closer to home, but today we'd agreed to go to the larger one Lisa attended on campus.

I finally found an open space on the far side of the soccer fields behind the church. Pulling out my phone from my pocket, I sent Sam a quick text and walked toward the looming gray stone building that had housed worshippers for over fifty years. Sam had better text back, or I'd never find him among the crowd.

My pocket vibrated, and I pulled out my phone.

We're on the right side, near the front.

I chuckled. Sam was one of the few people I knew who texted using proper grammar.

Shaking the hand of the greeter, I accepted a bulletin and pushed open the door to the sanctuary. The ceiling arched high and lofty, giving the spacious room a cathedral feel. The wood beams of the tall, peaked ceiling contrasted sharply with the royal-blue carpet beneath my feet. I walked down the aisle of the grandiose church, passing row after row of pews. I smiled at those who turned at the sound of footsteps passing their seats. Men and women dressed in their finest offered small smiles or dips of their head in return.

The sun shone through the stained-glass picture of Jesus at the front of the sanctuary. I tried once more to clear my mind in order to receive the blessing of the sermon. Sliding into the pew beside Sam, I whispered a hello and opened the bulletin, scanning the printed pages absentmindedly.

"What's with the scowl?" Lisa asked as she leaned around Sam. She looked pretty in a crimson-red dress, and she had done something different with her hair. Curled it maybe?

I tried to relax the muscles in my face and shoulders. "I don't know what you're talking about."

Evasion's not a lie. It's a survival tactic.

"Uh-huh," she said with a roll of her hazel eyes.

Fortunately for me, the pastor stepped out onto the platform, and I was saved any more of an explanation. Putting my finger to my lips, I shushed her and pointed to the speaker, sat back, and gave the pastor my undivided attention.

At least I hoped it looked that way. My thoughts still weren't cooperating. Becky's situation had me preoccupied. Would she be able to find someone in time? Would that man treat her right, or would my dream from the night before become a reality? Too many scenarios filled my mind, and not a one of them good.

But where did that leave me? It's not like I was willing to uproot myself and move to another state to marry a woman I'd never met. Unlike her, I wanted to get to know the person I was going to spend the rest of my life with. Goodness, I especially wanted to pick her myself and not let someone else do the choosing for me. So if I wasn't willing to be the man Becky was going to marry, then why did I spend so much time thinking about her—worrying about her?

Because no matter how hard I tried, I couldn't stop.

The sound of the organ and the shuffle of bodies as everyone stood roused me from my introspection.

So much for clearing my head to hear the message.

Lifting the hymnal from the back of the pew in front of me, I leafed through its pages to find the closing song. I could at least participate in one part of the service. I closed my eyes and lifted my voice, singing as a prayer. "Have thine own way, Lord! Have thine own way!"

The song washed over me like a cleansing rain. Out of all six-hundred-plus songs in the hymnal, this was by far my favorite. It held the most personal meaning for me. Every time I heard it, I felt a bit of the agony and all of the peace from when it first became my mantra two years before. When I was engaged to Leslie.

We'd had a whirlwind romance, and she'd awakened desires best saved for marriage. I was ashamed of what our relationship became, now that I looked back on it.

During the time we were together, I couldn't read the book of Song of Solomon because of the Shulamite's warning not to awaken love before its time. The caution poked at my conscience, and in the heat of the moment, I didn't want it being poked. I didn't read much of the Bible then, to be honest. My burning passions were battling against the quiet voice of my conscience saying such actions with a woman were better reserved for marriage.

Oh, I didn't jump into bed with Leslie, but we did skirt the line a little too closely. Taking the advice of Paul that it's better to marry than to fall into sin, I proposed and she accepted—for all of three weeks. She decided she wanted a little more fun out of life before settling down with one man. I was devastated. That is, until I gave all my heartache and guilt to God, finally releasing my hold on them and telling the Lord to have His own way—and He did. His way was and always will be better than my own.

The song concluded, and the pastor prayed a benediction over the congregation. People spilled into the aisle, causing major congestion. Instead of fighting the crowd, I sat back down on the hard wooden bench and waited until the flow of traffic started to move. The second my spine touched the backrest, Lisa leaned over Sam once more. Why didn't she switch seats with him instead of craning around his tall, thin frame? Maybe it had something to do with her hand and forearm resting on his thigh as she bent over to close the distance between us. Sam didn't look at all upset about his personal space being invaded.

"So what was with the scowl?" The police department

should've put her on salary as an interrogator.

The closing song, the one part of the service to which I'd actually paid attention, had managed to carry away the foul temper that had clung to me all morning. The lyrics *have thine own way, Lord* had reminded me that God did have a plan for people's lives. Just as He had a plan for my life two years ago. Just as He had a plan for Becky's life now.

As I was singing those words, it was as if I had put Becky back in God's hands. I didn't know when or why or how I had taken her out of His hands, but my preoccupation with the situation clearly showed I was trying to figure it out on my own. Which was absurd, since I'd never met her, and it wasn't any of my business to begin with. But I kept feeling drawn—no, pulled—back. But no more. God would have His own way.

"Nothing. It doesn't matter now." And it truly didn't.

"Tell me. I want to know."

She wasn't going to let it drop. I looked at Sam. "Is she always this nosey?"

"Always," he said with a grin.

"I had a bad dream last night that I couldn't shake. That's all."

"What about?"

Man, was she persistent. "Your friend, actually."

"Oh?" If possible, she looked even more intrigued.

Sighing, I told her my dream. "Your friend was kneeling in front of a grave—her grandfather's, I assumed—when a man storms into the cemetery and demands to know why she's there. Before she can say a word, he starts to beat her and doesn't stop until she can't move."

"Really."

The way she said it didn't sound like a question at all. I expected her to be a bit stunned that I'd had such a violent dream about her friend, but she didn't seem surprised. If anything, I was the one surprised. Surprised at the gleam that shone from her eyes and the cat-that-got-the-canary look that had taken over her entire face.

That look was never good for anyone. Especially the person on the receiving end. "Why are you looking at me like that?" I asked with suspicion.

"Like what?" She tried to mask her face in innocence, but her eyes shone with untold secrets.

Sam sat beside me, trying with all his might to hold back his laughter. Although no sound made it past his lips, his shoulders shook with his contained mirth.

"Okay, what's so funny? What aren't you guys telling me?" My wariness was rapidly turning to dread in the pit of my stomach.

Swallowing back his amusement, Sam clasped me on the shoulder and tried to look serious. He was failing, however, because his eyes still danced in merriment.

"You're the one," he pronounced as if that would clear everything up. Of course it didn't.

"The one what?" I tried not to sound as exasperated as I was feeling.

"The one Lisa has been looking for." His last word ended in a snort as he laughed through his nose.

We were starting to garner strange looks from the people milling around in the aisles, but at this point, I didn't care. Clearly Sam was enjoying himself, cackling like an idiot. I was about ready to wipe that smirk off his face if he didn't start making some sense

"What do you mean?" Surely I wasn't hearing right. Lisa had been looking for a husband for her friend. I couldn't be that man. These two must have lost their minds.

"You told Lisa that she should ask God for a sign so she

could know who He had planned to be Becky's husband."

"So..."

I looked to Lisa. Maybe she would make more sense than my addle-brained cousin.

"That was the sign I'd asked for."

I must have looked completely confused, because she continued.

"You see, so far all the guys I've told about Becky either laughed, got all weirded out, or made fun of her. I knew before I even started I'd need a sign from God just like Eliezer did. I know Becky really well, but I don't want to be responsible for choosing her husband. This way, it's more like God is the one responsible since He has to show me a sign. Becky may have a list of things she'd want in a man, but the main thing is someone with a heart for God. So I told God that the sign would be for the man who was supposed to marry Becky suggest I ask for a sign. This would show me that he knew the story from the Bible and that he had enough of a personal relationship with God to recommend I seek God's guidance."

She looked at me expectantly, as though this was some sort of algebra problem and only I had the right answer. I'd seen that look on Marty's face a hundred times. But this wasn't a+b=?

What could I say? I had sympathy for Becky. I felt bad that her grandfather was dying. Truly, I did. But that didn't mean I was ready to go and marry the woman! It was simply out of the question.

"Sorry"—I shook my head—"but you've got the wrong guy."

Chapter Eleven

Luke

Have thine own way, Lord. Have thine own way. The lyrics repeated themselves over and over again like a broken record. Was I letting God have His own way? I'd jumped the gun in a relationship once before without asking what His will was in the matter. But surely His plan didn't have anything to do with me moving to California to marry a complete stranger. Besides, what about love? Becky might be content with a loveless marriage, but that wasn't the kind of union I wanted for myself.

Love is a choice.

My uncle's words rang in my ears. I didn't want to admit the accuracy of the statement, but I couldn't deny it either. The statistics of divorce in this country were staggering. If a couple were in love on their wedding day, then what happened to end their marital bliss? Did they base everything on the flightiness of feelings instead of a lasting commitment to love their partner through thick and thin, richer or poorer, sickness and health?

Have thine own way, Lord.

What's Your way, Lord? What is it You want me do?

Love thy neighbor as thyself...

I couldn't have been more taken aback if I'd been hit by a battering ram. I talked to God all the time, but that was the first time I'd heard Him talk back.

I looked up at the sky, my hands stretched out in front of me, palms up in supplication. "What's that supposed to mean, love my neighbor? If that's Your answer, then I don't understand. I need a yes or a no. Am I supposed to go to California and marry that woman? Is that Your plan for my life?"

As if the words of 1 John 4:19 were illuminated in neon lights on a billboard, I saw them clearly—we love because He first loved us.

Was it really that simple? The reason followers of Christ love Him is because He loved us first. Deep in my heart I knew this was a promise from God as well as His divine direction. He was telling me to go to California. To marry Becky. To love her. And in loving her, she would love me in return.

Rebekah

"Stay, Lady," I commanded, although I'm not sure why I bothered. The way her head rested on Mr. Peddlemyer's leg, tongue lolled out the side of her mouth, eyes half-closed, I doubted I could have gotten her to move from that spot.

"Stop your worryin'." Mr. Peddlemyer waved a purple-veined hand at me. "Your dog and I will be just fine, won't we girl?"

I smiled at the pair before walking through Grandview's front door, nearly bumping into Rita.

"Hey, Rita. Is Poppy in his room?"

She bit her lower lip and hesitated before answering. “No, he no in his room right now.” She jerked her head to the left. “He in front room.”

My brows came together. What was with her nervous behavior?

The petite CNA scurried away before I had a chance to utter my thanks.

The front room was empty save my grandfather. He sat in the middle of the tufted sofa provided for guests and residents alike. The TV was off, and he held no book in his hands, but he stared straight ahead. Curious, I followed his gaze to the stark white wall.

“Poppy?”

My voice had no effect on his line of vision, so I stepped directly in front of him.

He didn’t look up.

I squatted to be eye level with him, but he seemed to look right through me.

“Poppy.” I placed my hand on his knee.

He blinked and focused on my face. I smiled.

“Evelyn?”

My smile faltered at my mom’s name. I forced it back in place.

“No, Poppy. It’s me, Rebekah.”

“Rebekah?”

I nodded and blinked back traitorous tears.

“Where’s Evelyn?”

“Poppy, Mom—Evelyn—died a long time ago. Remember?” *Please remember, Poppy.*

He closed his eyes tight and leaned his head back. When he opened them again, resignation showed in their depths.

“I remember. How could I forget?” His fingers brushed my cheek. “And I could never forget you, my Rebekah Anne.”

Time was running out. Its tick, tock, tick, tock clanged in my ear.

Lisa, please hurry!

Luke

One would think I'd be nervous as I sat next to Lisa and waited for the call to go through, but I wasn't. There was a peace I couldn't explain about my decision, except to say that it was the peace of knowing I'd made the right choice. I would choose to love Becky. And with time, she'd love me in return. My pulse raced, but it was more from anticipation than anxiety.

"Becky?" Lisa smiled. "Hey, I was just calling to let you know The Isaac Project was a success."

Lisa's gaze caught mine, and her smile grew. This girl must have been a handful for her parents growing up. Sam was a lucky guy.

"He's perfect." She winked at me. Good thing I wasn't the blushing type.

"In fact, he's right here, so I'll go ahead and let you talk to him."

Lisa offered me the phone with a little nod of encouragement. There wasn't any script or past experience, personal or otherwise, to help me know what to say. One of Sam's corny Christian pickup lines wouldn't work in this situation. Although, truthfully, I didn't know how they had worked in any situation.

"Hey, Becky. My name is Luke Masterson." I ran a hand over my head. "How're you doing?" Was that what you said to the girl you've agreed to marry?

No chipper response. No "I'm fine, thank you, and how are you?" No nothing. Just dead silence returned my greeting. Rocky start.

I tried again. "How's your grandfather?"

"Umm...yeah...uh...hi. I'm hanging in there, and so is Poppy, thanks for asking. We both have our good days and bad days, but that's to be expected."

Her voice was like a river in autumn. The waters had since receded from the deluge of spring rains and snowmelt from warmer weather. Where the river had once playfully rolled over rocks and fearlessly leaped over clefts, it now trickled sedately on its course, more focused on its destination than the joy of the journey. Had her voice had always been like—like an autumn river? Or had it once contained the playfulness of spring before some jerk broke her heart?

"That's good to hear. I've been praying for you."

"Thank you."

This conversation was awkward at best. What else was I supposed to say? The dead space actual felt painful. Thankfully, I was saved by the voice on the other end of the line.

"Is what Lisa said true?" she asked with a hint of shyness. Her vulnerability stirred a protectiveness inside me. It was a good thing Becky's cheating ex-boyfriend wasn't there right then, because I would've been tempted to use his face as my next punching bag.

"If you'll have me, then I'd be proud to be your husband." I was a little shocked to discover how completely true that statement was. Not twenty-four hours earlier I'd been close to mocking the whole idea of an arranged marriage in the twenty-first century. Now there I was, the prospective groom of one.

Silence once again grew thick over the line. I dragged a hand across the back of my neck. We should've had this conversation over Skype instead of a regular phone call. Then I'd be able to see her reactions, her body language, and, well, *her.*

"Are you okay?" I asked gently.

"Oh yes. Yes, thank you. You have no idea what this means to me," she said, then paused. "I'm a little embarrassed about what I'm about to ask you."

A thread of trepidation snaked down my spine. This was a woman who'd asked her best friend to find her a husband. If what she wanted to ask me embarrassed her...well...there was no telling what it could be.

"I was visiting Poppy today and talked to Rita, she's one of the CNAs that takes care of him, and she told me he was starting a downward spiral. He hasn't been eating much and sleeps most of the day. I'm really worried he won't last much longer. It seems like he's just given up."

Her voice was shaky, and she took a steadying breath before continuing. "In light of that...and I hate to ask this at all...but...would you be willing...I mean, would it be possible if..."

"You need me there ASAP."

"If it's at all feasible." The river became a trickle as uncertainty cut off its flow.

"Let me talk to my boss, but I promise I'll be there as soon as I can." She didn't need to face this alone.

Lisa's wild gesturing caught my eye, as did the concerned look on her face.

"Uh, Becky, Lisa is over here waving her arms like she's trying to land a 747, so I'll hand the phone back over to her. It was nice talking to you." Lisa snagged the phone from my ear as I said good-bye.

Chapter Twelve

Luke

My weight rested on my forearms as I leaned against the dollhouse-sized butcher block island in my modest kitchen. The blank, black screen of my iPhone resting on the pale countertop mocked me. Ironic how I hadn't been nervous to talk to Becky, a complete stranger I'd committed to marry, but the thought of picking up that phone and calling my dad made my palms sweat.

Mom had taken the news of my upcoming nuptials fairly well. At least she tried to hide her cynicism. Dad, however, liked to lay on the sarcasm as thick as icing on a birthday cake.

I wiped my hands on my pants and gritted my teeth before picking up the phone and dialing his number.

"Hey, Dad, how's it going?"

"Eh, I've been better." His husky baritone voice sounded defeated. Maybe it wasn't a good time to give him what he'd consider bad news.

"What's wrong? Trouble at work?"

"No, work is good. It's Regina."

"Is she all right? Are the two of you okay?" Regina was Dad's third wife. After mom, he'd married a buxom Italian named Rosa. When that relationship went south, he'd moved to Nashville and found Regina, a wanna be country music singer.

"I don't know what happened. We used to have such passion. We'd kiss, and fireworks would go off, you know? But nowadays...I don't know...there isn't even a spark. No sizzle. I think we've flamed out." He sounded so resigned. Like there was nothing he could do about the situation but walk away.

See, that's what happens when you treat marriage like it's a package of fireworks. The fuel always burns out, and there's a long, dark night left to follow. I paced the length of my apartment. Truth be told, it was too small for pacing, but I needed to expel some of the nervous energy that talking to my old man had created.

"Have you tried rekindling it?" I asked, exasperated that he was going to give up on yet another marriage. "Even when a flame goes out, there are still hot coals. All you need is a little fuel, and you can have a roaring blaze again."

"I know you're a fireman and all, son, but relationships don't work like that."

"How would you know? You've never stuck around long enough to give it a try." The words were out of my mouth before I could stop them. Facing the far side of the narrow apartment, I let my head hang, my forehead resting on the sun-warmed glass of the sole window in the studio. Deep down I still carried some hurt over my dad leaving. We'd talked it through and had built a relationship in spite of the past, but it didn't erase the pain of growing up without a father when I needed him the most. Or the agony of watching my mom's heart break because her husband had decided he didn't love her anymore.

"That's not fair." My dad's voice boomed in my ear.

I pinched the bridge of my nose. "You're right. I'm sorry. That was uncalled for. It's just that you seem to fall in and out of love more times than a kid who has his shoelaces untied. Did you ever stop to consider that love is a choice you make every day?"

"When you get married, you can give me advice, all right?" he snapped.

I swallowed the lump of dread lodged in the back of my throat.

"Actually, Dad, that was one of the reasons I called. I'm getting married."

"Married?" The surprise in his voice was evident. "I didn't even know you were dating someone."

And here was the tricky part. "Well, I'm not...I wasn't...exactly."

Dad huffed into the phone, causing static. "What are you talking about? How are you getting married if you haven't...aren't...dating someone?"

"It's a rather long and complicated story," I said and proceeded to give him a condensed version, bracing myself.

He started to laugh. I'd been expecting a lecture or a tirade, not the uncontrollable chortles of a man who deemed himself God's gift to women.

"I'm sorry, son," he said when he was finally able to contain his mirth. "But it's never going to work. Marriages are hard enough when you start out already in love. Begin one with someone you don't even know, much less have no romantic feelings for, and it's doomed from the start. Trust me. I've been married three times."

"Let me get this straight—you're giving me your notice,

and you don't even have the decency to tell me why?" Chief's booming voice resonated across the desk separating us. If I'd been a rookie, I would've been tempted to cower like an abused puppy, but I'd been around long enough to know that Chief's bark was much worse than his bite. That, and it had never been in my nature to cower.

"It's personal, Chief."

"Personal," he mumbled under his breath as he shuffled around some paperwork. "Can you at least tell me where you're going?"

"California."

He snorted and leaned back in his chair, interlocking his fingers and resting his clasped hands over his ample belly. I never did understand how Chief could do the daily physical training with the rest of the crew and still have the pooch around his middle. Granted it was rock hard, and a man could probably break a hand if he ever attempted punching Chief in his gut, but it was still a curious phenomenon.

"I like you, Masterson. Have always liked you. And so I'm going to do something that I wouldn't do for just any man out there in the bay." Sitting back up, he rummaged through his papers again until he found a small ledger-type book. Opening it, he took out a memo pad and started writing. He offered me the small piece of paper. There was a name and number written on it.

"That's the name of a good friend of mine in California. He's a captain of a firehouse out there. Now, California's a big state, so I don't know if that will even be useful to you or not. And as you know, firefighters can't just make transfers, but you tell him I sent you, and he'll find a place for you."

"Thanks, Chief." I stood to leave.

"One more thing, Masterson. This personal thing you've got—is it urgent?"

"Fairly urgent, sir."

"Finish out the week, and I'll cover your shifts for the rest of the month."

I couldn't stop the smile that spread on my face, nor did I want to. Firmly gripping the chief's hand, I thanked him and walked out of his office. My mind reeled with all the things I would need to accomplish in a short amount of time. Number one on that list being a call to Becky to tell her the news.

First, though, I had to finish my shift. Most people thought firefighting was a glorious and heroic job. All the movies and TV shows portray it that way, anyway. But most of the stuff we did was pretty mundane. I didn't remember the last movie about firefighters I'd seen that showed a brother or sister in uniform bent over the toilet scrubbing urine stains from the porcelain or pushing a mop around the tiled floors of the kitchen area. We didn't have a maid to come in and do those chores. Every day we were assigned some kind of cleanup detail. We had to keep the station in top-notch shape.

Thankfully, I'd already done my housekeeping detail for the day. The common room was tidy, and the carpets sported that nice just-vacuumed pattern.

Grabbing a bottle of water from the fridge, I ambled over to the weight room. We also had physical training scheduled during each shift as well as time for studying. There were some at the station who were taking courses to be EMT certified, and others were working on different classes such as search and rescue, water rescue, and wildfire containment. We didn't want to be caught unprepared in any situation.

Richard and Betty were doing some reps with the free weights in the corner, so I decided to get some bench pressing in before someone else showed up and stole the bench.

I checked the weights on the bar and added twenty pounds on each side. Straddling the bench with my back to the bar, I slowly lowered myself down until my back was flat against the bench and the bar was horizontal to my body. Gripping the bar firmly with both hands, I lifted it off its holder and brought it down a hair's breadth above my chest. I raised the bar and weights fairly easily when I straightened my arms. This wasn't the max I could press, but I wanted to work on endurance with the number of reps, and my arms would feel the strain after a few sets. I was just starting to feel the burn in my muscles when the tones rang throughout the firehouse. I rushed to the bay, running straight into my turnout gear.

Rebekah

"Hi, Poppy, it's me, Rebekah." I held my grandfather's aged hand in my own. His fingers seemed to have gotten longer with each pound he lost, making his hands look like skin stretched loosely over bone.

Poppy's eyes were closed as he napped. His even breathing was accompanied by a whistling in his nose.

"I have some good news. I'm going to get married. Can you believe it?" I forced a laugh, but it came out strangled. "I know it's something you always wanted, so you have to hang on a little longer, you hear me? I'm not going to walk down the aisle without you by my side. His name is Luke Masterson, and he's a firefighter. I know you'll love him."

Whether I loved him or not wasn't important. The only thing that mattered was the man lying in the bed beside me.

"So you have to start eating better, you hear? You have to be strong and fight." My voice cracked, and I let the tears flow unchecked down my cheek. "Please fight, Poppy. I'm not ready to lose you." I bowed my head, sandwiching his hands between my own.

Moments later, a rustling of the covers brought my head up, and I caught Poppy's eyes watching me. Eyes that once lit with mischief and shined with life now stared back at me dull and listless. His other hand came up and cupped my cheek. I leaned into his touch.

"I love you, my Rebekah Anne." His voice barely carried, but a soft smile crinkled his eyes before they drifted closed once again.

Rebekah

That week had been both the longest and shortest of my entire life. Luke had called on Monday to tell me the news. I still couldn't believe his boss was actually letting him leave without the customary two weeks' notice. My stomach twisted with the looming arrival of the man who would soon become my husband. There could be no second-guessing, no turning back. I just needed to keep Poppy in the forefront of my mind. Let his image be the reminder of why I was doing this in the first place.

Thankfully, Luke's call had come while I was driving home from Grandview. Seeing Poppy's health decline tore me apart. Every time I left him, the sand in the hourglass of time siphoned to the bottom—I was running out of time.

When Luke said he could be in Meadowlark in little over a week, I wanted to cry with relief. At least initially. My anticipation that Poppy's wish was going to be fulfilled, that I wasn't going to be too late to do this last thing for him, gave way to a gnawing anxiety that drove me to the pharmacy for some over-the-counter antacids.

Too many thoughts plagued my mind. What if Poppy took a turn for the worse and Luke didn't make it in time? What if Poppy saw right through the ruse? What if Luke came all the way to California, took one look at me, and hightailed it back to the Midwest? What if he married me like he said he would and then came to regret his decision later? Which, let's face it, was very likely. What if I ended up falling in love with him and he didn't love me in return? What if I lived my entire life and never got the chance to fall in love because I'd married a complete stranger? What if he turned out to be a criminal, a robber, or a psychopathic killer?

The breath in my lungs reached up and wrapped its murderous fingers around my throat. Everything around me seemed to hyper-focus as my eyes widened in panic. The colors were more vibrant, the lines sharper. I couldn't take it all in. My head spun. I reached out and grabbed the top plank of the arena. Squeezing my eyes shut, I blocked out my surroundings, focusing instead on drawing in even breaths. A paper bag would've been handy.

My hands climbed down, plank after plank, until I was squatting, my head in between my knees. *In through the nose, out through the mouth.*

Slowly the tightness in my chest loosened, and my head stopped pretending it was a toy top.

No use getting yourself all worked up. Too many of those what ifs were out of my control anyway. And Lisa would have never approved someone who was a criminal, robber, or psychopathic murderer.

God has a plan for your life, Rebekah. Get it together. A plan that includes good things like prosperity and hope.

I had to believe that He was the one who planted the idea in my head in the first place. I considered again the story that had started this whole thing spiraling. It was comforting to know God had brought Isaac and Rebekah together. That the two strangers fell instantly in love when they met. If it happened once, it could happen again, right? Perhaps? Possibly? It was a fledgling hope, but I held on to it with a tenacious grip.

One thing Luke and I had going for us that Isaac and Rebekah didn't was the advantage of modern technology. Luke and I might have never met, but at least we'd had the opportunity to talk on the phone a few times. The conversations were always a little awkward, but it did allow me to get to know him somewhat. And every time we talked, it helped chip away at my fears. Although there was still that little annoying voice in the back corner of my mind. Didn't friends and family of serial killers always say they would never have thought the person was capable of such a thing? I immediately tried to squash that voice.

Luke had texted a picture of himself, and he didn't look like a criminal. Granted, I couldn't see much detail on the four-inch screen, but the man in the picture didn't have any resemblance to Timothy McVey or Jack- the- Ripper.

In fact, he looked rather nice. He wore a navy-blue T-shirt with a fire-station logo stamped over his heart. The muscles in his arms bulged against the restraint of the fabric, and I couldn't help the little smile that turned up my lips, thinking of all the hay bales arms like that could help me lift. His stormy gray-blue eyes were only intensified by the contrasting frame of his short, cropped dark hair and five o'clock shadow along his chin and jawline. A dimple in the right cheek unsuccessfully played hide-and-seek with the man's stubble.

After one glance at the picture, I knew I didn't have to worry about being attracted to the man who was going to be my husband. Any woman with a heartbeat and active brain waves would think he was good looking.

I was a little nervous about what he would think of me though. Would he find me as attractive as I found him? Lisa told me she'd shown him a picture of me, and I racked my brain to think which one that could have been. Hopefully it was at least a little flattering, although it couldn't have been too bad. After all, he agreed to marry me *after* he'd seen it and not before. That ruled out the photo from last year's pie-eating contest when my face was covered in blueberry pie. Thank goodness. No one needed to see *that* picture.

Luke told me to go ahead and make arrangements for the wedding, but I couldn't bring myself to do it yet. I wasn't going to back out of it. I couldn't. I loved Poppy too much to disappoint him. But I still wanted to give Luke the chance to change his mind after he met me. I didn't want to rope him into anything he didn't want to do, and the added pressure of booked venues and wedding details seemed a little like coercion to me. Depending on Poppy's health, a wedding at Grandview might become necessary, and that wouldn't take much to set up.

The words *set up* snapped me out of my musings, and I pushed off the rail of the arena. I'd always been susceptible to daydreaming, my mind going a thousand miles a minute. But I needed to get in gear and set up the arena for Faith's riding lesson. Tucking a couple of ground poles under each arm, I dragged the long pieces of wood across the sandy ground and placed them parallel to each other, spacing them a few feet apart.

Lady's barking, combined with a horse-induced raucous in the back pasture, drew my attention.

What was that all about?

Leaving the poles where they lay, I dashed across the arena and ducked under the fence. I wasn't sure what had caused the commotion, but it was better to check now than have an injured animal later.

The new mare, Miracle, was back there with some of the other horses so she could get the most opportunities to graze. I'd chosen some of the calmer horses hoping they wouldn't challenge her as a new member of the herd. If one of them decided to show her who was boss... I quickened my pace. The poor little thing had been through enough already.

Raising a hand to shield the sun's bright rays, I squinted at the field. My heart leapt to my throat when I recognized the glossy black coat, dished nose, and high, arched neck of a purebred Arabian.

What was he doing there?

I sprinted the remaining distance, hoping I wouldn't be too late to avoid disaster.

One of the mares grazing on the late summer grass was in heat. That wasn't supposed to be a problem, because the only stallion on the ranch, Artemis, was safely in his stall in the barn. Except he wasn't. He was standing right in front of me, nipping at the mare's rump and about to get a hoof in the face in return.

Huffing and puffing, I slid through the slits in the fence. If anything happened to Artemis, any little scratch marred his shiny black coat, I wouldn't hear the end of it from Mr. Lockhart. Artemis was the only full-paying boarder I had, and even though his owner could be extremely tiresome, I needed the money.

"Now, Artie," I crooned to the lovesick four-legged beast as I approached. I didn't want him to bolt once he knew my plans to separate him from his lady love. "How in the world did you get out here? C'mon boy. We need to get you back to the barn."

Artie didn't put up much of a fuss as I snapped the lead

rope on to his halter and led him away. He nickered as if his heart was breaking but faithfully plodded along by my side. Once he was safely returned to his stall, I checked him over to make sure he hadn't suffered any repercussions for his forward behavior toward the mare. I breathed a sigh of relief at the lack of evidence of his little escapade.

Securing the latch on the stallion's stall, I looked for clues. I had shut the door properly when I'd fed the horses that morning, so how did Artie get in with the other horses? It was a mystery. Artie wasn't an escape artist. I definitely couldn't see him jumping over the pasture fence to get in. As much as Mr. Lockhart thought Artie a king because of his bloodlines, he was a bit on the lazy side. Probably because of all the baby treatment he received from his owner.

Glancing down at the watch on my wrist, I skedaddled back to the arena. It would have to remain a mystery for now because I didn't have time to play detective. I had to finish setting up for Faith's lesson. She was scheduled to arrive any minute.

I rolled one of the large blue plastic barrels, which had been used in yesterday's session with Jessica, across the arena. A second barrel and a few more ground poles crisscrossed on top made a small makeshift jump. I couldn't wait to see Faith's reaction when she saw it. She'd been begging me for something other than simple ground poles. The girl had worked hard, and she was ready for a new challenge

When she first started taking lessons, it was because her mom had forced her. A year before she'd had her left leg amputated below the knee, and she'd become one very angry thirteen-year-old. Her mom had confided in me that I was her last hope.

After her first lesson, I doubted I could do anything to help her. She wasn't responding to me or the horse I'd paired her with. The next time she came out, I didn't even bring out a horse for her. In fact, I was already in the arena riding. I had a couple jumps set up and a few barrels. Samson and I flew over the jumps and raced around the barrels and finished off with a few impressive dressage moves just to show off a bit.

Then I rode Samson right in front of her and, without saying a word, slipped my feet out of the stirrups. I pulled the iron up and crossed them over the pommel, letting my legs dangle on the sides of my mount. I turned, and Samson and I went through the course again. When I came back around the second time, I'd asked Faith's mom to let me have a minute alone with her daughter. I told Faith that I knew she was probably feeling sorry for herself, but that it was her and not the loss of her leg that was holding her back. I told her that if riding horses was something she wanted to do, then it didn't matter if she had two legs, one leg, or no legs at all—I could teach her. She'd been riding with determination ever since.

What a change from the girl so dead set against liking horses that first day.

But what about Luke? I smacked my head with the palm of my hand and groaned. How could I have forgotten to ask him if he liked horses? Especially since he was about to come live on a ranch.

Chapter Fourteen

Luke

It was a good thing I wasn't claustrophobic, because my Jeep resembled a clown car. Except instead of being stuffed with crazily clad people wearing oversized shoes and bright-colored wigs, it was filled with every earthly possession I couldn't live without or buy when I reached California. The down side, besides being incredibly cramped, was I couldn't see out of any of the windows except my own and the windshield. Not exactly the safest way to travel halfway across the country.

"C'mon, c'mon, c'mon," I urged the vehicle in front of me. Okay, so I wasn't the epitome of patience, but it was a long drive, and I didn't want to be stuck behind this slowpoke.

I drove westbound along I-80 and had, up until that point, made pretty good progress. But now I was stuck behind Mr. Ed and his family, staring at a horse's rump in a trailer and crawling along the interstate at fifty-five miles per hour. This guy was in the left lane, and a semi occupied the right, so there was no possible way to pass. My verbal encouragement did nothing to speed Mr. Ed's driver along or relieve my agitation.

Surprisingly, the semi pulled ahead first. I switched lanes to pass and finally continued my trip at a rate other than a snail's pace.

My phone's GPS said the trip would take just under thirty-one hours, but if I'd had to travel behind that truck the whole time, it would have taken at least twice that long. Although I would have loved to take my time and see some of the interesting things in the states I was traveling through, I knew Becky was anxious that I get there as quickly as possible. And I admit that my own excitement was growing the closer I got.

Having driven nearly two days and fifteen hundred miles along I-80, I felt like celebrating when I finally came to my exit and the next leg of this long trip. Turning off onto US-93, I still had roughly another five hundred miles to go. I'd hoped to make it into town in a decent-enough hour to meet Becky that night, but it didn't look like I would make that deadline.

My phone rested in the cup holder to my right, and I reached to grab it. Tapping on Becky's name in my contact list and then putting the call on speaker, I let the phone rest on my thigh so I could keep both hands on the wheel. I preferred not to use my cell phone in the car, having been called to the scene of too many accidents caused by texting and driving, but there wasn't a good place to pull off.

The sound of ringing rose, and I glanced down at the screen. The call went straight to voice mail.

"Hey, Becky, it's Luke. I just got off I-80 and will be getting into town late tonight. I'll stop by a hotel and meet you at your place sometime tomorrow morning. Call and let me know if that doesn't work for you. Otherwise, I'll see you then."

Rebekah

I groaned. Luke would arrive in the morning, and that left me with two options. I could wake up super early to get all the morning chores done and still have enough time to take a shower and put on something a little more attractive than barn clothes, or I could go about my regular routine and risk the chance of being dressed in ripped jeans and possibly having hay in my hair for our first meeting.

With the two options laid out before me, my mind went into hyperdrive, arguing for both sides with equal ferocity. The second option was my usual look, and if he did go through with the plan and marry me, he'd need to get used to that. Still, I didn't want to give him any reasons to turn around and head back to Michigan. Why not look my best? However, the more logical part of me reasoned that he should see what he was getting into—who I was on a day-to-day basis.

I closed my eyes and sighed, my shoulders slumping. I had to be myself and go about my regular routine. I argued with myself that it would've been okay to put on some nice clothes and do my makeup and hair. I mean, if I were going on a date I would try my hardest to look nice and make a good first impression. But the reality was that nothing about this situation was normal, and this was much more than a date. I needed him to see me for who I was and to make his decision based on the facts.

The decision made, I turned down the covers and crawled into bed. I tried to turn off my mind and fall asleep. If only it were as easy as flipping a switch.

Mittens curled up on the pillow beside me and flicked her fluffy tail across my face. Sputtering against the hair in my mouth, I tucked her tail under her and gave her long soft fur a few strokes, eliciting a satisfied purr from the feline. My eyes grew heavy, and I finally fell asleep.

Morning came with it a bundle of nerves.

I stuck to my guns and put on an only slightly stained pair of jeans and a green John Deere tank top. As far as work clothes went, they were some of my nicer ones. As I strode toward the barn in the crisp morning air, I determined I would try to at least remain as clean as I possibly could.

The water sprayed from the hose and sloshed into the trough as I cast a furtive look over my shoulder toward the driveway. What time was Luke going to show up? My stomach was starting to jostle around more than a novice rider on a bucking bronco. The splash of water spilling over the edge of the large metal tub, soaking the top of my muck boots, yanked my attention back to the task at hand. I turned the water off and grabbed the handles of a nearby wheelbarrow. Maybe if I hurried, I could get everything finished before he arrived.

I measured out the extra feed for the horses that needed a few more pounds put on them and balanced the buckets on the handles of the wheelbarrow. Tossing in a square bale of hay in the bed, I pushed the one-wheeled lifesaver toward the pasture.

Daisy poked her head over the fence, and I reached up to scratch her along the white blaze between her eyes. She nudged her nose against my chest and sniffed around to see if I had any hidden treats on me. Lady barked from where she was laying in the shade under the tree, alerting me to a vehicle coming up the drive before I could hear the crunch of tires on the gravel. As I turned, Daisy let out a huge sneeze, and I found myself covered in wet, dirty horsey mucus.

Just great.

I didn't have time to run into the house. I had no other option than to meet Luke looking like a human Kleenex.

You wanted him to see the real you. This is your own fault, Rebekah.

Dipping my arms into the water trough, I rinsed off as

much of the goopy mess as I could and wiped my hands and forearms against my pant legs.

Perfect. Now my shirt has gunk all over it, my arms and hands are damp from trough water, and my pants are streaked from their experience as a hand towel. So much for staying clean. So much for first impressions.

Walking to the parked Jeep and the man stepping out of the vehicle, I pasted on a smile and wished I'd decided to look my nicest instead of a cowhand hobo. But there was no turning back now.

Lady had run ahead to meet our guest, who was now standing next to his Jeep. He looked even better than his picture had portrayed, especially since he was bending down, both hands scratching behind my dog's ears.

What I wouldn't have done for a clean shirt and a hairbrush right then. My hand itched to reach up and check to make sure there weren't any flyaways from my ponytail making me look like Medusa, but I stifled the urge. It would finish off my horrendous look anyway.

Luke straightened, a hand still on top of Lady's head. I sucked in a quick breath, and my stomach took flight as if it were one of the birds Lady loved to chase around the ranch.

Goodness, he's gorgeous.

His dimple winked at me behind a measure of black stubble that ran along his jaw and halfway up his cheeks. His eyes sparkled against bronzed skin that told of hours spent in the outdoors.

I licked my lips and tried to add moisture to a mouth that had suddenly gone dry. "Glad you made it safely," I said as I approached.

If my hands were dry and my shirt clean, I would've had to decide on some sort of gesture of greeting. Shake hands? Quick hug? Instead, I stood there awkwardly without even my dog to hide behind.

Luke grinned and looked completely at ease. "I'm glad to finally be out of that suitcase on wheels. It was a long drive."

I glanced to the parked Jeep beside him. It was packed to almost overflowing. I cringed at how much this man must have given up for me.

Stay on task, Becky. I cleared my throat. "Why don't I show you around the place? Then, if you're hungry, I'll take a quick shower, and we can go to the diner for an early lunch."

"Sounds good to me. I could use a break from sitting."

Lady bounded ahead as our official tour guide but was soon distracted by a squirrel spiraling up a nearby oak.

As we reached the pasture fence, Luke placed a sneaker-clad foot on the bottom rung. My eyes trailed the length of him. Nike running shoes, jeans, and an untucked white button-up shirt. The sleeves were rolled, exposing muscular forearms, and the top button was undone and had aviator glasses hooked to the fabric. Okay, so he wasn't the quintessential cowboy. He was missing the boots, the Wranglers, and the Stetson. But as he looked at me with one side of his mouth quirked in a grin and slate-blue eyes that rivaled a stormy day on the Pacific, I couldn't remember why any of those things were important.

I pinched myself on the leg to get my mind back on track. "In this pasture we have Samson, Dakota, Daisy, and Miracle."

Luke's laugh was hearty beside me. "I don't think I need to ask which is Samson."

I grinned and put two fingers in my mouth, blowing a shrill whistle. Samson perked up from where he was grazing, his ears turned forward and his head high. He still held himself with regality from his short stint as a racehorse. He trotted over to us, nickering and tossing his head.

"Good boy." I patted his shoulder and stroked the length

of his neck.

"Impressive." Luke's voice held a note of awe.

"He is rather remarkable, isn't he?" I didn't even try to hide my motherly pride for the equine.

"Him too."

Luke was looking down at me. Heat rose to my cheeks. He thought I was remarkable? Really? Ducking my head, we continued to the barn for the remainder of the introductions.

Mittens weaved in and out in a figure eight between Luke's legs as he stood in front of Artie's stall. The tabby meowed for attention and pressed her body against his shins. I scooped her up and tucked her under my arm.

"This is Mittens." Nodding toward the stall, I added, "And that is Artie. His real name is Artemis, but I call him Artie for short. I think it fits him better."

Luke reached out to pet Mittens, and I could feel the vibration of her satisfied purr against my arm.

"It's a really nice place you've got here, Becky."

I looked around, and my lips turned up in a satisfied smile. It was no Olympic training facility, but it was mine.

Luke's stomach rumbled, and, call it reflexes, I put a hand over my own midsection. Crusty dried snot met my touch. Gross. I needed to clean up and salvage what was left of a first impression before Luke decided to do a Julia Roberts impersonation and become a runaway groom.

"Let me jump in the shower real quick, and then we can get some lunch."

I'd debated whether taking him to the diner on the first day was a good idea or not. The simple fact was, I wasn't a world-renowned chef like Gordon Ramsey. Instead of a perfectly cooked beef Wellington, my culinary repertoire consisted of peanut butter and jelly sandwiches and pasta, and usually I could scramble eggs without managing to undercook them. My mortification of serving the man sandwiches fit for a kindergarten class outweighed my fear of anything the town gossips would say.

Stepping out of the shower, I chose a light-pink eyelet sundress with spaghetti straps to make up for the horrible first impression I must have given Luke. Instead of muck boots, I pulled on a nice pair of calf length brown embroidered cowgirl boots. Deftly, I French-braided my still damp hair and added a bit of mascara to my eyelashes and gloss to my lips.

"Ready?" I asked as I stepped out of my bedroom and into the main room of the house. His eyes roamed over me, and his lips twitched upward.

Please let that be a twitch of appreciation. I could feel my cheeks begin to warm in a blush at his gaze. Now it was beginning to feel like a first date.

The most important first date of my life.

When we pulled up to the diner, I was happy to find a lot of empty parking spaces.. Maybe there wouldn't be too many prying eyes and listening ears.

Luke was a perfect gentleman and walked around to open my door. As we approached the diner, another couple stepped out. My eyes locked on the tall man in a Stetson hat, and my heart froze in my chest. There stood James Anthony and the blond bimbo who had stolen him from me.

To his credit, James looked as startled as I felt.

"Uh, hi, Becky."

"James."

Luke looked at me and then back at James, and James looked at Luke and then back at me and the blond just looked bored as she picked at her nails. I wanted to melt into a puddle on the ground, do a magic trick and make myself disappear, or quickly invent a time machine and program it for a time and place that wasn't then and there. Anything to get out of that awkward setting.

"Who's this?" James jutted out his chin in Luke's direction. There was an edge to his voice that he no longer had the right to have. If I hadn't known any better, I'd have said he sounded jealous.

Luke stepped a little closer and placed a hand to the small of my back. The warmth of the contact was surprisingly calming, although by the way James's eyes widened, I think it had the opposite effect on him.

I sighed. This day was not going at all like I'd planned. The first impression I made was that of a human Kleenex, and now this. Even though it was the last thing I wanted to do, I introduced the two men—the one from my past to the one of my future.

"James, this is Luke Masterson."

"Her fiancé," Luke supplied.

I snapped my mouth shut as I tried to recover from Luke's pronouncement. In the truest sense of the word, Luke was my fiancé. He'd just driven two thousand miles to move to another state with the express purpose of marrying me, but I never thought I would hear him say it the first day we met...in public...to my ex-boyfriend...and even before we had a chance to talk.

The hand on my back curled around my waist, and Luke gently pulled me close to his side, tucking me under his shoulder.

James glared at Luke a second longer before stalking off, his new lady following in his wake.

"Come on. I'm starving," Luke said.

The slight pressure on my back prodded me through the diner doors. My legs automatically propelled me forward, while my mind was still paralyzed from Luke's proclamation. I didn't know why I was so surprised. I guess a part of me just figured that before all was said and done, he'd come to his senses and hightail it back to the Midwest. He seemed too normal, too good to be true, to marry a complete stranger—to marry me.

We were seated at a booth in the corner of the diner. Luke watched me from across the table. Nervous and completely embarrassed about the scene that had taken place out front, I tried to avoid eye contact at all costs.

As intent as I was about not looking at the man across from me, I totally missed the outstretched arm until my hand was engulfed in a larger one and gently drawn to rest in his in the middle of the table. The gesture was less of an intimate one as much as it was to gain my attention. It was effective. I found myself peering into gray-blue eyes that were earnest in their regard.

"I was serious about what I said."

My throat worked as I swallowed and bought time to think of something to say.

Wendy approached our table, and I didn't know if I should kiss her for saving me from my tongue-tied response or be upset with her for interrupting a conversation upon which my future hinged.

I attempted to extricate my hand from under Luke's, but the pressure increased. Wendy stared at our joined hands. I cringed. Should I try to remove my hand? No. That would just create more of scene. I left it where it was, cradled in his large, warm, capable palm. Besides, it felt kind of nice. My life had seemed like it was unraveling faster than a ball of yarn in a kitten's grasp ever since I'd learned Poppy's leukemia was back. The hand holding mine was a bit of an anchor that, at the very least, slowed the unraveling down.

"You guys ready to order?" Wendy's pen was poised over her pad of paper. Her lips smacked the gum rolling around in her mouth. Ah, such fine dining.

We gave Wendy our order, and she left with one last pointed glance at our hands still clasped atop the table.

Needing to gain some composure, I tugged my hand free and demurely placed it in my lap with the other.

"Listen," I said, "I want to apologize for what happened out there."

"There's nothing to apologize for."

"James and I, well, we broke up not that long ago and, well..."

"It's okay, Becky. Lisa told me all about it."

My relief over not having to explain further battled my embarrassment.

"But Becky," he continued, "what I told him was true too. I'm not going anywhere."

Even though that was exactly what I wanted to hear, my self-doubt took ahold of my voice.

"How can you say that—know that? We've only met an hour ago, and you hardly know anything about me. Once you get to know me more, you might change your mind."

"I won't change my mind."

"How do you know?"

He studied me a moment. "If someone were to ask you to define love, what would you say?"

What *would* I say? With everything that had happened recently, I wasn't sure I knew what love was anymore. "I guess I'd say that, on the basic level, love is a feeling you have for another person. But it's an extremely powerful feeling. It can pick you up and wash you away faster than an undertow at Monterey Bay. It's so powerful it can change the world. Or break a heart. Or make you do things you never thought you'd do." That was my experience, anyway.

Luke nodded his head as he considered my answer.

"You're right. But I also think love is more than just a strong feeling. Love is in the words we say and the things we do for others, but most importantly, love is the choice we make to say those words and do those things. You say that I hardly know you, but I know you well enough to know that you are capable of great love. The love you have for your grandfather is enough to put others to shame." His smile was gentle as he regarded me. "Before I ever came here, I made a decision, a commitment, and that's how I know I won't change my mind. Besides," a teasing quality crept into his voice, "I don't think the Rebekah in the Bible ever imagined returning to her father and brother back in Padan-Aram after meeting Isaac, and isn't she supposed to be my mentor?"

Wow. Was this guy for real? I didn't know guys like him, with mind frames like that, even existed. He sounded so certain. Like there was no question things would work out between us. But I had to ask one more time. "Are you sure?"

A mischievous glint entered Luke's eyes as he scooted out of the booth.

Oh no. What's he going to do?

Straight-faced, Luke stood before me. Then, as if time moved in slow motion, he descended until he was down on one knee. He took one of my hands in both of his.

"Rebekah Sawyer, will you marry me?"

Leaning forward so our faces were close, I whispered harshly, "What are you doing? Get up."

Not even trying to hide his grin he replied, "Not until you answer me "Get up. Everyone is staring." I looked around the diner, and sure enough, every eye was focused on the two of us.

His grin was cheeky, and his eyes danced. "Then you'd better say yes."

"Yes, yes. Are you happy now?" I tried to pull him off the floor.

"Ecstatic."

Chapter Fifteen

Luke

Some decisions in life are hard to make, and others are easy. What was I going to have for dinner? Pretty easy. Even if I got it wrong, the consequences weren't that dreadful. What car should I buy? A little more difficult decision, but one I could make by gathering facts on various makes and models. Leave a job that I love, a comfortable apartment, and all my friends and family to come to a state where I'd never been to marry a woman I'd never met was definitely in the hard category. But now that I was here and had met Becky, it didn't seem all that arduous. In fact, every minute I spent in her presence only confirmed that I'd made the right choice. And any doubts or second-guessing I might have had faded into the background.

That morning when I'd met that two-timing louse Becky had once called her boyfriend, it had taken all my self-restraint not to use him like one of the punching bags at the Bunker. Seeing him had awakened a protectiveness within me that I hadn't felt for a long time. In my line of work, I was used to protecting people physically. But this time I wanted to protect the woman in question emotionally. I could feel her slight tremble when I'd placed my hand to her back in silent support. So I'd tucked her in closer, trying to shield her as much as possible.

Now we were on our way to meet the famous Poppy. The man responsible for bringing me two thousand miles to a new home and for introducing me to a woman I had already begun to recognize as someone special.

We pulled up to a nice ranch-style house with an inviting front porch and rocking chairs swaying gently in the afternoon breeze. The grounds were well maintained and sported many different colors, sizes, and variety of flowers. If not for the Grandview Nursing Home sign out front, I would've thought this the residence of a young growing family.

As we walked up the steps and onto the porch, the screen door opened and slammed shut as a petite young Hispanic woman wearing pink scrubs came barreling out and nearly ran Becky down.

"I so glad you here." Her accent was thick in her distress.

"Calm down, Rita. What's wrong?" Becky grabbed the woman's forearms in an attempt to steady the...nurse?

"I just about call you. Mr. Sawyer...he..."

Rebekah bent her head down, staring into the woman's face.

"What is it, Rita? What about Mr. Sawyer?" Her voice was strained. A vein running along her temple throbbed.

"Ten minutes ago ambulance take him to hospital. His *corazon.*" She placed her hand across her chest.

"His heart," Becky whispered, stricken. Stepping around Rita, Becky rushed through the door, calling out for a Dr. Henshaw.

I gave Rita a reassuring smile but left her on the porch to follow Becky. I wished I knew my fiancée better. A few hours' acquaintance didn't tell me a twit about how to handle this situation. Did she need space during a crisis to figure things out, or did she want someone to be there with her so she didn't have to face it on her own?

When I caught up to Becky, she was talking to a droopy-eyed older gentleman in a white coat.

"He's being taken to Northern Samaritan Hospital up in Bishop. Now don't look so alarmed, my dear," the gray-haired doctor soothed. "It was a minor heart attack and he was in stable condition when the paramedics left here. I'm sure in a few days he'll be back with us."

As Becky turned, the fear in her eyes made me jump into action.

"Come on," I said and took the keys that had been dangling from her limp hand. "I'll drive."

I found the hospital's address on my iPhone and let its GPS guide me. It took nearly forty-five minutes, but to Becky I was sure it felt like a lifetime. She sat up completely straight, her body making a perfect ninety-degree angle. Her back didn't touch the backrest, and her knuckles were white from gripping the faded striped material on her side of the long bench seat. I reached over and covered the hand closest to me with my own, giving it an encouraging squeeze before returning both hands to the steering wheel.

I had barely put the truck in park before Becky flung herself out the door and barreled toward the entrance of the hospital. I reached across the long seat and punched down the lock mechanism on the passenger door before hopping out the driver's side and sprinting across the parking lot.

The automatic doors opened, and I could see Becky at the registration desk. Before I could reach her, she turned to the left and dashed down the hallway, stopping in front of the elevators. Over and over she pushed the little round button, now illuminated with an arrow pointing up.

Finally, the elevator dinged and the doors opened. We stepped inside and silently rode to the third floor.

When the doors opened again, Becky continued to rush down hallways, even managing to dodge a nurse pushing a patient in a wheelchair. At last we came to the room we were looking for, and Becky stepped inside.

I let her go in alone. I thought she might like some privacy with her grandfather. I wasn't sure what she had told him about me. We hadn't been able to discuss that yet, and I didn't want her to have to explain the presence of a strange man.

I meandered down the hall and found a small alcove with some chairs. They weren't the most comfortable, but it was a place to pass the time. I picked up a copy of *Time* magazine and flipped through its glossy pages.

It wasn't ten minutes later that Becky found me. The corner of her lower lip was sucked between her teeth.

"He wants to talk to you. Alone."

She looked so uncertain, so vulnerable. I stood and reached out my hand, squeezing her shoulder.

"It's going to be okay."

Lord, don't make me a liar.

Mr. Sawyer was lying on his hospital bed as I entered his room. At least three separate soft beeps sounded from triplet screens on the opposite side of his bed. An IV line with two small and one large medicine bag dripped in his vein. An oxygen mask covered his ashen face. With his eyes closed, he appeared to be resting, except I could see the effort it took to draw in each breath, could hear the wheeze as air entered and exited his lungs.

"So," he rasped, opening his eyes and focusing them directly on me. He lifted the oxygen mask to talk. "Rebekah Anne tells me you two are to be married."

"Yes, sir," I replied. "With your permission, that is."

He waved aside my comment and indicated a chair that had been scooted up close to his bed.

Taking a deep breath, he pushed aside his mask once again. I opened my mouth to tell him to save his strength, but the man had a stubborn set to his jaw. Even though I hadn't known Becky all that long, I was pretty sure she'd already tried to convince him of that very thing, to no avail.

"Do you love my granddaughter?" No beating around the bush with this man. He cut out the fat and went straight to the point.

"Yes, sir. I do."

I didn't want to deceive the old man, but there were many different types of love. It was true that I wasn't *in love* with his granddaughter. I had only known her a few hours, and I didn't believe in love at first sight or the notion of soul mates. But I did love her in the way God calls us to love all His children. And I truly believed that with time I could love her another way. The way a husband loved his wife. The way I was sure Mr. Sawyer meant by his question.

"And just how long have you known Rebekah?"

I couldn't hesitate. I couldn't look away. I had to answer him honestly.

"I first talked to her a couple of weeks ago on the phone, but today is the first time we've met."

Mr. Sawyer harrumphed and shook his head.

"I know what she is up to, that girl of mine. Sweet child. I should be cross at her and tell her to stop all these shenanigans right here and now, but I'm not going to do that. I know she is doing it all for me, a silly idea about my final wish, no doubt."

He pointed a finger at me. "You can't tell her I know what she is up to. I don't mean for you to keep it a secret forever—husbands and wives shouldn't have secrets from each other—

but just for a little bit. I want her to have this. This idea that she did this last big thing for me. Can you do that?"

"Yes, sir. I can."

"Good. Good boy. You know I wouldn't let her do this if I thought you weren't right for her. But I can tell. I can see it in you. You are going to be good for her."

I didn't say anything but prayed he was right.

"My Rebekah though, she can be a stubborn girl. She is independent, and that James fellow hurt her pretty badly. I'm going to let you in on a few things, you know, just to kind of give you a head start to her heart."

And he did. In the few minutes that followed, I learned more about the woman who was to become my wife than I'd ever learned about any girl that I had ever dated in the past. I learned about the devastating deaths of her parents. How her mother had loved the ballet, and because of that, Becky was drawn to anything in a tutu and ballet slippers. I learned that her favorite comfort food was a grilled cheese sandwich dipped in ketchup with a pickle on the side. It was something Poppy had always fixed her whenever she had a bad day growing up. I learned that no matter how many abused horses she took in, she cried over every one. And I learned where Mr. Sawyer had kept his daughter-in-law's wedding ring since her car accident.

Mr. Sawyer's strength was completely zapped by the time he finished speaking. I insisted he rest for a while, and this time he didn't object. By the time I stepped out the door, he was already sleeping soundly.

I was nearly pounced on the second my foot stepped over the threshold.

"Is he okay? What did he say? Does he want to see me?"

"He's fine," I assured her. "He's resting now."

Becky took a deep breath, and when she exhaled it seemed all her strength left with it. The stress of the day was taking its toll on her, and she was wilting quickly before my eyes.

I touched her elbow. "Let's go get some coffee."

She didn't object, and I led her to the hospital cafeteria. It wasn't until we were seated with steaming cups of surprisingly decent coffee that she seemed to find the words that had been bogging down her mind.

"When you were in with Poppy, the doctor came and talked to me in the hallway. It doesn't look good, Luke. He said Poppy's body is beginning to shut down and that..." Her voice cracked, and her face was beginning to develop red blotches from the onset of tears. "That I should start to make any last-minute arrangements."

She turned her head and looked out the window. I wanted to tell her it was okay to cry, that she didn't have to put on a brave front for me. When she turned toward me once again, there was a sort of pleading quality to her face. My heart broke for the woman across from me. How could someone elicit such strong emotions after only knowing her a few hours? My arms ached to hold her. To crush her to my chest and reassure her that everything would be okay.

"I know we just officially met, and I had wanted to give you more time, but it seems time is something I no longer have to give. If you're still willing—"

I looked at my watch. "The county courthouse is already closed for the day, but we can go first thing tomorrow and get a marriage license. I'm sure the hospital has a chaplain on staff who can marry us right here in your grandfather's room, and a nurse can act as a witness."

She smiled, and this time a tear seeped past her protective barrier.

"Thank you," she whispered.

We finished our coffees and headed back to Mr. Sawyer's room. It was understandable that Becky wanted to spend as much time with him as possible.

A hand on my forearm stopped me, and I turned in the long white hallway to face Becky once again.

"If you want, you can go back to my place for the night, but I think I'm going to stay here. I don't want to leave Poppy right now."

"I know Rebekah is the one I'm supposed to be imitating, but I'm not too manly to borrow from another woman in the Bible. In the words of Ruth, where you go, I go. Your family is my family. I wouldn't think of being anywhere else but here."

The harsh hospital lights reflected off her damp cheeks as she lifted up on her tiptoes and pressed a kiss to my bristly cheek.

"You're a good man, Luke Masterson," she said, her voice tight and strained. "A good man."

I wasn't so sure she was right about that or not, but this woman made me want to be better than I was.

Chapter Sixteen

Luke

Blinking a few times to rid the sleep from my eyes, I lifted my head and winced at the stiffness in my neck. The waiting room at the hospital was definitely not the most comfortable place on earth to sleep. The weight on my shoulder reminded me that every ache and pain was well worth it, however. Becky's dark-blond hair tickled my nose as she continued to lean against me, my shoulder her pillow. Was this the way it was going to be from now on? Would I wake every morning with this woman by my side? As I breathed in the sweet scent of her, my pulse quickened with the thought.

Becky stirred beside me. It was probably a good thing she was waking up. As much as I was enjoying her snuggled against me, I ached to stand and stretch some of the kinks out of my own stiff muscles. She lifted her head to reveal a bright-red circle marring her cheek where it had pressed against my shoulder.

"Morning," I said, restraining myself from cupping her smooth cheek and trying to erase the red mark with my thumb.

"Morning." She shook out her disheveled hair from an elastic band and refastened it in a ponytail.

"So I checked on my phone last night, and the courthouse's website said they open at nine this morning."

Becky nodded and looked down the hall toward the room Mr. Sawyer occupied.

"We both have to be present for the clerk's office to issue the license, but I double-checked, and there isn't a waiting period in Inyo County. We can get the license and be married today, no problem. After we go to the courthouse, I'll bring you back here so you can be with Poppy, and I'll go and take care of the rest. What do you say?"

Her head remained turned away from me as she stared down the hall. If I hadn't been standing so close, I would have thought she hadn't heard me at all. Then she slowly turned, eyes glistening with unshed tears. She took one of my hands in hers and gently squeezed. "You don't know how much this means to me." She whispered, her voice cracking with emotion.

This probably wasn't how she had imagined her wedding day when she'd dreamed about it as a girl. It wasn't what I'd imagined the few times I'd stopped to think about it over the years. A hospital room wasn't exactly a dream venue, and Becky would be missing the big white floofy gown all girls envisioned themselves wearing when they said "I do." I was sure she never thought she'd feel the need to keep thanking her groom for marrying her, either. But then, those were most likely the least of her worries at this point.

Becky checked on her grandfather, and I went to get us a couple cups of hot coffee. When she returned, she accepted the steaming liquid with a small smile. The strain of the last few days was showing in the dark circles under her eyes, even though she was attempting to put on a brave front.

We got to the courthouse just when it was opening, so

thankfully, we didn't have to wait in a long line. We stepped up to the counter and were greeted by Rainbow Brite herself. Except the rainbow was on her face—bright-red lipstick, pink circles of blush on her cheeks, and some sort of indigo-blue eye shadow. And the smile she directed at us was bright enough to rival the sun. I should have been happy for the cheerful demeanor of this woman, since most civil servants were anything but civil, but I was too shocked at the display before me to sift out gratefulness.

"And how may I help you this bright and cheery morning?" She beamed.

Trying to hide my amusement, I cleared my throat and swallowed the laughter that was brimming and threatening to spill out.

"We'd like to apply for a marriage license."

"Oh, well, isn't that divine! Two little lovebirds. I knew it the moment I saw you walk through that door. Gladys, I said to myself, if those two aren't in love and coming for a marriage license, then you ain't no wiser than a screen door on a submarine, I said. Yes, sir. You done got that twinkle in your eye. So when you two plannin' on tyin' the knot?"

I could sense Becky fidgeting nervously beside me. When I glanced over, her cheeks were warming into a becoming shade of pink. I tried once again to hide my smile. I didn't want her to get the impression I was enjoying her discomfort. Only, I guess I was. Not her discomfort really, but I did quite enjoy the color the blush brought to her face.

"Today," I answered as I pulled my gaze away from Becky and back toward the clerk. "We're planning on marrying today."

I didn't think the woman's eyes could have gotten any rounder or brighter, but I was wrong. Her red lips formed a perfect *O* before widening into a smile that almost had me reaching for my sunglasses.

"Oh, isn't that romantic," she gushed. "So in love you can't wait another day. You hear about that all the time over in Vegas, but folks around here are so practical, it takes them months to get hitched. Well, practical ain't romantic, I say." Then she placed her hands over her heart and squealed. Actually squealed. I thought she might do a little happy dance right there on the spot.

For the first time since stepping foot into the building, Becky spoke, or I should say, croaked. "The papers?"

"Ah, yes. The papers."

Turning her back to us, the clerk rummaged through a filing cabinet looking for the forms that would get us on our way and one step closer to our apparently oh-so-romantic nuptials.

"Here we go." She placed the documents in front of us. "Fill out this application and make sure you both sign it here." She indicated the lines by marking an *X* in front.

"Thank you." I took the clipboard, and Becky and I sat down in the waiting room, hunched over the papers and huddled together. It didn't take long to fill out the necessary questions, and then we were handing the forms back over to the grinning clerk.

Thankfully, she didn't give us any more flowery speeches on how romantic we were, but gave us knowing looks and a conspiratorial wink when handing back a few papers.

"These need to be signed by the person performing the ceremony and two witnesses. Then all you need to do is mail them back in, and it will all be finalized."

"Thank you so much," I said as I cupped Becky's elbow and steered her in the direction of the exit before we could be gushed over anymore.

With Becky back at the hospital with her grandfather, I made my way down the interstate toward Meadowlark. I had managed to pick up a couple of toothbrushes at a convenience store near the hospital for this morning, but there were a few things Becky needed from the house and I needed from my Jeep. All of her animals needed to be fed and watered as well. I also needed to swing by Grandview and find Becky's mother's ring.

I sighed. I wished there was something I could give her from myself to show her that I viewed this as a real wedding, a real marriage. That even though I'd only known her two days, I was committed to her and to this union. Most guys bought an engagement ring to signify their commitment, and I would have been more than happy to have done that, but I thought Becky would want her mother's ring.

What can I give her, Lord?

Even though this was her idea, there was an uncertainty in her eyes every time she looked at me. It was as if she was just waiting to see how long it was going to take for me to turn tail and run.

Fast food and gas station signs loomed ahead, and I glanced down at the gauges on the dashboard of Becky's truck. Driving across the country taught me one thing: always fill up when traveling through rural areas. The needle pointed more toward empty than full, so I put on the blinker and took the off-ramp. Sitting at the stop sign, I looked left and right, checking for oncoming traffic and a place to top off. I squinted past the Exxon sign to another with red letters. One with a heart as an apostrophe. A grin broke out across my face as I yanked the steering wheel left and pressed the gas pedal to the floor.

Visions of Becky from this morning filled my mind. I could see her in her cute but rumpled sundress that she had put on yesterday and slept in last night. I could pick up something fresh for her to wear while at her house. In fact, that was what I had planned on doing. But this was her wedding day. I couldn't give her a big church wedding with all her friends and family and all that other stuff that girls dream, but I could at least get her a dress.

Stepping into the store, I was immediately blinded by all the yards of white fabric that hung from the displays. Were the fabrics all different? Every woman would know the difference between that gauzy see-through material and that shiny, silky material, but my head was spinning. Not only did the dresses have different fabrics, they were all in different styles too.

"Can I help you?"

Boy, did I need it. "I'm looking for a dress."

Her lips curled up at the ends.

"A wedding dress," I amended.

Her eyes perused me from head to toe and back again.

"For my fiancée." Man, I guess you had to clarify in California.

"Ah, I see. And what size is your fiancée?"

Size? Oh boy. "Well, she's about this tall." I held my hand under my nose. "And about this big." I held my hands slightly apart, guessing at the size of Becky's waist.

"I see. And style?"

"Style?" I rubbed a hand over my short-cropped head.

She sighed, anchoring an impatient hand on her hip. "Was your fiancée interested in tea length or floor length? A-line, empire waist, mermaid? Tulle, satin, lace, silk?"

"Ummm..." This was going to be harder than I'd thought.

"It might be easier if your fiancée comes in and tries on a few different styles. Then she can decide what she likes and what fits her."

Yeah. Only that wouldn't work. I needed something

today. But how...Lisa. She'd know what Becky would like.

"Can you give me just a minute while I make a phone call?"

Without waiting for a reply, I whipped my phone out of my back pocket.

"Hello?" Lisa answered.

"Hi, Lisa. It's Luke."

"Oh, hey, Luke. I didn't expect to hear from you today. How's everything going?"

"Not so good, actually."

"Really? I was so sure Becky would love you."

Love me? I doubted Lisa meant that the way it sounded. "It's not Becky. It's Mr. Sawyer. He had a minor heart attack and is in the hospital. Becky wants to have the wedding today. She's afraid if we wait any longer, it will be too late."

"Oh no. I had no idea."

"Listen, Lisa, the reason I'm calling is because I'm standing in David's Bridal. I wanted Becky to at least have a nice dress for her wedding, but I have no idea what size she is or what styles she likes. Can you help?"

"Is there a salesperson there?"

I handed the phone to the saleslady, who was pretending she hadn't been listening but who was definitely looking at me much more tenderly than before.

"My fiancée's best friend is on the phone and might be able to answer all those questions you asked me."

She accepted the phone and without a by-your-leave walked off with my cell toward a rack of wedding gowns near the back.

I found a seat by the dressing rooms and waited, but not nearly as long as I'd expected. Soon the saleslady was back, a white garment bag draped across her arms.

I jumped to my feet. "Can I see it?"

"Tsk, tsk. The groom is not to see the wedding dress before the ceremony."

And so I dished out more money on one dress that I'd never seen than I would have spent on clothes for myself in a two-year period. And yet, despite my sticker shock, it would be worth it. I couldn't wait to see Becky's face when I gave it to her.

Or how she'd look in it.

Chapter Seventeen

Rebekah

"How could you do that to me?"

"Now don't scold a dying man, Rebekah Anne."

"You're no more dying than I am." Oh, how I wished that were true, but the evidence lay before me in that hospital bed. At least he was looking better and no longer required the use of an oxygen mask.

"Come here, sugar." Poppy patted an empty spot on the bed next to him. "Tell me about your fella."

I propped my hip on the mattress and took Poppy's hand in mine.

"What would you like to know?" I asked, trying to keep the trepidation out of my voice. I had no intention of telling Poppy a bold-faced lie, but I also didn't plan on telling him the complete truth. I was walking a fine line, which was why I'd hoped this conversation wouldn't take place.

"Where did you two meet?"

"Lisa introduced us a while back." As in, two weeks ago. Over the phone. Being vague was not lying.

"When did you know you were in love with him?"

I swallowed hard. Love? This would be a tricky one to answer. "Does anyone ever know the exact moment they fall in love?" Answering a question with a question seemed the safest bet.

"How did he propose?"

Finally, a question I could answer for real. I smiled. Even though Luke had just proposed yesterday, with all the events that took place since then, it felt like forever ago. When I'd first asked Lisa to find me an "Isaac," I thought having someone propose to me was something else I was giving up. But I was wrong.

"Well, he took me to a restaurant"—no reason to tell him it was the diner—"and in front of everyone"—about five people— "got down on one knee and asked me to marry him."

I caught Poppy staring at me, and the pressure on my hand increased.

"Are you happy, sweetheart? You sure this is what you want to do? You and James just broke up not that long ago."

I tried not to blink. Or twitch. Tried not to gulp down the saliva that was gathering in my mouth, or wipe away the sweat beginning to form on my palms. Nothing that would give me away. How could I tell him I wasn't sure? That I had only met Luke the day before, and even though I felt God's guidance, there was still a sinking sensation in the pit of my stomach? That my chest felt like it was in an ever-tightening vise, and I couldn't take a full breath? That I was scared spit-less, but I was doing it all because of him? For him.

I could never say any of that, so I plastered on what I hoped was a believable smile and a lovesick expression.

"I'm sure."

Poppy was once more resting, and I had just finished talking with the doctor as he was doing his rounds. He told me they were going to keep Poppy one more day for observation, but it looked like he was doing better. He assured me there wasn't anything they could do for him there at the hospital that they couldn't do for him back at Grandview.

As I was thanking the doctor, I noticed Rita strolling down the hallway toward me, a big grin stretched on her face. She held a stark white garment bag reverently in her hands. The bag was so long that Rita risked tripping on the edge that was trailing the ground.

"What are you doing here? What do you have?" I asked, my curiosity getting the better of me. She was still in her scrubs and appeared to have come straight from work at the nursing home.

"It your wedding dress." She stretched out the garment bag for me to take.

My wedding dress? Like an out-of-body experience, my arms reached out and took the bag. How did Rita have money to bring me a wedding dress? Was it a family dress? Wait. How did Rita know I was getting married today?

Moisture gathered in the corner of my eye, and I blinked it back. The kindness Rita was showing me, especially since we'd been friends for only a short amount of time, humbled me. My throat tightened with emotion. I had resigned myself to the fact that my wedding would not have even a hint of anything traditional. No white dress, no bouquet of wedding flowers, no wedding cake to cut and feed to my groom, no first dance. Rita had changed that. I would be able to wear a gown and at least look like a real bride.

I realized I had been staring at the gift in my arms and had not yet expressed my deepest gratitude. Lifting my head, I looked Rita in the eyes and opened my mouth to try to articulate how much this meant to me.

"It from Mr. Luke," she said before any sound passed my lips. "He ask me give to you."

"Luke?" I struggled to wrap my mind around that thought. "Luke asked you to give this to me?"

"Yes." She said the word on a sigh, and I could tell she was halfway in love with my groom already.

"He say he get chaplain and to meet in Mr. Sawyer room in *veinte minutos*." Shaking her head, she clarified, "Twenty minutes."

"Twenty minutes?" I yelped.

"I help." She slung off her backpack and withdrew two bags. One looked like a makeup case, and the other held a brush and some pins and other hair accessories.

Luke

Standing in Mr. Sawyer's hospital room, I chatted with the chaplain. Some of my married friends told me about how nervous they were as they stood at the front of the church and waited for their brides to walk through the door and down the aisle, but I didn't have a single butterfly in my stomach. All I felt was peace and anticipation—as if I had just won a great prize in a raffle I hadn't even realized I'd entered.

I tried to give the chaplain my full attention as he droned on and on about the theology of marriage starting at creation with Adam and Eve. Normally I would have thought the conversation stimulating, but there were other things on my mind. I kept checking the door, waiting for the first glimpse of Becky.

I wasn't disappointed.

When the door began to open, a hush fell in the room, and every eye turned. Rita came in first, her smile stretching from ear to ear. A rustling of fabric, a flash of white, and a picture of bridal perfection graced our presence. I had no idea if the dress was A-frame, dynasty, or whatever other style the saleslady said. All I knew was the dress was nice, but the woman wearing it took my breath away.

Rebekah

I felt like a princess. I had been astounded that Luke would know my size and pick out such a beautiful gown. The bodice, with its built-in corset, hugged my body, while the skirt, with its many yards of material, flowed out from my hips in a bell shape. Rita had curled my hair into loose ringlets and attached a single flower to the side of my head. She'd thrust a bouquet of flowers into my hand, telling me that they too were from Luke. Looking in the bathroom mirror, my breath caught. I was a bride, and I was about to get married!

My pulse raced as Rita opened the door. Would Luke like what he saw? In my attempt to keep my hands from shaking, I might have squeezed the stems of the bouquet a little hard. Would he think I was pretty in his beautiful gift?

Taking a steadying breath, I stepped through the door after Rita. My gaze shifted nervously between the three men and one nurse who occupied the room besides Rita and me. Like a magnet, my focus was drawn to Luke. Everyone else faded. My groom stood tall and proud. The broad shoulders that I was sure had carried their fair share of people out of burning buildings cut a fine figure in his white buttoned-up shirt. Perhaps those shoulders would carry me through my own emotional emergency. His gaze never wavered, and his eyes darkened. My breath caught at the intensity of his gaze. Instead of shuttering his manly desire and admiration, he was completely open, as if he wanted me to see what he was thinking.

In place of the wedding march, I walked toward my

groom to the cadence of the *beep, beep, beep* of the monitor registering Poppy's heartbeat. It was the best sound in the world. Better than a string quartet any day. The sound meant the man who raised me was still living and breathing.

"You look absolutely beautiful Rebekah Anne." Poppy's words stole my attention from Luke, and I turned to face my grandfather. Moisture had formed in his eyes. His hand was shaking as he held it out to me. "You look just like your mama."

Pressing a kiss to Poppy's saggy cheek, I blinked rapidly against the threat of tears. No use ruining all of Rita's hard work by having my mascara run.

As we began the ceremony, the sound of my own heartbeat and the beeping of the monitors were all I could hear, even though I could see the lips of the hospital chaplain moving. Luke reached out and grasped my shoulder. He let his fingertips trail down the length of my arm in a featherlight touch before clasping my hand and bringing it up waist high.

"I, Luke Masterson, take you, Rebekah Sawyer, to be my wife, to have and to hold from this day forward, for better or for worse, for richer, for poorer, in sickness and in health, to love and to cherish, from this day forward until death do us part."

From his other hand, he produced a ring and began to slip it on my finger. I couldn't pull my eyes away from the circle of white gold as it slowly descended down my finger toward my knuckle. My mother's ring. I remembered sitting on Poppy's lap as a child, and he'd let me try the ring on. He'd tell me all about my parents and how, someday, when I met the man God had chosen for me, it would be mine. I hadn't seen that ring in I didn't know how many years. I wasn't even sure where Poppy had kept it. But there it was. Perched on my finger. I didn't bother trying to stem the tears this time. I let them flow freely as I looked first at Poppy and then at Luke, mouthing *thank you* to them both for this gift.

"I, Rebekah Sawyer..." My voice quivered. Luke's focus stayed on me, and I felt we were having a conversation with just our eyes. I began to lift my hand to wipe away a stray tear, but before my hand was barely raised, Luke's was already there. The pad of his thumb was rough on my skin, but the gentleness with which he wiped away the moisture moved me.

"I now pronounce you husband and wife. You may kiss your bride."

His gaze, which until that moment had held mine, shifted to my lips. His eyes narrowed, and his large hands wrapped around my waist and gently tugged me closer to him. I placed my hands on his chest to steady myself and could feel his heartbeat through his shirt. Was it just my imagination, or was it beating rather quickly? My own breath was becoming more rapid and shallow by the second, straining against the formfitting bodice of the dress.

His lips hovered above mine a second before descending in agonizing slowness. The kiss was chaste and sweet, full of tenderness and promise...but not a hint of passion. I tried not to feel disappointed when his mouth left mine. Luke looked me in the eye once more before pressing his lips to my forehead and pulling me even closer, crushing me in a hug and pinning my arms between us. I could feel his lips once more as he kissed the top of my head.

Once Luke released me, congratulations were had all around, and the papers were signed to make our union final and binding.

"And what is a celebration without a cake?" Luke asked as he pulled out a small sheet cake decorated with pink and purple flowers made out of frosting from the serving cart one of the nurses had wheeled in.

"I do believe," he said as he cut the cake, "that the tradition is for the bride and groom to feed each other. What do you say, Becky?"

He handed me a plate. Picking up the piece of cake, I daintily held it up in front of his face. He opened his mouth but didn't even bother to look at the cake as I brought it closer. I tried to look as sweet and innocent as I could while his teeth sunk into the fluffy cake. Just when he had almost bitten off a piece, I propelled the sweet treat up and smeared it over his face. Giggling, I retreated to the other side of Poppy's bed before Luke could retaliate.

Fragments of cake and frosting rained down from Luke's square jaw. Grabbing a napkin, he swiped at the sugary mess that had painted him like a rodeo clown.

"Just wait your turn," he warned.

"Ah-ah." I shook my head. "I've been feeding myself since infancy, and I'll continue to do so, thank you very much."

"Hmmm...This is not the end, little wife."

The title sent shivers down my spine.

"Rebekah, can you come here a moment?" Poppy asked from his perched position on the bed. His eyes were twinkling once more, and if it weren't for the surroundings, I would have thought he was back to his old self before the leukemia came back.

"What is it, Poppy?"

"Closer, dear."

He must have a secret to share with me.

Boy was I mistaken. For a man who was supposedly weak from a recent heart attack, he was surely quick as he brought his plate of cake that he had been holding up and—*splat*—shoved it in my face. I couldn't have been more shocked. The room erupted in laughter, but my mouth hung open in surprise. I turned my face to Poppy and couldn't help laughing out loud at his look of mock innocence. Giving him a cakey kiss, I accepted the napkin Luke held out and wiped away the mess before it got all over my dress.

Luke met me by the trash can and took the napkin from my hand.

He pointed to my right ear. "You missed a spot."

"Here?" I asked as I tried to wipe away a spot I couldn't see.

"Let me get it for you."

I tilted my head to the side, angling it so that Luke had a better view. Instead of using the napkin in his hand to wipe up the mess, his head lowered. I could feel his warm breath against my skin. Before I could react, the lobe of my ear was in his mouth, his teeth taking tiny nibbles.

My stomach summersaulted, and my knees trembled as the strength went out of them. Every nerve of my body stood at attention. Gooseflesh showed on my arms. When I didn't think I could stand another second, Luke stood up straight and smirked at me.

"All clean."

Chapter Eighteen

Rebekah

Poppy was recovering, at least from the effects of the heart attack, and was in much better spirits as well. He had the nursing staff laughing at all of his corn[illegible] and had licked his dinner plate clean.

I chose to think about these things and these things only. I would *not* feel anxious. I would *not* worry. I would only celebrate this day and my grandfather.

No matter how many times I told myself this, I couldn't help the uneasiness that mounted with every mile we drove closer to home. Even though Luke was now my husband, he was still practically a stranger—albeit a very attractive stranger. I wasn't sure what he was expecting from me, and I was too embarrassed to ask.

Luke had given me a real wedding with a dress and flowers and a cake. Things most girls dreamed of. Did he expect a real wedding night? That was the only part of the wedding most men cared about anyway, wasn't it? I wanted to give him something to show him how much I appreciated everything he had done for me, but could I really do...that? Could I give myself to someone I had just met and who I didn't even love yet? The Rebekah of the Bible comforted Isaac in that way, but just the thought of it terrified me.

"I don't think I've ever seen a whole pasture of horses lying down at one time," Luke said from the passenger's seat as soon as we turned into the driveway.

I looked to the pasture, and sure enough, four bulging bellies rose ominously from the ground.

"Something's not right." Throwing the truck into park, I jumped from the cab and raced to the field.

Dakota was the closest, and I slid to my knees beside her. Resting my head on her stomach, I listened for any sounds in the gut. Not a gurgle or a groan met my ear. Frantically I stumbled to Dakota's head. Taking her muzzle in my hands, I lifted her upper lip and looked at her gums. A healthy horse's gums are a nice pink color, but Dakota's looked quite pale.

Samson, a few feet away from me, started to roll. Daisy stood up and pawed at the ground.

No, no, no. This can't be happening.

I hadn't even realized Luke was there until I felt his hand on my shoulder. "What can I do to help?"

"Go to the barn and get four lead ropes. They're hanging from a peg in the tack room. We have to get these horses up and on their feet." Samson had already been rolling, and that was not a good sign. All the symptoms pointed toward colic, and rolling was the last thing I wanted the horses to do. Samson was only trying to alleviate the pain in his abdomen, but rolling could cause him to twist a gut.

Luke ran back with the ropes in hand.

"What's wrong with them?" he asked.

"Looks like colic. What did you feed them this morning?"

"Just what you told me to."

None of this added up. The horses' normal feed wouldn't

cause them to colic.

"I'm not sure why they're sick, but they are, and we have to do everything we can to save them."

His forehead creased as he frowned. "Is it that serious?"

"It can be deadly." I clipped the lead rope to Samson's halter and tugged to get him to start walking.

Luke placed his hand on my arm as the large horse took one step forward. "Tell me what to do, and I'll do it."

"In the barn there is a small organizer hanging from a peg in the tack room." My words came out clipped as I alternately pulled, pushed, and cajoled Samson to keep moving. "In one of the slots on the organizer, you should see a few white syringes marked Banamine. Grab one for each horse."

Luke turned and raced back to the barn. Now that Samson was at least on his feet, I left him to work on Daisy. She was the last horse still lying on the ground. Trying to get a nine-hundred-pound animal to stand up when she didn't want to was an impossible task, but I refused to give up. Sweat beaded on my upper lip and dripped from my hairline. No matter how much I tugged and coaxed and pleaded, Daisy barely raised her head.

Leaving her nearly broke my heart, but the other horses needed to start moving, and they weren't going to do that without my help.

Luke returned, his hands full with large plastic syringes. I grabbed the medical supplies and uncapped the first dose. Dakota was the closest. Her head skimmed the ground, and it looked like she was about to lie down again. I pulled up on her halter, straining against the dead weight. Luke went around to the other side and helped lift. The white paste left the syringe and made it into the corner of Dakota's mouth, the mare's tongue thrusting in and out. I wasn't sure if the Banamine tasted good or not, but I didn't care. It would hopefully save the horses' lives.

"Should we call a vet?" Luke asked. His eyes reflected concern as he braced the weight of Dakota's head on his shoulder.

"I'd love to, but there's no way I'd be able to afford that kind of bill." I patted Dakota's neck before moving on to the next horse.

We dosed all the horses. Luke and I began to pace the pasture with a lead rope in each hand, a horse on either side. As dust clung to my Wranglers and sweat stained my pink camo top, I felt anything but the beautiful princess Luke's dress had transformed me into. My fairytale clock had struck midnight, the magic fading and the real world coming back in to focus.

The sky turned more dark than light as our wedding day came to a close. The barn had lights, but unfortunately the pasture did not. Our vigil would have to continue by the light of God's creation on the fourth day.

As I made my way farther down the field, I began to notice bits of leftover bright-green hay strewn about the ground.

What's this doing here? I feed the horses grass hay, not alfalfa.

Bending down, I grabbed a bit of the mysterious stalks and leaves and brought it up to my nose. Sniffing, I nearly choked from the strong musty scent permeating the dried alfalfa. How did moldy alfalfa hay end up in my pasture?

Samson stopped walking on my right, and I turned to give him a pat of encouragement. I nearly jumped for joy when I spotted his tail held high and at an angle. The smell coming from his rear, which would normally wrinkle my nose, smelled better than a perfume shop in Paris.

"Praise God," I breathed.

Luke walked up beside me from the other direction, one

brow quirked as he pointed to Samson's backside. "This is a good thing?" Luke asked.

"Yes." I grinned. "It means the horse's intestines are no longer blocked and he's out of immediate danger. The release of gas is a good sign as well."

It took a few more hours and who knew how many miles before I was convinced all the horses were out of danger. By that time, I was tired and dirty and wanted nothing more than a shower and my bed.

Luke

I wasn't sure if it was the optimist in me, believing that every gray cloud had a silver lining, but I couldn't help feeling just a little satisfied with how the night had gone. Granted, I wasn't glad Becky's horses had been sick. She was still worried about them, and rightly so. But I took pleasure in the fact that Becky and I were able to work together so well, even under the stress of a small crisis.

I could tell something had been bothering her the closer we got to home. I was about to broach the subject, when I noticed the horses. I had my suspicions as to what was on her mind, but I wanted to ask her about it. A marriage needs to be based on trust and communication. I didn't want her to be afraid to talk to me if something was bothering her. I knew it was all going to take some time and adjustments on both of our parts, but I was confident it was going to work out in the end.

Yawning, I stretched out on the couch. I would only close my eyes a moment. I didn't want to go to sleep without talking to Becky first. If my guess was right, she was worried about the physical side of married life. I wanted to reassure her that I wouldn't force myself on her in any way. When we came together, I wanted it to be what it was meant to be—an expression of our love.

That didn't mean I wasn't going to woo my wife, however. I smiled to myself as I remembered the shocked look she gave me when I "helped" her get the cake off her ear. She needed to know that even though our relationship was new, it was in no way going to have a platonic foundation. I found her desirable, and I wanted her to know it. James had shaken something deep within her, and it was going to take some time and care to heal those wounds.

"Luke?" The sound barely reached my ears. Had I only imagined it?

I strained to listen.

"Luke?" A little louder this time. Becky was definitely calling me, although her voice sounded timid and unsure.

Becky had been in the bathroom taking a shower, but I couldn't hear the water running anymore.

I moved through her bedroom to the bath and stood in front of the door. "Becky?"

"I, uh, I forgot a towel."

Her voice dripped with embarrassment. I could just imagine her there, water sliding down her creamy skin, biting her lip trying to decide what to do. Hmmm...better not dwell on that picture for too long.

I shook my head to dislodge the image. "Where are they? I'll get you one."

"The bottom half of the pantry in the kitchen serves as a linen closet."

This house really was tiny. The one bedroom would make sleeping arrangements a little uncomfortable, but I was willing to sleep on the couch—even if my legs hung over the edge by at least a foot. Grabbing one of the two towels from the shelf, I went once more through Becky's room to stand in front of the bathroom door. The layout of the house was a bit awkward.

I tapped on the door before opening it. A wet arm reached

out from behind the shower curtain. That was it. Just an arm with an open palm ready to receive the towel. I was tempted to stand there until her head popped around the curtain too, but decided to have mercy on her in her embarrassment instead of indulging my own mischievousness. I settled for allowing our hands to graze in the transfer of the towel. Her arm trembled slightly, whether from the chilly air on her wet body or from my touch, I wasn't sure.

I'd noticed an extra set of sheets and a blanket in the pantry/linen closet. Sometimes actions spoke louder than words. If I went ahead and made up a bed on the couch, then maybe Becky would see that I respected her and would never ask her for something she wasn't ready to give.

I was just shaking the blanket out over the couch when Becky came out. She wore baggy sweatpants and a plain black T-shirt. Her hair was still damp and her skin glowed from a good scrubbing. She looked absolutely adorable.

Becky stilled when she saw the couch and my obvious plans to use it as a bed. One emotion crossed her face followed immediately by a second before it took on a look of neutrality. As if she hadn't a care in the world, her emotions were hidden behind a lovely mask.

"I thought I'd sleep out on the couch."

Becky nodded, though her eyes refused to meet mine.

The weight of frustration pushed down on me. I'd hoped Becky would trust me enough to share what was on her mind, but it didn't look like that was going to happen.

Sitting down on the couch, I patted the spot next to me. The stiffness of her spine and the way she held herself rigid when she sat belied the look of nonchalance she was trying so hard to plaster on her face. Taking her hand in mine, I interlocked our fingers and began tracing small circles on the back her hand with my thumb. We sat like that for some time.

The small motion of my thumb was the only movement in the room. Lady's intermittent snoring from where she slept in the corner the only sound. I let the silence stretch until I felt Becky start to slowly relax next to me.

"Becky," I said quietly, gently. "What do you want out of this marriage?"

She jerked a little, stunned, I thought, but she still allowed me to hold her hand. She glanced at me for a split second and then cast her eyes around the room with a weak laugh. She fidgeted, cleared her throat, and then shrugged. "To be honest, I didn't really give it much thought. I was too consumed with trying to find someone who would just marry me for Poppy's sake that I didn't really think of anything else."

I nodded. "Can I tell you what I want out of this marriage?"

Becky looked at me, her bottom lip held prisoner between her teeth.

"I want a real marriage and everything that goes with it." The hand in mine twitched, but I continued. "I want to be able to work beside you on a common goal. I want to be able to encourage you on the road to fulfilling your dreams, and I want you to encourage me with mine." I gave a self-deprecating chuckle. "Of course, we'll need to know what each other's dreams are for that to happen."

Standing, I began to pace in front of the couch where Becky sat. I pulled a hand along the back of my neck. "I want to be able to come home from a stressful shift at work and hold you in my arms and know that everything is going to be okay. If you are hurting or having a hard time, I want to know that you trust me enough to come to me and let me comfort you. I even want us to argue, and then I want us to make up so I can show you that, even if we disagree, I will always love you."

Shifting on the couch once again, I faced Becky more fully.

I took both of her hands in mine.

"Now let me tell you what I don't want." I waited for her eyes to meet mine before I continued. "I don't want to have to guess about what is going through that pretty little head of yours. I don't want walls put up between us because of misunderstandings due to lack of communication. I don't want you to think of me as a stranger anymore—I'm your husband."

Becky looked away. I crooked a finger under her chin, raising her face until she once more looked me in the eye. "I don't want you to be afraid of me in any way, or think that I mean to take advantage of you. That's what this is about." I gestured to the blankets on the couch.

Becky didn't say anything but fidgeted with her hands. I wanted to have mercy on her. She was obviously uncomfortable and somewhat embarrassed. But the subject was too important.

"I noticed that you were getting a bit, well, nervous, when we were coming back from the hospital and I was waiting for you tell me what was on your mind. I figured it had something to do with the sleeping arrangements. Was I right?"

Becky nodded once.

"I thought so. Look, I'm not going to lie to you. I find you desirable, and I will probably have to take my fair share of cold showers." I grinned at her to lighten the tension. "But I won't force myself on you. The act of lovemaking is just that—love. When the love between us blossoms, then we can consider showing each other that affection in a physical way."

I nudged Becky in the shoulder. "What do you say?"

She laughed lightly. "I don't know what to say." She turned her big eyes on me. "Thank you."

Taking her face in my hands, I tipped her head down and pressed a kiss to her forehead.

"Go get some sleep. It's been a long day."

Becky walked toward the bedroom, her hips swaying. I gulped and forced my eyes up. I'd meant every word I'd said to her, but it might prove harder than I'd originally thought. The door clicked shut. I shook my head and chuckled. If my teenaged self were there, I'd owe him a big apology. Never in my wildest dreams had I thought I'd be spending my wedding night sleeping on a couch...alone. And yet I was pretty sure reality was going to turn out better than anything I could have ever dreamed up.

Chapter Nineteen

Rebekah

The morning sun filtered through sheer curtains hanging in front of the window opposite my bed. I swung my legs over the side and sat on the edge, head in hands. Coffee. I needed some, and fast. It would evict the fog clouding my mind. Maybe then I could form a coherent thought, even plan out my day.

I stood and padded into the next room, tunnel vision and a one-track mind making me oblivious to my surroundings. Sweet elixir of life, I cradled a warm cup in my hands. My vision widened, and my eyes snagged on the neatly folded sheets and blankets tucked in the corner of the couch.

My breath hitched, and I looked around. How could I have been such a ninny? Had I really forgotten, even for a moment, everything that had happened? Where was Luke? I looked down at the dark-brown liquid sloshing in my mug. My shaking hands and jumbled nerves were an accident waiting to happen. I set the cup on the counter.

If it wasn't for the proof right before my eyes, I'd think yesterday was some sort of surreal out-of-body experience. I looked at my left hand. My mother's ring sparkled, and I slid my thumb along the underside of the band. Married. Not a concept I could easily wrap my head around. Where was that husband of mine anyway? There wasn't exactly space in my small house to hide a man of his stature.

My stomach grumbled. Hide-and-seek would have to wait. I needed some breakfast.

As I made my way over to the cupboard to grab the Raisin Bran, I noticed a note waiting for me on the table. I chewed on my bottom lip. Did I want to read it? Maybe he had come to his senses and hightailed it back to the Midwest. Who could blame him really? Baby steps brought me closer to the folded paper. A deep breath and I picked it up.

> *Becky,*
>
> *I have to go in and report at the fire station this morning. I meant to tell you last night, but it slipped my mind with all the other excitement. I should be home tonight, but if something comes up, I'll call you. I hope you have a great day!*
>
> *Love,*
> *Luke*

The note was nothing special really—just telling me where he was and when he'd be back. But even so, it sent my brain flying in all directions. Why did he sign it "Love, Luke"? Did he sign all his letters that way? Was I reading more into it than he meant to put there, or did he really mean love? Impossible. We'd only known each other for two days. His voice gonged through my head: "I don't want you to think of me as a stranger anymore—I'm your husband."

Of course, both were true.

He was a stranger.

But he was also my husband.

I massaged my temples. Somehow I was going to have to start training my brain to think of him as only my husband and not as a stranger.

Lord, I am confused and not just a little scared. I thought I knew what I was doing, but I had only planned on getting *married and made no plans on* being *married.*

I paused in my prayers, hoping for some response. Nothing. Wouldn't it be handy if God sent e-mails? With a sigh, I pushed off the table and strode out the door, Lady ever faithful by my side. I might have been confused in my relationships, but I was confident with my horses, and they needed my attention right now.

A quick check assured me that all the horses that had been out at pasture yesterday were still on their feet and appeared to be recovering nicely. I didn't waste any time starting the morning chores and mixed all the horses' feed with the finesse of someone who had done it hundreds of times before. Which I had. Being the prince that Artie was, he took up more of my time than any of the others, but even he didn't detain me too long.

With the feeding done, I was free to finally head out to the pasture and investigate a little more. There was no way what I'd told Luke to feed the horses the day before would have caused them to colic. Plus, the remnants of moldy hay had been a mystery. I only fed my horses hay in the winter when the grass wasn't as plentiful, and I would never have moldy hay kept on my property. As a precaution, Luke and I had moved the horses into the south pasture last night.

Opening the gate, Lady darted through, and I followed at a more reasonable pace, pushing a wheelbarrow with a rake inside. Even at a distance, I could see a few mounds of hay along the back fence line. Thankfully, the horses hadn't eaten all of it, or I might have been hiring a backhoe to dig a few graves this morning.

The sun hadn't even made it to the peak of its ascent before I was, for the second time that day, asking myself questions that I had no answers for.

Who would throw moldy hay into my pasture? Did he or she mean to just scare me, or did the person really mean to kill my horses?

I couldn't think of a single person who would do something like that, much less have a reason for doing it. No matter who it was that did it, or why, the fact remained unchanged that every single strand of hay needed to be removed from the pasture. Raking the putrid stuff into a pile, I bent down and gathered as much as I could in my arms before dropping it into the wheelbarrow.

It was like hugging a porcupine. The strands poked into the tender flesh of my skin and left a residue that had me itching and wishing for a shower. Unfortunately, a shower was nowhere in my immediate future. As soon as I scooped up the remainder of the offending hay and picked up the handles of the wheelbarrow to push it out of the pasture, Mrs. Steinbeck's spotless red Prius pulled into the driveway.

She stepped out in pristine black slacks and stiletto heels. Her designer jacket hugged her curves and accentuated her every attribute. It didn't matter how ridiculous it was that she stepped foot on a ranch in four-inch heels—a surefire way to break an ankle—the sight of her refinement instantly made me feel like a frump. Lifting my hand, I waved until she saw me, then I pushed the wheelbarrow through the gate. Leaving it there, I ambled over to Mrs. Steinbeck. The force of her glare and the tension emanating from her person slowed my steps.

"What a pleasant surprise to see you today, Mrs.

Steinbeck." I forced friendliness into my voice, although the wariness welling inside nearly choked out any amiability.

"Is it true?" she demanded.

A piece of hay on my shoulder caught in my peripheral vision, and I lifted my left hand to brush it away. Before I could ask Mrs. Steinbeck what in the world she was talking about, she reached out and grabbed my hand faster than a viper striking at its prey.

"It is true." Accusation seethed from every word as she inspected my mother's ring on my finger.

To say I was speechless would be an understatement. Mrs. Steinbeck had never shown any personal interest in my life. Our relationship was purely professional, and I couldn't imagine why that had changed. And why the change came with such a negative reaction.

She dropped my hand as if stung and crossed her delicate arms. "I can't believe you got married. The little mishap with James just happened. You didn't even give him time to come to his senses. He would have, you know. He loves you very much."

This conversation was something out of a dream. No, a nightmare.

"James? He cheated on me, Mrs. Steinbeck. He made his decision long before I did." I hated the fact that just thinking about it brought a pang to my chest.

She waved her hand as if swatting at a pesky fly. "A little misjudgment is all. Every man's head is turned by a pretty face and feminine figure. It's our job to turn our men's heads back again." Pivoting her weight back to give herself a better view, she tilted her head and let her eyes roam over me from the top of my hair to the tip of my toes and back again. "You, my dear, could do a lot better in that department."

My hands balled into fists so tight I could feel my nails

biting into my palms. Even so, I tried not to let Mrs. Steinbeck see how her remark had cut me. If I'd been thinking a little more clearly and a little less emotionally, I might have actually felt sorry for the woman. I might have seen the real reason behind the designer clothes and perfectly arranged hair. All I saw was red.

"Why do you even care, Mrs. Steinbeck?" I ground out the words in the most even tone I could muster.

"James is my cousin, and you broke his heart."

"*I* broke *his* heart?" My voice rose, and Lady trotted over to my side to comfort me in my obvious distress.

"Yes. And family comes first. From now on, Jessica and I will go someplace else for her hippotherapy sessions. I'm sure you understand."

Without another word, she got in her car and drove away.

Hours later, I still fumed. No longer able to ignore the protests of my hungry stomach, I'd come into the house to find something to eat. The pantry and countertops took the brunt of my foul mood as I slammed down a jar of peanut butter and used more force than necessary to close the pantry door.

Lady darted from her typical napping place and ran barking to the door. A sharp reprimand coated my tongue as the front door opened.

"Honey, I'm home."

The sing-song male voice reached my ears a second before the smell of Chinese takeout tickled my nose. The spicy chilies of a good Szechuan sauce would match my mood perfectly.

"I hope you like Chinese food."

Luke sauntered up behind me, bent down, and placed a very quick kiss on my cheek. At least I thought his lips touched my skin. It was so feathery light he could have just kissed the air near my cheek. It didn't really matter either way. I wasn't in the mood to play June Cleaver and the happily-in-love married couple.

"How was your day?" Luke removed the takeout containers from the plastic bag.

"Fine." I returned the peanut butter to the pantry, careful not to let the door smack shut. Although, I wasn't sure why I bothered.

The crinkling of plastic stopped, and I could feel the full force of Luke's appraisal. "From my very limited experience, when a woman says she's 'fine,' that means she's anything but fine."

I ground my teeth. "I said I'm fine."

Luke stood in front of me, but I refused to look up at him. I was trying to put a lid on my anger, and if I looked up, it just might boil over. Of course, Luke had no idea that he might get burned. He crooked a finger under my chin, gently lifting until I was forced to look in his eyes.

"I heard what you said, but I'm going to ask you again anyway. How was your day?"

My eyes narrowed, and I jerked my head away from his touch. Stalking over to the food, I finished taking the rest of the containers out of the plastic bag, each one landing with a thud on the counter.

"I thought we agreed to communicate. That I wouldn't have to guess what you were thinking." Luke's patient voice held no condemnation, which only infuriated me more.

Swinging around to face him, I let my words fly like poisoned darts. "We didn't agree. You told me what you wanted. Well, I'm sorry to have to be the one to tell you, but we don't always get what we want."

I regretted my words the second the left my mouth, but

there was no taking them back.

Pain flashed in his eyes as the words hit their mark. "I'm going to the barn." I turned, not wanting to look at his hurt-filled eyes. "Don't wait up for me."

I stayed in the barn until every last visage of fury drained from my body. Everyone always said life wasn't fair. Boy, were they ever right. James cheating on me certainly wasn't fair. I snorted. There was no way Mrs. Steinbeck blaming me and punishing me for it even remotely came close to being fair. A heavy weight sunk in my gut, and I hung my head. Was it fair that I'd taken out all my anger and frustration on a man who didn't deserve it? My throat worked as I swallowed a lump the size of gold rush nugget. I needed to apologize.

Had the dirt walk between the barn and the house turned to quicksand? My legs felt heavy as I trudged up the path, the small cottage looming before me. I paused in front of the front door and took a deep breath. Big-girl words. That was what I needed if this marriage was going to work. I turned the knob and walked in.

Luke sat on the couch with his Bible open in front of him. He looked at me, the soft light of the floor lamp casting shadows across his face.

I swallowed hard. "I wasn't sure if you'd still be awake."

The lines around his mouth softened. He picked up his Bible and read, "Do not let the sun go down on your anger." His voice was quiet and controlled, but his jaw ticked. Was he clenching and unclenching his teeth? He must be more upset than he was letting on.

"But you weren't angry. I was."

He gave me a small, sad smile. "That's where you're wrong. I was angry at whoever or whatever it was that had you so worked up. Very angry, actually. And more than a little perturbed at you for trying to pick a fight with me instead of just telling me what was wrong."

I hung my head. "I'm sorry. I shouldn't have come at you like that. I just had a bad day and took it out on you, and that wasn't right or fair."

"Ready to talk about it?"

With a sigh, I lowered myself onto the couch beside him. "How much of my job do you understand?"

Luke looked puzzled. "You board horses and give riding lessons, right?"

"Yes, but I also work with people who use horses as therapy. The professional term for it is hippotherapy. I was working with a physical therapist, Mrs. Steinbeck, to help a little girl named Jessica who has cerebral palsy. Well, Mrs. Steinbeck paid me a visit today. Come to find out, she is James's cousin."

"James, your ex-boyfriend?"

"The very same. In essence, I was canned because apparently it was my fault that James's eyes wandered to another woman, and Mrs. Steinbeck must remain loyal to family."

Luke's mouth hung open, and his eyes refused to blink. I couldn't help but laugh.

"Yup," I said. "That was pretty much my initial reaction as well. Until I got so mad I only saw red."

"You never know what the future holds. Six months ago, did you ever imagine being married to another man besides James?"

"Point taken."

Silence descended upon the small space, and I picked at the cuticle of my thumb with my fingernail. What did the future hold? Every aspect of my life was a question mark. I glanced at Luke out of the corner of my eye. Would there be a happily ever after for us?

He caught me staring, and I cleared my throat, looking at my hands. What had we been talking about again? Oh, right. Mrs. Steinbeck, Jessica, and my dreams of a therapy ranch being squashed like a bug. My shoulders slumped. "The sad part, though, is that Jessica is going to be devastated. I have no doubt Mrs. Steinbeck will find another horse handler to work with, but Jessica had a special relationship with one of my horses."

Luke covered my hands with one of his own. "Who's to say that relationship has to end?"

His touch was warm and the callouses on his palm rough. "What do you mean?"

"Mrs. Steinbeck may not be coming back here to have her sessions, but you could tell Jessica she is welcome to come without Mrs. Steinbeck to spend time or ride her special horse."

I felt my first genuine smile of the whole day blossom, and I looked up into his eyes. "Luke, I'm so happy, I could kiss you."

One side of his mouth lifted in a grin. "Well, who's stopping you, woman?"

Heat surged to my cheeks, and I looked away from his teasing eyes. My stomach churned like a dryer drum. Just the mention of kissing, and I was a mess. Great reaction.

My eyes flicked back to his face, to his mouth stretched over white teeth. What *was* stopping me? He'd kissed me yesterday at the ceremony, but that had been short and sweet. If I leaned forward, invited him in, what would his kiss be like today?

Luke stood and walked to the kitchen. My window of opportunity slammed shut in my face. He took a glass from the cupboard and filled it from the tap.

"Want some?" he asked.

I shook my head.

He drained his cup, set it in the sink, and then came back and sat next to me again, his arm stretched over the back of the sofa. Such a casual gesture. Did he not feel nervous energy zinging through his body like I did?

I bolted to me feet. "Want to see something?"

His eyebrows rose, but he leaned forward. "Sure."

I grabbed my keys from the hook by the door. Luke followed and shut the door behind us.

"So where are we going?" he asked as he buckled his seatbelt.

My shoulders began to relax, and my lips tilted in a smile. "One of my favorite places."

Luke settled into his seat, and the silence that filled the cab was comfortable. The high beams from my truck illuminated the road ahead of us. No one else was out on the small back-country road.

"So, what was one of your favorite places back home?" I asked.

He thought a moment before answering. "Lake Michigan. I know it's not the ocean or anything, but I used to pretend it was when I was a boy. Standing on sandy beaches and looking out over the water as far as your eye can see." He chuckled. "My cousin and I would see who would jump in first each year. One year he waded out waist deep through a filmy layer of ice. Crazy, if you ask me."

"Have you ever seen the ocean then?"

"I've been to the Atlantic a few times. It's weird how warm the water is though. Like bath water." He shook his head. "Lake Michigan never gets that warm. Not even in July or August."

"The coast is a few hours away. I've never been to any of the Great Lakes, but I imagine the Pacific is like them—frigid."

I shivered just thinking about it.

Luke peered out the window as I turned on yet another switchback. "So where are we going exactly?"

I didn't answer but drove the truck into a pull-off and put it in park.

I looked at him and grinned and then slid out of the cab and closed the door with a thud. Luke met me at the back of the truck as I let the tailgate down and hopped on, my legs dangling. I patted the spot next to me and then laid back. The bed of the truck dipped under his weight.

Millions of stars dotted the night sky. I took in a deep breath and let it out slowly.

Hello, God.

Heat melted the frigidness of the night air along my left side, making me all too aware of the body next to mine, but the nervous ball didn't return to my stomach.

"This is my favorite place," I said, my eyes never straying from the celestial masterpiece illuminated above us.

"I can see why." Luke's voice held awed appreciation.

"When I'm here...I don't know...I just experience this special connection with God. I feel small compared to the vastness of the universe, but instead of that making me feel insignificant, I feel treasured." I turn my head to look at him. "Does that make any sense?"

His eyes looked into mine. "Like God must think you're special because even though He created all of this, He still cares what happens to you and wants to be a part of your life?"

"Yeah." He got it. Warmth spread from my center.

I turned my gaze back to the stars. Luke shifted, and the back of his hand grazed mine. My stomach lurched. Awareness tickled my skin, and I bit my lip.

I snuck a look at Luke out of the corner of my eye. Husband, not stranger.

My heart thundered in my chest. Then why was I reacting to him like a hormone-dazed teenager? It was now or never. I swallowed hard and skimmed a finger over his hand and hooked it around one of his fingers. His hand moved away, and my heart plummeted. Maybe I had just imagined the attraction, the connection. I balled my hand in a fist as rejection lumped in my throat.

Luke's arm crossed over mine and his calloused fingers coaxed mine from their curled position. My breath hitched as his fingers interlaced with my own. His thumb slowly stroked the back of my hand in small circles. The breath I had been holding whooshed out on a contented sigh.

I laid my cheek against his shoulder. "So what made you decide to become a firefighter?"

"Most boys dream of being a firefighter at some point in their childhood." I could hear the smile in his voice. "To hear my mother tell it, I was obsessed. Firefighter themed birthdays were requested every year for a while, and I think there was about a year period when I was two or three that I insisted on only wearing my fireman costume, hat and all. I guess you can say I never grew out of the phase."

"Cute."

"I am, aren't I?"

I rolled my eyes but couldn't help the grin that spread on my face. The grin turned into a yawn, and I brought my free hand up to cover it.

"Tired?" Luke asked.

My eyelids were starting to get heavy, but the moment was too perfect to interrupt. "Let's just stay a little while longer."

His arm rose like a gate opening, welcoming and inviting me in. I scooted closer and rested my head in the crook where his shoulder and chest met. His arm came down and wrapped around me.

The day might have been crummy, but could there be a more perfect night?

Chapter Twenty

Luke

"Please don't tell me you're a Niners fan." I groaned.

Becky looked adorable in her football jersey with her hair pulled back in ribbons. Too bad she was wearing the wrong team colors.

"What? You don't like football?" She said the words like they were impossible to comprehend. Which, of course, they were.

"I'm an American male with a pulse. Of course I like football," I growled.

"Then what's the problem?"

"Problem is you're a Niners fan."

"I don't see why that's a problem. They are the greatest team in the NFL. The only reason that would be a problem would be if..." She blanched. "Oh no. Don't tell me you're a Rams fan."

"Blue and gold all the way."

Becky sat down hard, and the look on her face was so comical I had to laugh. One would have thought I'd told her something earth shattering by the way her mouth hung open in shock and her eyes flitted back and forth. I could almost see her brain trying to catch up and categorize the new information.

"That's okay," I said reassuringly, allowing a hint of team rival condescension in my voice. "I'll forgive your lapse of judgment."

Her head snapped up at that. "*My* lapse of judgment? My team is going to crush yours in today's game."

I snorted a laugh. "We'll ram you back all the way to when your team was actually a challenge to play against."

Becky glared at me, and I thought the carpet might catch on fire from the sparks in that look alone. I smothered a chuckle. The woman was downright adorable when riled. I didn't really take the team rivalry to heart, but it was more than evident that she did. And with great passion too. What would it be like if she turned even an ounce of it on me? My heart tapped a little harder. Better put that thought away for another day.

"If you're so sure your team is the best, then why don't we have ourselves a little wager?" Becky challenged.

"What did you have in mind?"

A little smirk played on her lips. "If the Niners win, then every Sunday for the rest of the season you have to wear a Kaepernick jersey." She looked smug.

"Okay," I agreed. "But *when* the Rams win, you'll have to wear their jersey for the rest of the season. I'll even let you choose the player."

Her eyes narrowed. "You're on." Then she turned on her heel, head held high. Walking toward the door, she only stopped long enough to grab a rain jacket and put on a pair of muck boots. It was an unusually rainy day for mid-September, but thankfully, our plans were to spend the day inside watching the game at Grandview with Mr. Sawyer.

About a half an hour later, Becky reentered the house, shaking off the water that clung to her slicker. When she turned around from hanging the jacket on the peg by the door, her hands were shaking, and she refused to look at me.

"What? Afraid your team is going to lose?" I goaded.

Her chin trembled as her eyes briefly met mine. She gave a small shake of her head.

Maybe I was taking this a little too far. Sports fans can be a little touchy. If she was getting this worked up, maybe I had better back off. I was just about to apologize, when Becky breezed past me and scooped up the keys that had been lying on the table.

"Ready to go?" she asked without looking back at me.

Not waiting for a response, she dashed out the door and ran to the truck, trying to dodge the falling raindrops. I followed at a more sedate pace. I'd seen an episode of a show on the Discovery Channel where these two guys conducted an experiment to see if a person would get more wet running in the rain or walking. Surprisingly, they found that a person actually became wetter when running in the rain than just walking.

Climbing into the truck, I buckled my seat belt, and the noisy diesel engine revved to life. Between the noise and the vibration the truck made, it's no wonder Lady fell asleep every time Becky let her ride in the cab.

"So why the Rams?" Becky took her eyes off the road momentarily to ask the question. "I would've figured you'd be a Lions or a Bears fan, coming from Michigan."

"My dad was originally from Saint Louis and went to their first game when they transferred there. When he packed up all his stuff and moved to Michigan, he took his love for the Rams with him. It was only natural that he bestowed that love to me.

Call it a sports inheritance."

"Hmmm..." She still wasn't happy. Was this really that big of a deal to her?

We made it to Grandview just in time for kickoff. Becky sat on the edge of the couch next to Mr. Sawyer, who definitely looked more comfortable as he lounged against the back cushions. Becky's focus was intense as she stared at the TV, its reflection casting a glow on her eager face. I could barely make out the "go, go, go" she muttered under her breath as Kaepernick threw it long and deep, her body rising off the couch as the spiraling ball rose in the air. Unfortunately for Becky and the 49ers, the intended receiver couldn't quite shake the man-to-man coverage, and the ball was batted harmlessly to the turf.

"No!" Becky sank back down to the couch, deflated. "C'mon, guys!"

My lips twitched in a smile. While I was happy for the great defensive play from my team, I found watching Becky even more entertaining than the game.

"I see that smile, Luke Masterson. Just don't get too cocky over there. This is only the first half, and we're only down by a field goal."

I held up my hands but did nothing to hide my broadening grin.

The game was pretty much a deadlock after that. Neither team was able to move the ball much, nor put any more points on the board. The game clock read fifty-nine seconds left in the game, and the Rams had possession of the ball. Becky was tense. She had the edge of her jersey between her thumb and index finger, and she was rubbing the fabric. It didn't look like she would get the chance to wear that jersey for the rest of the season. I kind of felt bad for her, but a bet was a bet.

"Yes!" Becky shouted at the TV as she leaped off the

couch. “Run!”

Wait. What? Didn’t we have the ball? Quickly, I looked back to the screen only to see Eric Reid, the Niners safety, running down the field. Thankfully, Rams tight end Jared Cook pushed him out of bounds before he scored a touchdown.

My mouth hung open. What happened? We had the game in the bag. Instant replay showed Sam Bradford’s mistake as he hurled the ball toward a receiver trapped in double coverage. The ball was picked out of the air by Reid in a game-changing interception.

The game clock now read thirty-three seconds with the 49ers lining up at the Rams seven-yard line. With both teams in formation, the 49ers center hiked the ball, and the Rams blitzed, forcing Kaepernick out of the pocket and scrambling. With no receivers open and hulky linebackers charging him, the 49ers quarterback had two choices—throw the ball away or tuck it in close and run it himself. With the left side of the field conveniently open, the athletic quarterback lengthened his stride and sprinted to the orange pylon and the end zone. Once his feet crossed the white painted line indicating the end zone, he quickly slid to the ground to avoid a tackle and possible injury.

“Touchdown!” Both Becky and Mr. Sawyer yelled as they gave each other a high-five.

Now it was the Rams turn to be down by three. And if the Niners made the extra point, they’d be down by four. With less than twenty-five seconds left on the clock, they might as well have been down by a hundred. There was no way they would come back after that.

“Ah, don’t look so dejected.” Becky came over and patted my shoulder. The gleam of victory in her eyes contradicted the comforting action. “You’re going to look really good in red and gold."

"Okay, rub it in. Have your fun."

"Look on the bright side," Mr. Sawyer supplied from his seat. "At least we aren't Packers fans and Becky's not making you wear a cheese head all season." He laughed until the shaking of his shoulders was no longer from mirth but a dry, hacking cough.

"Help me get him back to bed, will ya?" Becky nodded her head in Mr. Sawyer's direction.

Becky brought over a wheelchair, and I slid one arm around Mr. Sawyer's shoulders and the other under his knees. My heart dropped at his light weight. I glanced at Becky and tried to block her view as I placed her grandfather in the wheelchair. She was still riding a high from a team victory. She didn't need a reminder of the present reality.

Once Mr. Sawyer was comfortably in bed, we climbed back into her truck to head home. Home. I rolled the word around in my mind. When had Becky's house become home? It felt good.

"So you ready to trade in your blue for crimson? Join a winning team?" Becky glanced at me with a cheeky grin before returning her focus to the road.

"I'm not a fair-weather fan. Win or lose, I'm in it for the long haul." I looked over and inspected her profile. A becoming blush tinged her cheeks. She'd caught my double entendre.

"I'm a size large, by the way."

"Excuse me?" Her voice squeaked.

"The bet. I guess my new Sunday uniform will be sporting Kaepernick's name on the back."

The rumble of the truck died as Becky killed the engine. As we walked toward the house, I wrapped my hand around her small one. She looked up at me, and I winked. I opened the door and let Becky walk through. The door closed behind me, and Becky's rain jacket fell to the ground. A crumpled piece of paper tumbled out of the pocket. What was that? I bent to pick up the paper, and Becky lunged at me.

"I got it!"

Too late. I'd already seen what was written on the note, and my heart iced over faster than the shores of Lake Michigan in December.

Chapter Twenty-One

Rebekah

"It's not what you think."

"And what is it that I think?" Luke's jaw pulsated.

"It's nothing, Luke." I reached out to touch his arm, but he took a half step back. "There's no reason to get so upset."

"No reason?" He waved the paper in my face. "Becky, have you even read this note?"

"Of course I've read it." And it scared me to death, but there was no way I was going to tell him that.

"Obviously you haven't if you think it's nothing. Let me refresh your memory. 'Horse thieves should be lynched.' Lynched, Becky. And you think it's nothing?"

"It's probably just teenagers out for a good laugh. I've never stolen anything in my life, much less a horse."

The tension radiating off Luke could be picked up by a Geiger counter. His arms were crossed over his chest, and he was regarding me with a look that made me want to go hide behind the couch.

"Were you even going to tell me about it?"

The question sounded more like an accusation.

My first instinct was to say, yes, of course, as soon as we got home. But it was a lie, and I could feel my own defenses rise in the face of his disapproval.

"No, I wasn't going to tell you, because it's nothing." I crossed my arms and scowled. "Just a silly little prank by some bored teenagers."

If Luke had been a cartoon, his face would have been beet red and steam would have been coming out of his ears. As it was, his nostrils flared and his jaw ticked. I waited for the explosion.

"Well, that's just fine, little miss independence." Sarcasm and anger mixed in his voice. "You just keep your little secrets and keep telling yourself it's you against the world. As a matter of fact, I have a secret of my own. But, unlike you, I was planning on telling you mine. I was waiting for the right time, but, like they say, there's no time like the present." He practically stomped the two short steps to the table, reached in his back pocket, and withdrew an envelope and threw it on the table. Without a word, he turned and stormed out of the house, slamming the door in his wake.

I sunk onto the couch and blew out the breath I didn't know I'd been holding. That hadn't gone well at all. Honestly, I wasn't even sure why Luke was in such a huff. Granted, when I'd found the note on top of the feed bins that morning, it had scared me too, but I truly believed what I'd told Luke. It was no big deal. Just some prank. I wasn't in any real danger. And it wasn't his problem anyway.

My justifications finished, I allowed my curiosity to take over. Inching over to the edge of the couch, I took the envelope off the table. Turning it over, I opened the flap, and two tickets fell onto the floor. I leaned over and picked them up, reading them as I settled back into the couch again, tucking my legs underneath me.

My hand flew to my mouth.

Luke had bought tickets to the Sacramento Ballet Company's production of *Swan Lake*. How did he know about my obsession with ballet? I looked to the door, willing him to open it and step through. I wanted to apologize for our misunderstanding and say thank you for such a gift. Ballet tickets. I was finally going to go see a real ballet.

But Luke didn't step through the doorway. I guess he needed more time to cool off. In the meantime, I had horses to feed. Maybe I'd run across him on my way to the barn.

I scanned the yard between the house and barn, but the only living things I saw were Lady and the squirrel she'd chased up a tree. The horses trotted to the fence line and nickered at me.

"Hey, ol' boy," I crooned as I stroked Samson on his broad forehead. He shoved my chest with his nose.

"Okay, okay, I hear ya. No need to get pushy. I'll be right back with dinner, your highness."

I grabbed the wheelbarrow by the barn and pushed it over to the lean-to that housed the hay. The bale I had opened that morning was nearly gone, so I climbed up the bales I had stacked as stairs to reach the top of the pile. When I reached the pinnacle, I gasped.

A doll with a rope tied around its neck dangled from the rafters. Hanging in midair, it swayed gently in the evening breeze.

The flesh on my skin crawled as goose bumps formed. My heart pounded. I looked around to see if anyone was in sight. I half expected a boy from town to be lurking behind one of the posts, ready to point and laugh at my frightened reaction. I didn't see anyone, but that didn't mean they weren't there.

"Ha-ha, very funny, guys."

Taking out my pocket knife, I reached up and cut the doll down. There was no reason Luke needed to see this. If he'd overreacted to a little note, I couldn't imagine how he would react to a lynched doll.

I rolled the bale of hay I needed off the top, and it landed with a thud on the ground. I loaded the flakes of hay into the wheelbarrow and pushed it back out to the horses. Lady ran over to "help" just as I reached the fence.

"And just where were you, oh mighty watchdog, when someone was stringing up a doll to the rafters of the lean-to, hmm?"

All I got in response was slobbery panting and a wagging tail. She was more likely to lick someone to death than anything else.

I threw the doll in the outside garbage before going back to the house.

"Luke? You back yet?"

Silence.

"Guess not."

Removing a pot from the cabinet, I filled it with water, some olive oil, and a pinch of salt and set it on the stove to boil. The store-bought can of spaghetti sauce went in another pot on the stove to warm. When the water began to boil, I put in the noodles and began chopping vegetables for a salad. The sauce was starting to make tiny bubbly explosions when the front door opened.

"Something smells good." Luke sniffed the air.

I stirred the sauce and turned down the heat and then turned to look at Luke.

"What happened to you?" I blurted out. His face was red, and his hair was damp.

"Well, when I usually have a lot on my mind or need to blow off some steam, I head to the gym and a punching bag.

But since there was nothing around here I could punch, I went for a run."

"Feel better?"

He shrugged. "A bit, I guess."

I wanted to apologize for not telling him about the note, but images of a swinging doll filtered through my head. I couldn't apologize for one secret when I was still hiding another.

"Luke." I picked up the envelope with the tickets off the table. "How did you know? Thank you so much."

The corners of his lips turned up slightly, but his eyes still remained shuttered. "Your grandfather told me about your love of ballet. I'm glad you like your gift."

"I do. I love it. Thank you."

The cliché of crickets chirping during an awkward silence was surprisingly true. The late summer song of the cicadas out the window grated against my nerves as the thickness in the air threatened to suffocate me. I missed the camaraderie we'd shared earlier in the day. I turned back to the stove and finished getting dinner ready.

After a quick blessing for the food, Luke turned toward me. I steeled myself for anything he might say. I had hoped he would let this whole thing go, but it didn't look like that was going to happen.

"I think we should file a report with the police."

"The police?" He was taking this all too seriously.

"Yes, the police. Becky, whether you realize it or not, someone threatened you. I know you think it's all some big joke, but, even still, the police should know. They need to have it on file. If you don't think it's a threat, at least consider it harassment. You never know what they might do next to scare you."

Oh yes, I did. They'd hang a doll from the rafters above

my hay.

"You're not going to let this go, are you?"

"No, I'm not."

I sighed. "Fine. Tomorrow I'll head over to the police station and file a report."

Luke's shoulders relaxed. "Thank you."

A week later I sat across from Luke at a fancy restaurant in downtown Sacramento. The crystal water glasses reflected the dancing light from the candles in the middle of our table, the low murmur of conversation harmonized with the strands of Chopin coming from the baby Grand piano in the corner. I ran my hand along the lace overlay of my gown. The night felt so surreal, so Cinderella-like. Could the man across from me be my Prince Charming?

"So why did you do it?" Maybe it was the euphoric state I was in—the ballet company's excellent performance of *Swan Lake* and the ambiance of the upscale restaurant mixing to form an elixir that left me with little inhibitions. Or maybe I felt like tonight, defrocked of frumpy jeans and my ever-present ponytail, I was a different person, and if I didn't seize this moment to satisfy my curiosity, then I'd wake up tomorrow plain ol' me with the nagging question still unanswered.

Luke dabbed at his mouth with his napkin. "Why did I do what? Take you to the ballet?"

"No. I mean, yes. Yes to all of it." The cloth napkin twisted in my grip. "Why did you marry a complete stranger? Why did you buy me a wedding dress when we had only known each other a day? Why did you go to all the trouble to make tonight so special?"

"I'm glad you think tonight is special." He reached over

and touched my hand. "I think you're special."

I blushed. "Seriously. I really want to know. You know why I asked Lisa to find me a husband, but why did you say yes?"

He took a drink of water from a crystal goblet and leaned back in his chair after he set it back on the table. "When Lisa first told me about her friend who had asked her to find her a husband, I thought you were both crazy. I thought you must be this really unattractive woman who was so lonely and desperate that you would do anything to get married." He pushed his plate to the side and leaned forward. "But I was wrong. You are very beautiful, Becky."

It was hard not to squirm. "Thank you, but stop stalling with your flattery."

He laughed and shifted positions in his chair. His foot brushed against mine under the table, so I moved it to give him more room. His foot followed mine. Was he flirting? Should I flirt back?

A lazy smile stretched across his face. "My aunt thought it was romantic, and my uncle thought it was logical. He said feelings come and go, but a person must make a choice to love. I asked Lisa if she'd asked God for a sign, you know, like the Biblical Eliezer did." He paused and then chuckled. "Apparently that was the sign."

"Really?"

"Yep. But it wasn't until God spoke to me that I quit my job, packed up my car, and headed out here."

"God spoke to you?" I couldn't help but lean forward in my chair. "What did He say?"

"He quoted scripture to me. He told me to love my neighbor and that we love Him because He first loved us. He told me that, in the same way, if I loved you first, then you would love me in return."

Do you love me? Even as I thought it, I knew I would never actually ask him. That wasn't a question you asked someone. That was something you were told. But the silence that followed spoke volumes. He didn't say the three little words. He didn't say any words. The clock struck midnight in my head, and my Cinderella dream crashed around me. Luke may be my Prince Charming, but would I ever be his lady love?

Chapter Twenty-Two

Luke

"Masterson, get in here!" Captain Freeman bellowed as I passed his small office.

"Yes, sir?" I stepped over the threshold into the captain's immaculate space. Where Chief had had papers scattered all over his desk, Captain Freeman seemed to have a master's degree in organization. Not a memo out of place.

"Take a seat, son." Captain Freeman tipped his head toward an empty chair. He bobbed a pen between his fingers like a manic seesaw. I'd never seen the man completely still.

"We need to talk about your future here at station four."

My shoulders notched back. He paused, but I refused to break eye contact. I'd done good work, and if he was dismissing me, I would go with my head held high.

"As you know, it is very unusual to transfer to a new state, especially California. I took you on a trial basis as a favor to Chief Noles."

Another pause. This time, however, the lines around the captain's eyes softened.

"And I'm glad I did. You're an asset to the team. I want to offer you a permanent place here, but in order to do that, we need to get you caught up with all the qualifications the other firefighters have when they graduate from the academy. Namely, you need wildland fire training."

"That won't be a problem, sir."

"Glad to hear it." He extended some papers to me, and I took them. "Here are the registration forms for the course. It's offered in Sacramento in a few weeks, and I want you there. The sooner we get you trained, the better I'll feel."

"Yes, sir." The ball uncurled in my gut. I wouldn't have to trade my bunker gear for hedge clippers.

"That will be all, Masterson."

Thank you, Jesus. It seemed God was working everything out. Becky and I had a great time the other night at the ballet, and even though we were taking things slow, our relationship was headed in the right direction. I felt she was slowly coming to see me not as a complete stranger, but as her husband. And now my job was secure, which, to be honest, I'd been worried about. If the United States were a family, California would be the snobby cousin. Certified professionals such as firefighters and teachers had to pass California's specific tests. The state wouldn't accept out of state licenses.

The rest of my shift passed quickly. On the way home, I stopped by a video store and picked up a John Wayne classic. I wasn't sure what type of movies Becky liked, but I assumed since she was the cowgirl type she would enjoy a good Western. I hoped I wasn't stereotyping.

By the time I reached the house, the long shift was beginning to take its toll on me, and a few hours of sleep sounded like a good idea. I was surprised, however, by the excitement that mounted with every step I took toward home.

Becky. Five more paces, and I'd see my wife. I felt like a

seventeen-year-old picking up his date for the prom and wished I had flowers in my hand instead of a goofy old movie.

I walked into the house and set my keys on the table. Becky stood by the stove with a daisy-print apron tied around her waist. Better than a prom dress. She looked up and smiled.

"Lucky me. I married a looker and a cooker." I winced as soon as the words left my mouth. Apparently corny lines were a family trait.

She turned toward me, her eyes light with laughter. An eye roll is what I deserved, but I'd take the laughter any day.

What would she do if I walked up behind her, wrapped my arms around her waist, and buried my nose in the crook of her neck? I'd breathe in her essence—sunshine and wide open spaces. She'd turn in my arms, face lifted to receive my kiss. Our lips would meet and...

My heart thumped against my ribs. I shook my head to dislodge the picture from my mind. What was I thinking? Becky needed time, and I wasn't some teenage girl. Men didn't daydream. We acted.

I remembered the way she'd worried her lip on our wedding night.

We also exhibit self-control. The last thing I wanted was to scare my wife with physical contact before she was ready.

Becky spooned out runny scrambled eggs and burnt toast on a couple of plates and brought them to the table. After a quick prayer, we began to eat.

"Thanks for making breakfast," I said as I dredged an almost black piece of toast through the undercooked eggs, hoping to soften the bread before consumption. I appreciated Becky's efforts, but her talents definitely lay elsewhere.

"No problem. I know you must be tired," she said. "Speaking of which, I was thinking. I don't think you need to sleep on the couch."

I didn't? But the only other place to sleep was the... My pulse raced. Was she really saying what I hoped she was saying? I never thought—

"Today, I mean," she rushed on. "Or the days you come home after a long shift. I won't be in my room anyway, and when you're on the couch, I'm afraid I'll wake you up with all my comings and goings."

I swallowed the disappointment. It tasted bitter. And lingered. "Thank you."

Time to change the subject. "Do you like John Wayne?"

The corners of her mouth slid up. "Who doesn't like John Wayne?"

I forced a smiled. "Good. I rented *McClintock* on my way home. I thought maybe we could watch it this evening after I've gotten some sleep and you're finished with your work for the day."

"Sounds good. And nice choice, by the way. *McClintock* is my favorite John Wayne movie."

"Do you have any popcorn?" Becky had barely made it into the house before I pounced on her with a question, my head still buried in the cabinet-turned-pantry.

"Yes, but it's the air-popper kind, not the microwave kind."

I ducked my head out. "Where? I've looked everywhere and can't find a single kernel."

She waved me aside and peeked in the cabinet. It took her less than a second to pull out an Orville Redenbacher container of yellow kernels.

"That wasn't there a second ago. I swear I looked in every nook and cranny."

Becky just smiled. My mom had called it "looking like a

man" when my dad and I couldn't find something and it took her no time at all to locate it. I thought it was some kind of conspiracy.

Becky made the popcorn while I put in the movie. As soon as the previews started, Becky sat next to me on the couch with a large bowl of popcorn in her lap. I reached over for a handful but grabbed only air. Becky had moved the bowl to the other side of her.

"This is mine, cowboy. Make your own."

I might have been offended if I hadn't seen the teasing glint in her eye.

Knowing my arm was longer than hers, I simply reached over her for the bowl. She swatted my hand away and jumped off the couch.

Eyes glued to hers, I slowly stood. She was slightly crouched, ready to spring if I made a move toward her. "Didn't Pops teach you to share?"

"Oh, do you want some?" she asked innocently.

"Yes, please." I edged toward her.

"Then open up," she said as she took a step back for every step I took forward.

I laughed but obediently opened my mouth.

The popcorn bounced off my forehead.

"I think you need to work on your—"

Another piece pelted me on the chin.

"I'm going to starve at this rate," I growled.

"Oh, we can't have that." Becky reached into the bowl and withdrew a handful of popcorn.

I held up my hands. "Now Becky, don't do anything you're going to regret."

She laughed but raised her hand behind her head in a throwing position. Just as she released her ammo, I lunged. I was hit by at least a dozen kernels but was able to pin Becky's arms to her sides before she made her escape. The bowl dangled in her grasp, about ready to spill.

"Care to share that bowl now?"

"Let me go, you brute." Becky wiggled in my arms and I tightened my hold. Even with her arms pinned, she was still able to twist her body just enough that I couldn't grab the bowl. Although, I admit, I wasn't trying all that hard.

"Since you won't willingly share," I said, mock seriousness lacing my voice, "I can only see one solution." With my arm still wrapped around her and her back to my chest, I lifted her feet off the ground and carried her to the couch. I pulled her down onto my lap and let my hand rest on her hip. If she tried to dart back up I could easily haul her back down.

She turned to give me a dirty look. I winked as I bit into a satisfying handful of Mr. Redenbacher's finest.

My cell phone rang just as the Duke made his entrance. Bummer—but not because I'd miss the scene. I allowed Becky to slide off my lap and walked to where my phone lay on the table.

"Hello?"

Chapter Twenty-Three

Rebekah

Luke's face fell. Only minutes before we'd been laughing and teasing, and now he looked like someone had just killed his dog. I had to admit it scared me.

Luke was silent as he listened to whoever was on the other end of the line. I wished he'd respond so that I could get some idea as to what the call was about. Obviously the news was not good, but there were so many possibilities, and I didn't know him well enough to make an educated guess.

"Okay, thanks for calling. Hopefully you can get ahold of his mom soon, but I'll see what I can do." He ended the call, his head still in his hands. He pushed one hand through his hair before looking up at me with glossy eyes.

"What is it? What's wrong?" I asked.

"It's Marty," he breathed. "He's in the hospital."

Who's Marty? I hadn't heard Luke talk about a Marty before, but clearly he was someone very important to him. I groaned silently in frustration. These were things that wives knew about their husbands. They knew the people closest to the man they'd married and didn't have to guess or ask who a person was in a time of obvious distress. But I wasn't that kind of wife. I had no choice but to ask.

I walked over to Luke and knelt in front of him. I took one of his large hands in mine and looked into his eyes. "Who's Marty?"

"Marty is this kid that I used to tutor back in Michigan."

"Was that his mom who called?" I gently probed.

"No. It was the hospital."

The hospital? But why would the hospital call a nonrelative?

My confusion must have been evident on my face, because Luke said, "Marty is in surgery right now. I wrote down my name and number on a piece of paper before I left and I guess a nurse found it in his pocket. The hospital couldn't reach his mom, and one of the doctors recognized my name. Being a firefighter, I knew a few of the doctors there. Anyway, they called me as a courtesy. The doctor thought maybe I could come and stay with Marty until they could get in touch with his mom. He didn't know I wasn't in Michigan anymore."

"Oh." It was an inane thing to say, but I didn't know what else *to* say. Luke had left a life midstride for me. People he cared about, family...what else?

I managed to gather my wits. "Is it anything serious?" My own concern mounted for this boy I had never met.

Luke nodded. "Apparently he was in a hit and run. He was riding his bike home from school, and a car hit him and drove off. His leg is broken in several places, and they're concerned about internal bleeding."

We sat there in silence a few minutes, each of us absorbed in our own thoughts.

I rubbed his thumb with mine. "So what are you going to do?"

"Is it crazy that I want to go see him? Make sure he's okay?" For a man who usually spoke with such confidence, he was showing a vulnerability I hadn't imagined existed.

Yes! "No, not crazy at all."

"I have the next four days off. Maybe I'll see if I can't catch the red-eye tonight or something early tomorrow morning."

I opened my mouth to respond, but Luke practically jumped from his seat. The sudden motion caught me off guard. I lost my balance where I knelt and landed hard on my rear. Luke didn't notice. His head was buried in his phone as he walked to the door and out of the house. I watched him go from my position on the floor.

I wanted to bang my head against the wall. Why now? I was just starting to get...comfortable with him here. And he seemed, uh, comfortable too.

Stop being so selfish.

Picking myself up off the ground, I went to retrieve the vacuum from the closet. I felt incompetent to help Luke, and, honestly, he seemed to have the situation well in hand anyway. While he was capable of helping himself, my house was not. The small appliance roared to life, and I passed it back and forth over the carpet, picking up the tiny pieces of popcorn that only a short time ago served as ammunition.

I felt like a traitor as a smile crept to my lips. A child, one very close to my husband, was about to undergo surgery, and I had a stupid grin on my face. I couldn't help it, remembering Luke chasing me while I pelted him with popcorn, the feel of his arms around me when he finally caught me, the warmth of his hand on my hip as he sat me on his lap. My stomach did an odd little flip-flop. It was easy being attracted to the man I'd married, but the way I was reacting to him made me both nervous and excited. I wasn't sure I could trust myself and my judgment. It wasn't that long ago that another man had made my insides quiver, and he had turned out to be about as trustworthy as the devil himself.

Luke wasn't James. All men didn't consider women just playthings. Still, a niggling of nervous doubt made my insides a little sick. With conscious effort, I turned my introspection to the bubbling excitement in the pit of my stomach. Instead of worrying, I should be thanking God. Maybe it was possible that Luke was a part of God's perfect plan for my life, after all. I had to admit my own plan had been just to get married for Poppy's sake. I hadn't expected to feel my heart skip a beat whenever I looked at the man I'd married. Dates to the ballet and food fights before John Wayne movies hadn't been on my radar. Maybe I could fall in love with my husband after all, and I wouldn't have to settle for a glorified roommate.

Luke walked back into the house, ripping me out of my perfect fairytale hopes.

"Okay. That'll be great. Thank you so much." He pushed the End Call button on his phone.

I looked at him expectantly.

"That was the airline. It took all my frequent flier miles, but I was able to book a flight for tonight. I have to leave in an hour to get to the airport on time."

"I'll drive you," I offered.

Why were my eyes burning? I wasn't a ninny, and he'd been a part of my life all of a month. No crying.

"Are you sure? I could just leave my Jeep in long-term parking."

"It's silly to pay for parking when I can take you." I was going to miss him. I didn't want to admit it, but it was true. How had I become attached to him being around so quickly? I pinched the outside of my leg. This wasn't about me. It was about Marty.

"Thanks."

"Hmm? Oh. No problem."

It turned out the ride to the airport didn't afford much opportunity for conversation. Luke was on his phone most of the trip, informing family he would be in town and setting up a place to stay. Curiosity had my nerves zinging when I heard him ask his aunt and uncle if he could stay with them. Weren't his parents still in Michigan? Why wasn't he staying with them? Just another part of my husband's life I didn't know anything about.

We pulled into the airport, my truck rumbling beneath large signs indicating which airlines were serviced in each terminal. Technically, it wasn't a fantastic time to start a more-than-superficial conversation, but my curiosity got the better of me.

"You must be really close to your aunt and uncle." I hedged around the real topic of my inquisitiveness. After all, his parents might be dead like mine, and I didn't want to put my foot in my mouth.

"Yeah, they're real great folks. Kind of like a second set of parents." Luke's voice held a warm quality as he spoke of his family.

"What about your mom and dad?"

"They're great too."

I huffed. This was getting me nowhere. At least I knew they were still alive, or he would have talked about them in the past tense. So why not stay with them?

"Do they still live in Michigan?" I changed lanes to avoid a car stopped in front of me. Cars were only allowed to park in the right lane for drop-offs, but that didn't stop vehicles from congesting the other lanes as they stopped to let their passengers disembark.

Luke turned his head to look behind him, pointing with

his thumb over his shoulder. "I think that's where I needed to get out."

I groaned and then flushed, offering a sheepish smile and small shrug. "Guess we'll have to go around again."

"I don't mind," he winked. "But to answer your question, no, my parents don't live in Michigan anymore. My mom was tired of the cold and retired to Florida. My dad was tired of my mom, divorced her, and now lives in Nashville with his new wife."

The comment was made as a matter of fact, but the residual bitterness was etched in Luke's tone.

As the truck looped around again, and I took in the same scenery I had just witnessed minutes before, I chastised myself for letting my curiosity get the better of me and starting this conversation when there wasn't enough time to see it through.

There were so many new questions now. How old was he when they got divorced? How come he decided to stay in Michigan instead of moving closer to one of his parents? Logically, I knew I could answer that question—because he was a grown man with a steady job and a life of his own. The sentimental side of me, the side that still remembered what it was like growing up without a mom or a dad, couldn't quite grasp living so far away from one's parents. Did he resent them for their decision to split up? Did he still have a good relationship, or any relationship for that matter, with either one of them? I certainly hadn't heard him talk about them before.

"You can just drop me off at the curb," Luke said.

I pulled the truck over when an opening appeared, and we both hopped out. As Luke grabbed his bag from the back, I walked around to the passenger side to join him. The low but loud hum of twin jet engines flying overhead shook the air around us.

"I'll be praying for Marty," I said, bringing the conversation back to the reason he was leaving.

"And me too, I hope?" he asked with a half smile.

I nodded as I looked up at him and he looked down at me. I was beginning to feel awkward and self-conscious. Should I shake his hand? Give him a hug? A little wave and drive away? All options were a far cry from a Hollywood good-bye scene.

Luke set down his bag and cupped the side of my face with his hand. His thumb caressed my cheek bone. "I'll miss you," he whispered.

You will? My heart fluttered.

"Will you miss me?" he asked.

I couldn't speak past the lump in my throat. I nodded again.

His smile seemed satisfied, and the dimple in his cheek peeked out. His hand inched backward into my hair at the nape of my neck. With gentle pressure he pulled me forward. I watched in slow motion as his lips descended. My eyes closed involuntarily the moment I felt the fullness of his mouth on mine. With one hand still in my hair, he draped his other hand around my waist and pulled me close to his body until there was no space left between us. Angling his head, he deepened the kiss. My arms rose of their own accord and wrapped themselves around his neck. Besides the few brotherly kisses to the forehead and the one chaste kiss at our wedding, this was the first physical contact we'd shared as man and wife.

A car horn blasted nearby, and I jumped back. Peeking around Luke's arm, I spotted a black Mercedes with its blinker light on waiting to pull in to the spot my truck occupied. The driver looked none too patient as she tapped her manicured nails on the steering wheel, the shine from the diamond on her ring nearly blinding me.

I looked back at Luke shyly. "Guess I better go."

He kissed me once more. A quick peck on the lips.

"To remember me by," he said with a cheeky grin.

Like I'd forget.

"You rogue!" I hollered to his retreating back. No one would have believed my words. The smile on my face told a different story.

The black Mercedes honked again. I jumped back in the truck, and pulled away. Something white in my peripheral vision snagged my attention as I merged onto the freeway. Reaching over, I grabbed the small piece of paper lying on the passenger's seat. I unfolded it on the top of the steering wheel. My eyes flitted back and forth between the words on the paper and the road. The note was in Luke's handwriting, a quote from the Bible.

I am my beloved's and my beloved is mine.

Usually I would balk at such possessiveness, my independent streak running deeper than the San Andreas Fault. Normally I wouldn't want anyone saying I was theirs, like some object to be obtained. I was my own woman. Or so I'd thought.

But as I read those words, instead of recoiling at the idea of being owned, my soul seized the feeling of belonging. I was not so naïve as to think this note did not hold some significance. The knowledge of its meaning and the memory of his kiss warmed me and sent shivers through my body at the same time.

Chapter Twenty-Four

Luke

Once I'd retrieved my carry-on from the overhead compartment, I whipped my phone out and sent a quick text to Sam while waiting in the narrow, crowded aisle of the plane.

Just landed. C u soon.

Seven hours in a cramped seat had left me stiff. It felt good to be able to stand up, even pressed as I was by bodies on either side of me. The line of people shuffled forward, and I followed, waiting impatiently till I got off the aircraft and could stretch my legs in a normal stride.

Sam stood waiting in front of security. He thumped me on the back. "So how's married life, old man?" The corners of his eyes crinkled with the upturn of his lips.

"Just wait and see," I teased back. "I'm sure Lisa is more than willing to make an honest man out of you."

Curiosity oozed out of Sam, but I remained tight lipped. I wasn't kidding myself to think I'd survive the few days among family and friends without getting grilled about my new wife and the life we were starting to share together. But I also wasn't prepared to have such a conversation in the South Bend Airport.

"Lisa wanted to come with me to pick you up, but she had an early class she couldn't miss this morning."

I nodded.

"Don't think you'll be able to blow her off like you did me though, man. She won't let you off the hook that easily."

"I didn't blow you off."

Sam raised his eyebrows. I chose to ignore him.

I tossed my bag in the back of his sedan and slid into the passenger's seat.

"Do you want to stop for a bite to eat first, or do you want me to take you straight to the hospital?" Sam asked as I buckled my seat belt.

"I can always grab something in the hospital's cafeteria. I want to see Marty as soon as I can. I'm not sure if they've been able to reach Mrs. Stabler, and I don't want Marty to be alone if they haven't."

Sam rolled down his window and paid the airport parking attendant.

"Speaking of Mrs. Stabler..." Sam let his sentence die.

"What about her?" I tried not to get defensive but could feel my hackles rise.

"Two questions. One," Sam held up one finger in the space between us. "Did you tell Becky about her? And two"—a second finger rose—"what are you going to do about her if she's there?"

"I hope for Marty's sake she is there."

"It would save you some trouble if she wasn't."

"True, but this isn't about me."

Sam nodded and glanced at me before returning his eyes to the road. "You still haven't answered either of my questions."

I sighed and pushed a hand through my hair. I couldn't wait to see Marty. His mom, on the other hand, was a different story. "I guess I'll do what I always did—try to keep my distance."

Sam harrumphed his disapproval. "And Becky? Did you tell her about Colleen?"

"There is nothing to tell about *Mrs. Stabler.*"

Sam turned and gave me the same look my father used to give whenever he was disappointed in me. I used to wish he'd yell at me, or slap me on the back of the head, or call me stupid. Anything besides regarding me with that look and the small shake of his head. Guilt and shame washed over me as I sat in Sam's sedan, the same way it had when I was a kid.

"What was I supposed to tell her?" I asked weakly in my defense.

"The truth." Sam snorted.

"What? That the woman came with her own theme song, which so happened to be 'Maneater,' and she wanted me as the next course?"

"I don't know if I'd have been that dramatic, but, yeah, something like that."

We drove into the hospital parking lot, and Sam pulled up beside the curb to let me out. I was opening the car door when he spoke again. "It's not too late, you know."

I didn't pretend not to know what he was talking about. I was sure he meant well, but I didn't see his logic. Why would I needlessly worry Becky about a woman that I couldn't even stand? If Mrs. Stabler had been an ex-girlfriend or something, sure, I would have seen the need to inform Becky about her. But Marty's mom was nothing more than a nuisance I had to deal with in order to try and make a difference in her kid's life. Becky had too many other things to worry about that were real concerns. Like people leaving threatening notes. She didn't need anything else on her plate.

"I'll see ya tonight," I said right before I shut the car door and walked through the automatic doors of Lakeland Hospital.

I felt a little out of place in the sterile environment of the hospital without my uniform. Shaking off my discomfort, I walked past the semi-circle desk with a sign marked Information hanging above it. I'd had enough stitches and burns tended here that I knew my way around fairly well.

I strode purposefully down a long corridor and turned to the right. When I reached post-op, I stopped in front of the nurses' station. A plump nurse with her hair tied back in a tight knot and wearing Scooby-Doo scrubs was hunched over some paperwork, a pen in hand.

I cleared my throat and she looked up at me over thick-framed glasses.

"Can you tell me which room Marty Stabler is in, please?"

Without a word she rolled her chair over to a computer. The *click, click, click* of nails on a keyboard drifted through the space between us.

"Marty Stabler. Room 1672." The nurse read off the illuminated screen.

"Thank you."

The room was almost at the end of the hallway. I knocked on the door, opening it only after an adolescent answered "Come in."

Marty's hospital bed was raised in a sitting position, with its patient propped up with extra pillows for support. The only color contrasting the white of the bed was the bright-blue cast that started on the boy's left foot and covered his leg all the way up to his thigh. Even the pallor of Marty's skin matched the starkness of the sheets he lay on. It reminded me of the vanilla ice cream cones he liked to eat in the summer.

Marty's arm rested palm up next to the top of his cast. A small tube, secured with clear medical tape, protruded from a vein in the soft underbelly of the boy's elbow. An IV dripped clear liquid into Marty's arm.

"How's it going, squirt?" I made my voice light.

Mr. Luke!" Surprise etched Marty' features as he leaned forward in his bed.

"You know, you didn't have to go to such drastic measures to see me. You could have just called."

A faint smile touched Marty's lips, but there was no light in his eyes. I wasn't sure if he was in pain, tired, or just plain bored of being cooped up in bed.

"Where's your mom?" I kept my tone casual.

A conspiratorial sparkle entered his eye. "I talked her into sneaking me a cheeseburger."

I made a show at looking at my watch. "It's only eight thirty in the morning. You're more likely to get an Egg McMuffin than a Big Mac this time of day."

Marty shrugged his shoulders. A hint of a smile tugged at the corners of his mouth.

Pulling up the only chair in the room to face the same direction as Marty, I sat. The phone in my back pocket was uncomfortable to sit on, so I leaned to the side, withdrew it, and set it on the small side table by the very stiff-looking love seat.

"So what are you watching?" I inclined my head toward the mounted television.

"iCarly."

"Oh yeah? I've never heard of it before."

For the next hour I learned more than I ever wanted about the Nickelodeon Channel's apparently very popular TV series. It was just my luck that it was having some sort of iCarly marathon. I could feel my IQ dropping with each episode.

The door opened, stealing both mine and Marty's attention.

"Sorry it took me so long. I was finally able to—" Mrs. Stabler's eyes widened in surprise when they landed on me. She blinked, and the woman changed before my eyes. Upon entering she had seemed a concerned, if distracted, mother. Now she sauntered languidly forward with the brazen look of a seductress. I was grateful for the cooler turn of the weather. Early for September but it necessitated the woman cover some of her...uh...more voluptuous attributes, that she usually liked to display. As it was, her short sweater dress hugged every curve of her petite form.

Self-preservation kicked in. I stood and ruffled Marty's hair. "Well, squirt, I should probably get going."

A female hand came to rest on my arm, and I turned toward red, pouty lips. "Leaving so soon?"

The air around me suddenly thinned, and the overwhelming scent of perfume sickened my stomach. Mrs. Stabler audaciously pressed closer until her soft body melted into my side. A buzzing began in the back of my head. I tried to take a cleansing breath, but my nostrils only filled with more of her store-bought fragrance.

"Mom? My food?" Marty's voice, laced with impatience and disdain, rescued me.

I shook off the restraining hand and took a wide step around the woman. At the door, I stopped and looked back at Marty. "I'll come back and see you again, squirt." Before the she-cat could sink her claws into me, I exited the room and shut the door behind me.

I breathed a sigh of relief and continued down the hospital halls. It wasn't until I reached the exit that I touched my back pocket and groaned. I'd left my phone on the table in Marty's room. I turned and walked grudgingly back into the dragon's lair.

Rebekah

I lifted my hand to my brow, casting a shadow over my eyes to protect them from the glaring sun. Even so, I still had to squint against the brightness of the day. It was a picturesque morning. In fact, nothing marred the blue expanse except the brilliant golden orb in front of me and the waning crescent of a moon to my back.

"Good job, Faith," I called to the girl on horseback.

She beamed at me, her cheeks rosy from exertion.

"I need to make a phone call real quick. Go ahead and enjoy your time with Daisy."

Faith clucked to the horse and trotted off.

Leaning against the fence, I pulled out my phone and called Luke. I wanted to make sure he'd arrived safely and everything was all right with Marty. I couldn't help the quickening of my heart as the phone rang in my ear.

"Hello?" A female answered.

I jerked the phone away from my head and stared at the screen. The name Luke Masterson glared back at me, proof I had dialed the right number.

Putting the phone back up to my mouth, I stumbled over my words. "Um, I was looking for Luke Masterson?"

"Well, this is his phone, sweetie." Her voice dripped. With what I wasn't sure, but it wasn't sweetness.

I know this is his phone, but who are you?

"Can I take a message for him? He is, how should I say it—" the woman giggled "—indisposed at the moment."

"Well...I..." All coherent thoughts fell out of my head, and my heart plummeted to my stomach as I saw my life, for the second time, come crashing down around me. I might as well have been in front of Ernie's Feed and Farm once again, watching in horror as another woman claimed the man I thought belonged to me. My hands began to sweat, and I had to grip my phone more firmly to keep it from sliding to the ground.

"I couldn't believe he'd come all this way to see me, but—"she giggled again and lowered her voice as if sharing a secret with a friend "—don't worry. I rewarded him well for the effort."

My voice strangled in my throat. I punched the End button with more force than necessary and barely restrained myself from flinging the suddenly offensive piece of technology across the pasture and into the water trough. Angry tears rolled down my cheek. Sniffing, I swiped at them with the back of my hand.

How stupid could I be? How did that old saying go? Fool me once, shame on you. Fool me twice, shame on me. Well, shame on me indeed! I was obviously too thick skulled to have learned my lesson the first time. The pain of James Anthony's betrayal hadn't even healed before I stabbed myself in the heart again by falling in love with another handsome face.

I stopped dead in my mental tracks. I loved him. The discovery rocked me to my core. My anger drifted away like dandelion puffs on the wind. I wished I had been able to hold on to it. What took residence in its place was a heartrending sense of loss. Emptiness covered me like a heavy cloak. Choking sobs racked my body, and I gasped for breath against the pain.

Faith and Daisy trotted over to me at the fence.

"Ms. Becky? Are you okay?" The girl's brows furrowed in concern, and her eyes held a hint of fear.

I used the fence rail to straighten from my hunched-over position. My lips trembled as I tried to tame them into the form of a reassuring smile.

"I'll be fine, Faith." My voice quivered. "Do me a favor, will you? Just leave Daisy tied to the fence when you leave. I'll take care of her later. I'm going to saddle Samson and go for a ride."

"Sure thing, Ms. Becky." She slipped her foot from the stirrups as I turned toward the barn.

By the time I reached the tack room, I'd changed my mind about the saddle. I wanted to be on the horse as quickly as possible. I snatched a bridle from a hook on the wall and hurried to the pasture where Samson grazed. Lifting two fingers to my mouth, I let out a shrill whistle. His head snapped up, and he trotted over to me. I gave him a quick scratch on his broad forehead before slipping the bit into his mouth. Gathering the reins and a handful of mane at the peak of his withers, I swung my leg up and over his rump and hoisted myself onto his back. Slight pressure to the horse's side put him in motion.

My spirit chafed against the slow pace as Samson plodded along through the woods behind the property. I was itching for a run but didn't dare increase the pace until we hit the meadow. Low-lying branches from towering oak trees reached out to scratch my arms and face. I didn't care.

As soon as it was safe, I leaned low over Samson's neck and kicked him into a full-fledged run. The horse's long legs ate up the distance as we flew over the long grass. But no matter how fast or how far we ran, I couldn't outpace my troubled thoughts or broken heart.

I allowed Samson to slow and rewarded him by dropping the reins so he could munch on the overgrown vegetation. Lifting my face to the azure sky, I poured out all my grief and frustrations.

"Is this your idea of a perfect plan for my life, Lord?" I railed at the heavens. While common sense told me I should have guarded my heart more closely, I felt deceived by God. Hadn't Lisa and I prayed that God would show her the man I was to marry? Hadn't she asked for a sign like Eliezer? How could it have worked out so flawlessly for Isaac and Rebekah, yet so dismally for me?

I gave a mirthless laugh. Last time, at least, I had the support of friends and family. Who could I turn to now? Poppy thought I was happily married to the love of my life, and Lisa was the one who had arranged the marriage. I couldn't disappoint Poppy by telling him the whole thing was a sham, cooked up for his benefit alone. And telling Lisa would only make her feel guilty for choosing a cad. God had promised that I would never be alone, but that was exactly what I was.

Utterly alone.

Chapter Twenty-Five

Luke

Familiarity enveloped me in its warm embrace. The outdated wallpaper that hung in Aunt Margaret's dining room wouldn't be featured on the woman's favorite HGTV show any time soon, but it imbued in me a feeling of nostalgia.

I was seated at the family's large oak farmhouse table. Years of meals eaten at its surface had left their loving marks in the form of scratches and dents. Uncle David sat at the head of the table. The top button of his shirt was undone, and his tie hung loosely around his neck. Beside him sat Aunt Margaret. She still wore her kitchen apron, but even with the protection, a small stain of barbeque sauce was splattered on the sleeve of her light-purple blouse. Sam and Lisa occupied the seats across from me. The way their arms angled toward each other, I surmised they were holding hands beneath the table.

I had never felt the emptiness of the seat beside me so keenly. This room, these people, should have filled me to overflowing. I hadn't expected to feel an unequivocal void in my life, in my heart. The hole was not ambiguous either. It had the definite shape of a certain blond-haired, blue-eyed cowgirl. Becky had taken a chisel and carved a place for herself in my heart.

As if those around me were privy to my inner thoughts, the conversation died down.

Lisa regarded me with intent.

"So how are things going with Becky?"

I was surprised it had taken her this long to ask. I'd expected to be bombarded by inquiries as soon as I stepped through the door, but the lady had shown marvelous self-control.

Knowing these questions were going to come, I was able to think about my answers ahead of time. I decided I had two options. I could either be vague about where Becky and I were in our relationship, or I could lay it all out on the table, so to speak. My first instinct was to keep my private thoughts and feelings just that—private. But wisdom told me that we needed the prayers of our friends and family, those who knew us and loved us best. So I decided to be as honest and open in my responses as I could. No matter how much discomfort or embarrassment it might cause me.

"Let's just say that if we were in *Aesop's Fables* we'd be styled the tortoise and not the hare."

Uncle David tapped his finger to the side of his nose. "Slow and steady won the race, my boy."

I inclined my head. It was true. I just hoped real life followed the story line.

"Any second thoughts?" This came from Sam.

I would have thought I'd need more time to weigh the answer to that question, but the response came unexpectedly swift. "None." I forked a heap of mashed potatoes into my mouth.

My aunt joined the conversation. "How's her grandfather

doing?"

"He seems to have rallied some after the wedding. He hasn't had any setback since then at least. I think Becky is secretly hoping he will go into remission again."

"Is that a real possibility?" Aunt Margaret asked.

I shrugged. "I haven't talked with his doctor, but I don't think so."

Everyone was quiet as they absorbed the somber news.

Lisa broke the silence. "So you've been married for over a month now."

It was a fact she well knew, so I waited for the inevitable question to follow, spearing a few green beans in the process.

"And you've told us where your head is. That you don't have any regrets."

I chewed as Lisa took her time getting to the point.

"But where is your heart?"

I set down my fork and leaned back in my seat, glancing to the empty chair beside me. "In California."

Lisa squealed, grabbed Sam's arm, and started shaking him in her excitement. We all laughed at her exuberance, but she didn't seem to care.

"You love Becky, don't you? Tell me you love her. I know you love her." Lisa's eyes were as wide as saucers, and she sucked her bottom lip in between her teeth. All her frantic shaking had stopped, and she sat as still as a ladder truck with an empty gas tank as she waited for my response.

I laughed. *Do I love Becky?* The question barely had time to resonate in my mind before my heart answered with a resounding yes.

"I do."

Lisa bounded out of her chair so quickly it went flying out behind her and tumbled to the ground. I thought she would launch herself right over the table at me, but instead she ran around the oak top. She flung her arms around my shoulders and bounced up and down. Sam laughed at my predicament from across the room while I tried to keep my teeth from rattling in my head.

Lisa released me and plunked down in the empty chair by my side. "What about Becky? Does she love you too? Of course she does." She gave me an appraising look. "What's not to love?"

"Hey!" Sam objected.

Lisa waved away his protest as if it were an annoying gnat. "Oh, don't be jealous, Sam. You know I love you."

Sam harrumphed and crossed his arms over his chest. He made a show of being hurt, but the edges of his eyes were soft as he gazed at his girlfriend.

"Well, son." Uncle David drew our attention. "What do you say? Do you think Becky returns your feelings?"

My confidence waned. I might have known where my heart was, but I was lost when it came to knowing where my wife's heart was. Images of our good-bye kiss flashed through my mind, and my doubts faded a bit. But did a kiss, sweet and passionate though it was, evidence the love in Becky's heart? I wasn't sure.

The sigh that escaped seemed to have taken all my energy with it. I leaned heavily on my forearms, which rested on the table. "That's just it. I don't know. She has this annoying habit of making me guess what she's thinking and feeling instead of just telling me outright."

Uncle David guffawed and slapped his knee. I didn't know I had said anything funny, but my uncle wiped a tear from the corner of his eye, and his shoulders shook.

"Ho, ho, sorry about that, Luke." Uncle David gasped as he regained his composure. "It's just that you seem to be experiencing something that men have been complaining about for generations."

Aunt Margaret slapped her husband on the shoulder. "Don't listen to this old man, Luke. He wouldn't know what a woman was talking about even if she spelled it out for him."

"It would be nice if you'd do that every once in a while," my uncle mumbled under his breath.

"You have to remember that Becky is pretty independent," Lisa said. "She lives alone and owns her own business that employs exactly one person, herself. She doesn't have the experience or the need as others do to communicate what is on her mind. Plus, she's recently been burned in the romance department. I'm sure she's dealing with some trust issues right now."

I nodded. "You're right." But where did that leave me? What was I supposed to do? Should I confront her? Press her until she told me where she stood, how she felt? Or should I give her space, let her move at her own pace and hope she'll eventually come to the realization on her own that I could be trusted, that I was committed to her, and that I loved her?

Dear God, show me what to do. The path was as hazy and obscure as any burning building I had run into.

Rebekah

It had been three days since Luke boarded a plane for Michigan. Two days since learning about his nefarious character, his duplicity, his treachery, his unfaithfulness. I shook my head. What was the use of listing his act of betrayal in the form of synonyms? Dwelling on the hurt he had caused would never solve anything.

Besides, yesterday I had come up with a plan. Not that strategizing had served me well in the past. In fact, it was my last plan that had landed me in this predicament. But what else was I to do? I wasn't going down without a fight. It was my life after all. A girl deserved at least a shred of happiness in this pitiful existence, and it looked like my sliver came in the form of a nice quiet life on a ranch by myself. Alone. No one to turn my life upside down with deceit and crush my heart with deception.

Luke was a class A actor. He had me fooled from the get-go. I considered making him a mock Oscar from the Academy Awards of cheaters. Well, he could just continue his little charade. For now anyway. No need to upset Poppy and dash his dreams when he had so little time left.

Originally, I'd thought to cut Luke loose as soon as his feet hit California soil again. That strategy went up in smoke at Grandview yesterday when I went to visit Poppy. I had no medical degree, but even I could tell he was getting worse. Just another knife wound to my already bleeding heart.

But we had a saying out here in the country, and I needed to heed it and cowgirl up. Get back on the horse of life that seemed to enjoy bucking me to the ground. Well, I'd pull my boots up and dust myself off. Life went on, and so would I.

Why had Luke married me in the first place though? It's not like marrying me gave him wealth, power, or prestige. I was a nobody from a small town who barely made enough money to pay the bills every month. What was in it for him? If he had a woman back in Michigan, then why leave her for me? I never did understand men. Especially cheating scoundrels. I guess some things never change.

It didn't matter. All I needed to understand now was how to push my feelings aside and live an undetermined amount of time in marital bliss—I choked on the thought—then, when the worst happened, when Poppy left me for good, Luke could pack his bags and take a hike.

Chapter Twenty-Six

Luke

I'd spent seven hours on two different planes and two hours at a layover in the Minneapolis airport, giving me plenty of time to think of a way to win Becky's heart. Or, if I'd already won it, to get her to tell me I had. And what did I have for my trouble? Nothing. Zero. Zilch. I was right where I was when I had left Michigan, with no idea how to proceed.

The people in the terminal ebbed and flowed around me. Some headed toward the exit I recognized from my flight. Others were going in the opposite direction, to various gates and departing aircrafts. I dodged a man sprinting down the corridor, obviously running late.

My heart rate increased the closer I came to the exit. I'd see Becky again in a few minutes.

As I passed the security checkpoint, my eyes scanned the people milling around for my blond-haired cowgirl. She leaned against the far wall, her arms crossed in front of her chest. Her jeans were tucked into a pair of brown leather cowboy boots, hair pulled up in a ponytail. She was looking down at the ground and didn't see me until I stood in front of her. She pushed herself off the wall and uncrossed her arms.

I couldn't wait another second. I enveloped her in a warm hug and swung her around in a circle. It felt good to have her in my arms again. Although, as I rotated around again, I noticed the limpness of her body.

No, not limp. That implied softness and fragility. Becky was more like dead weight. As unresponsive and hard as a brick wall.

I set her back down on her feet, moving my hand up to her shoulder. I looked at her, confused. She refused to meet my eyes.

"Becky?"

"We better go," she said as she started to walk away. "We have a long drive ahead of us."

I caught up to her and touched her arm. She stopped but still didn't look at me. "Becky, what's wrong?"

"Nothing." She started walking again. "I'm fine."

I didn't bother stopping her this time. Instead, I matched my stride to hers and walked beside her. "Nothing? Fine? So in other words, something and you're upset."

She spared me a glance out of the corner of her eye but continued walking.

I caught a growl in the back of my throat and tempered my growing frustration. *Patience, Luke, patience.*

We approached Becky's truck, and I jerked open the door, making the rusty hinge creak. Stepping up on the runner, I plunked down in the passenger's seat and set my bag at my feet under the dashboard.

I waited until we reached the freeway and my head was cool to broach the subject once more. "So are you going to tell me what's bothering you?"

"How was your trip? Did you have *fun*?" Becky evaded

my question by changing the subject. And what was with the emphasis on the word fun? It wasn't like it had been a pleasure trip.

"It was nice seeing my family, if that's what you mean."

Becky gave an unladylike snort. What was up with her?

"Lisa says hi, by the way."

Some of the icy facade melted.

It was really eating me up, this change that had come over my wife. Three days ago we had shared a moment of passion, and now I was getting a frigid blast from the Arctic Circle. I wanted to explode, to shake the answers from her if necessary. I contemplated pressing her until she unlocked whatever secret she was harboring, but the quiet voice of caution still whispered in the recesses of my mind. Maybe all Becky needed was some space. Most of the time these things worked themselves out, right?

I sighed, deflated. Leaning forward, the seat belt cut into my shoulder. I unzipped my bag and pulled out a small wooden box. My finger traced a line around its edges. I wasn't sure what type of wood the box was made out of. I only knew it held a rich honey hue. The three ballerinas etched on the lid sparkled as the sun caught the gold overlay poured in their grooves.

I placed the box on the center console between Becky's seat and my own. "I got you something."

She looked over but edged away as if she was afraid the thing would bite her. "What is it?"

"I know I probably should have waited till we got home. Especially since you're driving. But I couldn't wait." I let my enthusiasm tinge my voice. Maybe it would rub off on her, and she would stop making furtive looks of revulsion at my gift.

I opened the lid, and the strands of Beethoven's "Moonlight Sonata" wafted through the cabin, accompanied by the ever-present hum of the truck's diesel engine. The ballerina inside sprang up and twirled, one arm raised gracefully above her head and the other poised in a curve in front of her waist. Her legs were pressed tightly together, one crossed in front of the other, her feet perfectly arched, and all her invisible weight placed on her pointed toes. Below her, the box was covered in soft blue velvet, waiting for priceless trinkets and keepsakes.

"Do you like it?" I asked, my eagerness giving way to uncertainty.

Becky looked like she was struggling. Her mouth opened and then closed without any sound passing her lips. I thought I saw the sheen of unshed tears, but then she blinked, and I wasn't so sure. Her spine went ramrod straight and her shoulders pushed back.

"I can't accept that."

"What?" Her words hit my heart like shards of ice. "Why not?"

Becky let out a gust of breath and her shoulders slumped. "Oh, Luke, don't make such a big deal about it. It's just a...a...a stupid box."

A stupid box? My lungs collapsed. Granted, it wasn't the Hope Diamond or some priceless family jewels, but I thought she loved ballet. All things with those fluffy skirt. I thought I knew at least something important about my wife.

I didn't know anything.

With a heavy heart, I softly closed the lid to the music box, cutting off the sweet notes drifting through the vehicle. Returning the unwanted gift to my bag, I leaned back in the seat and stared out the window. Trees and buildings whizzed past my vision. The tension in the cab intensified with each mile. Becky jumped out of the truck a split second after she rammed the transmission into park and stalked toward the barn without a word.

I trudged toward the house with a tornado of confusion and frustration blowing inside my head. I really needed to find a local gym. The muscles in my shoulders bunched as the tension in my body increased. My fists itched to release the tightly wound stress on a punching bag. Pounding the pavement in my running shoes would have to work for now.

I quickly changed into a pair of gym shorts and a wicking shirt. As I stepped out of the house, I looked toward the barn. I considered informing Becky that I was going for a run, but shook my head. She didn't care where I was or what I was doing. Conversation with her right now seemed pointless, and I didn't care to be on the receiving end of another scornful look or scathing retort.

I didn't bother stretching. I needed open road, and I needed it now. I lengthened my stride and set out at a fast pace. With every slap of my foot on the asphalt, the cacophony booming between my ears died. Soon, the only sound I was conscious of was the cadence of my feet and the rhythm of my breathing. Sweat, hot and salty, burned my eyes. I blinked back the sting, refusing to lose the tempo of the run.

My legs ate up mile after mile. My lungs burned and my heart pounded, but still I pushed myself forward. The sun was setting behind me, giving way to the twilight that was beginning to ascend in my path. To my right and left, the sky was a soft, light shade of blue, ever darkening across the horizon toward the center of my vision. The first stars of night began to dot the sky.

When I reached the driveway, I finally allowed my body to slow. My chest heaved in my lungs' attempt to take in more oxygen. My wet shirt clung to my skin, and I shook out the exhaustion from my arms.

The lights in the house and barn were off, and the

property was getting darker by the second as the husky glow of twilight faded to the stark blackness of night. Becky's truck was gone, and I kicked myself at the relief I felt.

A jiggling of the knob revealed the front door locked. Thankfully we'd had a key made when I first moved in. Unlocking the door, I stepped inside and turned on the light. First thing I needed was a shower. I was sweaty and tired and just wanted to stand under the steady stream of warm water.

I grabbed a towel from the cabinet and turned the knob on Becky's door. My shoulder bounced off the wooden barrier when it refused to open. Locked. Really? I didn't even know the door had a lock on it. Becky had never used it before.

A growl tore from the back of my throat as my fist slammed against the door. If I ever met the person who built this poorly designed house, I'd have a few choice words to say to him. Whoever heard of having to go through the bedroom to get to the only bathroom?

Running out of options and patience, I called Becky. It went straight to voice mail.

Dried sweat left a stiff white ring on my skin. I wasn't sure when Becky would be home and I was running out of time. I had to leave early in the morning for training and still needed to pack for the weeklong trip.

Not liking my options, I grabbed some soap and stalked out of the house, slamming the door behind me. The air was cooling without the heat from the sun, but it felt good against my warm skin. My blood was still pumping hard from my run and now, also, from my rising temper.

A coiled hose lay on the ground opposite a water trough. Turning the spigot, water gushed from the opening of the green rubber tube. I pulled my shirt up over my head and tested the water by letting it run through my fingers. It was as if someone had dumped chunks of ice into the well. I leaned over and lifted the hose, letting the water run over my head and through my short hair. A small stream of liquid snaked down my back, sending an involuntarily shudder through my muscles. Man, it was cold. Better to get the process over with as quickly as possible.

I contemplated stripping off my shorts, but my sense of modesty held me back. I hastily worked up a sudsy lather and then rinsed with the spray of glacial water, watching the bubbles glide off my skin, which, even in the light of the moon, I could see was turning a pinkish color. I vigorously rubbed the plush towel over my shivering frame, hoping the friction would return some circulation to my body. Wrapping the long cloth about my shoulders, I jogged to the house.

Once I was in dry clothes again, I checked my phone. No messages. Becky hadn't called or texted. I was at a loss. If I hadn't known where my wife's heart stood before, then I was as good as in a foreign country with no map now. What could have caused the transformation? I had no idea, but I was determined to find out, one way or another.

Chapter Twenty-Seven

Rebekah

The blood in my veins didn't pump red. It pumped yellow. I couldn't even call myself a scaredy-cat. That wouldn't be fair to cats. I had once seen Mittens jump from a ten-foot branch of an oak tree, a feat I deemed courageous. Nevertheless, I found myself driving to Grandview less than an hour after picking Luke up at the airport. And it wasn't Luke I was afraid of.

I was afraid of myself. Or, rather, the reaction I had when in Luke's presence. I'd thought the sight of the man would fill me with loathing. And it did, for a while. But the bitterness soon mixed with unwanted compassion as I saw the hurt and confusion in his eyes in response to my rejection. The yearning of unrequited love mingled in the swirling vortex of my emotions.

When he had tried to give me that gorgeous music box, I'd almost been undone. The threads of my resolve nearly severed. I'd waivered and come close to giving in to his masculine charm.

So in a dire effort to protect myself from my own

imprudence, I was cloistering myself away in hiding for the night. If Lisa had been in town, I would have gone to her house. But, even though I got along well with her parents, I didn't want to have to explain why I, a grown woman with her own house, needed a place to stay for the night. It just wasn't a conversation I was willing to have with them. A hotel would have been the obvious choice for an alternate sleeping arrangement, but Meadowlark didn't boast such an establishment. More's the pity.

As it was, I was silently praying Rita would be on duty at Grandview. The nursing home didn't exactly allow overnight guests. I felt somewhat ashamed at taking advantage of my newfound friendship with the innocent and obliging CNA, but I didn't see any other options either. Besides going back home and facing Luke, that is. And in my book, that wasn't an option.

Grandview's parking lot was nearly empty. The only cars present were those of the staff. I parked near the entrance, rotating the key in the ignition and sliding it out. Turning off the truck's headlights, the darkness of the evening enclosed around me, nearly suffocating me with its despondency. The only light, the only reassurance, came from the fluorescent bulbs illuminating Grandview's front porch.

Stepping out of the truck, sound of hundreds of little wings rubbing together serenaded me. The mellifluous cadence of the country—crickets. The decreased speed of their song testified to the cooling weather. So did the tiny pinpricks on my skin. I should have grabbed a sweatshirt. I wrapped my arms about myself and hastened inside the nursing home.

"Ms. Becky!" Rita's thick accented voice was a whole octave higher in her surprise at my presence. "What you doing here?"

"Umm...well...you see..."

"Everything okay?" Her eyebrows knit together in concern.

I started to nod but then shook my head. "Not really. I know it's a bit unconventional, but can I stay here tonight? I can sleep on the couch in the front room."

"What wrong? Why you need stay here?" Her perplexity showed in the tilt of her head.

I sighed. I wasn't going to get off the hook without an explanation. "Things with Luke have turned a little...complicated."

"Compli—" The word tied her tongue. It obviously wasn't in her everyday vocabulary.

My shoulders slumped. I might as well tell Rita the whole sordid story. My soul yearned to confide in someone anyway. So with words that left a sour taste in my mouth, I spewed the truth of my marriage, the unexpected love I came to have for my husband, and, worst of all, my recent discovery of his disreputable character.

"I do not believe it," Rita exclaimed. "Mr. Luke, he a good man. I do not think he do this thing you say he do."

I frowned. I should have just kept my big mouth shut. "Look, can I sleep on the couch tonight, or what?" I couldn't quite keep the bite out of my voice. "Luke's leaving in the morning for training, and I'll figure something else out then."

Rita bit her lower lip, her eyes darting around. "I guess so?" It sounded more like a question than a statement as her shoulders rose to reach her ears.

"Thanks. I'll be out of here before the first resident wakes up." I turned my back on my friend and left without another word.

The couch in the front room was comfortable enough as I snuggled down into its springy cushions. I pulled the crocheted afghan from where it hung over the back of the sofa and cocooned myself in its warmth. Emotional exhaustion soon pulled me into a fitful sleep.

The clearing of a throat registered through the sleep-induced fog clouding my brain. I grunted, turned on to my side, and pulled the cover up closer to my chin.

The throat cleared again. This time followed by a deep voice that called my name. "Miss Sawyer."

I squinted against the morning sun and blinked rapidly to dislodge the sleep that was clinging to me much like a toddler to his mother.

"Miss Sawyer," the voice said again with more persistence and impatience.

I managed to collect enough of my faculties to look up and recognize that the voice belonged to Dr. Henshaw. Bolting upright, I extricated myself from the blanket and hopped off the sofa.

"Dr. Henshaw, how good to see you. How're you doing this morning, sir? I wanted to talk to you about Poppy. He seemed to be getting better, but now he looks like he's going downhill again. Is that normal? Should I be worried?" I spoke with the speed of a great thoroughbred racehorse. Secretariat wouldn't have been able to catch the words flowing out of my mouth. As I spoke, my hands worked in a frenzy folding the afghan and replacing it to the back of the couch.

I glanced at the clock on the wall. "Well, it was good seeing you, Dr. Henshaw, but I really must be going now. We'll have to discuss Poppy another time. Hope you have a good day." I dashed to the exit, leaving behind a befuddled, droopy-eyed physician in my wake.

I breathed a sigh of relief upon entering my truck. I could've kicked myself for oversleeping. Hopefully, Rita wouldn't receive any repercussions for my actions.

Not in a hurry to return home, I stopped at a coffee shop and leisurely sipped a caramel Frappuccino, watching the minutes on the clock tick by. Getting caught off guard once in a day was enough. I wanted to make sure enough time passed that Luke would be gone from the house before going back.

My phone vibrated in my pocket. Withdrawing it, I squinted at the screen. The sun was streaming through the coffeehouse window, producing a horrendous glare off the screen. Tilting the phone, I was shocked to find so many missed calls and texts. I opened the messaging service and began reading the texts I had slept through the night before.

Where are you? We need to talk.

It's getting late and I'm worried about you. Are you coming home?

Rita just called and told me you are at Grandview. I thought about coming but decided you must need your space. Do you want me to come?

Becky, I don't know what is going on, but whatever it is, we can talk about it.

Hey, I've got to go to training. I'll be back in a week. I hope that is enough time for you to figure out whatever it is you're going through.

I miss you and I'll be praying for you.

All the texts were from Luke. All the missed phone calls as well, although he didn't leave any voice mails. I resisted the urge to slam my head against the table. What was his game? What was his angle? It didn't make sense to me. But no matter what, I couldn't let his smooth talking dissuade from the hard facts of what had transpired in Michigan.

"Is this seat taken?"

My head snapped up at the sound of the voice that had haunted me day and night only a few short months ago.

So much for not getting caught off guard a second time that day.

I leaned back in my chair, crossed my arms, and glared. "Depends on who's asking."

James slid into the seat across from me despite my not giving him permission, much less an invitation. "Now, Becky, don't be like that."

"And how exactly do you expect me to be?" My voice was clipped.

"Civilized. A Christian. You are still a Christian, aren't you?"

Ouch. That hurt. "Yes, I'm still a Christian." Although I felt anything but Christ-like at that particular moment.

"Then what about loving your neighbor and forgiving seventy times seven and all that other junk you used to spout off about?"

I sighed and uncrossed my arms. "What do you want, James?"

He leaned forward and tried to take my hand.

I practically sat on them to keep them out of his reach.

He shrugged and pretended my reaction didn't bother him.

"Honestly, babe? I don't know. I saw you sitting here all alone, and I thought I'd come over and—"

The sounds of *Swan Lake* coming from my phone interrupted whatever it was James had planned to say. Which was fine by me. I didn't want to hear it anyway.

Dr. Smuthers's name registered on the caller ID. I stood and grabbed my almost empty Frappuccino and still-ringing phone.

"I've got to go, James. See you later." Hopefully much, much later.

I answered the phone as I stepped outside. "Hello, Dr.

Smuthers."

"Becky, we've got an issue. Mr. Bronson is having another horse confiscated, but animal control doesn't have a trailer available for transport. Are you free to lend a helping hand?"

I climbed into the truck and revved up the engine. "I can be there in about an hour. Will that work?"

"Perfect. There should be an animal control agent there to oversee the pickup. Thanks, Becky."

"No problem." I flung the phone onto the passenger seat and fired up the engine.

Fifty minutes later, I pulled up to a long driveway with overgrown grass hedging both sides, ending at a rundown house. The paint was chipped off the wood siding and the roof sagged in certain places. To the left of the house, a rusted Oldsmobile Cutlass hid like a ravenous lion in the tall vegetation. The place looked deserted. There wasn't an animal control vehicle anywhere on the property that I could see.

Curiosity pushed me out of my truck, but life didn't stir as I glanced around. Maybe I had the wrong place. I pulled out my cell, ready to make a call to Dr. Smuthers, when a soft whinny lured me past the house. My spine set rigid as I rounded the corner. Stuffed in a round pen meant for a pony, a full-grown Clydesdale pawed at the dust. His skin sagged from his back. Brown sugar-colored fur stuck out in dull patches. What was happening here? A draft of this size should be full, his coat should gleam in the sunshine, and he should not be shut up in a cage like a stuffed animal in a retail supply warehouse.

The metal pen was so corroded, the original color was impossible to decipher. Running a finger across the oxidized surface, I wasn't surprised to see the tip turn orange. Upon closer inspection, the desperate horse's neck and shoulders also sported orange stripes.

The ground in and around the pen was barren, made up of pulverized rock and settled dust. Not a single green shoot colored the harsh brown of the inhospitable earth. The horse, desperate for a morsel, tucked his enormous head between two rungs of the pen and stretched his neck, his lips extending even farther in a vain attempt to reach a blade of grass.

I scowled as I speared the area around me with a searching glance. Where was the owner? How could people treat animals this way? Compassion and anger pulled me in different directions.

I wrapped my hand around a fistful of grass and heaved. The ripping of California flora was like a dinner bell to the near-starved equine, and he lumbered to me, his upper lip curling around my offering, and his teeth grazing my open hand.

"And just what do you think you're doing, missy?"

I turned and met the outraged glare of a man twice my size. While he didn't have an overwhelming height, a few inches taller than me at the most, his girth was that of what the horse beside me should have possessed. His sweat-stained John Deere hat shadowed his eyes and the rest of his face was covered in an unkempt bushy beard. Dark crescents stained his shirt under his arms. His overalls could have once been a denim-blue color but were now nondescript. A spray of brown tobacco-filled saliva shot from his mouth in a long stream and landed inches from my foot.

He took a menacing step toward me. "This here is private property."

Where was animal control? Sent me here without backup? This could get ugly. I couldn't take the horse without the proper authorities present, and there was no way I was going to leave without that poor emaciated creature loaded safe in the trailer.

I pushed down the trepidation that gurgled in the pit of my stomach and squared my shoulders. Best to show no fear. "My name is Rebekah Sawyer, and I'm here to—"

"I know who you is." Another jet of chew juice ejected from the crude man's mouth, this time landing a bulls-eye on top of my boot. "And you've no right to be here."

I opened my mouth to object, but the man, I presumed Mr. Bronson, took another ominous step forward. "If I was you, I'd get my skinny little behind back in my truck and hightail it out of here, or I might just think you were here to steal another one of my horses. Are you here to take Big Ben from me, missy?"

Mr. Bronson pulled out a hunting knife from one of the side pockets of his overalls. With a quick flick of his wrist, the knife snapped open, the sun glinting off the steel of the blade. He caressed the knife's edge between his thumb and forefinger, all the while looking at me in a way that set my teeth on edge.

"Animal control." The words were strangled by my rising fear. I cleared my throat and grasped at confidence I didn't feel. "Animal control has asked me to come, Mr. Bronson. Big Ben obviously needs some help, and I am willing to give it to him."

Mr. Bronson snarled like a wild beast as he advanced upon me. Like horses, I possessed that natural survival instinct of fight or flight. And like the beautiful prey animals I loved, the muscles in my legs coiled, preparing to flee from the onslaught of impending danger.

"Ho there!" A voice rang out. "This is animal control."

Mr. Bronson cursed under his breath but quickly folded his knife and put it back in his pocket.

Relief washed over me in a torrent strong enough to rival Yosemite falls. "We're over here." *Get over here.* I waved my arms in a wide arc. I didn't want to be left alone with Mr. Bronson for a second longer.

The officer high-stepped the overgrowth. My knight in shining armor. Except instead of shining armor, he wore black slack and a khaki button-up shirt with a name tag over his chest and a badge patch on his shoulder. He didn't have a gun at his hip, but he did have the power of Inyo County behind him.

I left the officer to deal with Mr. Bronson and went back to the trailer to get a halter, lead rope, and a bucket of feed.

When I made it back to the round pen, Mr. Bronson was gone, and the officer nodded to me, indicating all was well to proceed. The gate pin was nearly rusted shut. I grasped hold of the metal rail and shook. All I got for my effort were copper fleck and streaks on my hands. Grabbing the pin again, I planted my feet and pushed, using all my weight to coax it open. A little more pushing and jiggling and I was finally able to step inside the round pen.

Big Ben's nostrils flared as he smelled the food at my side. I opened the halter above the bucket, and the Clydesdale obliging placed his nose through in order to get to his meal. After buckling the strap behind the horse's ear, I snapped the lead rope beneath his chin and lifted the bucket in the circle of my arm. Big Ben was more than happy to follow me wherever I led, even into the dark, scary cave of the trailer. Of course the few flakes of hay I'd thrown in there probably helped as well.

As I drove back up the long gravel path to the main road, I was incensed. Granted, it didn't look like Mr. Bronson had a lot of extra money. If he had, then I was sure his house wouldn't have been in the condition it was in, and his own personal appearance would've been a bit more presentable. But the man's land itself was a variable smorgasbord for any livestock, including horses. Why didn't he just let his horses out of the pen to eat down some of the grass that had taken over his property? It didn't make any sense.

I shook my head. Mr. Bronson was just another man I didn't understand.

Chapter Twenty-Eight

Luke

The expansive land extended before me. To the left the ground was black as a moonless night, smoke drifting like dragon's breath and floating away on the breeze. Dotting the shadow of the earth sprang hot spots of glowing red flames. A marked blazing line separated the scorched land from that of the living prairie grass to the right. That column moved at an incredible rate, consuming life in its wake.

My job in today's exercise was that of a spotter. I watched, my eyes ever scanning, for outbreaks of hot spots, new fires that start outside the perimeter of the main fire. Not far in the distance, another line etched the terrain. Instead of red flames, this queue was made up of fellow firefighters, clothed in sunny yellow Nomex jackets and hard hats, bent at the waist, brandishing their weapons of shovel and brush hooks upon the ground at their feet. They were creating a barrier, removing all burnable fuels in the fire's path.

Another group of men and women were even closer to the approaching flames, setting a burnout fire of their own. Their objective was to consume all the fuel between the control line and the edge of the fire.

We each had our assignments, although I chafed that mine was not all that exciting. The lack of adrenaline wasn't entirely to blame for my dreadful mood, however. A whole week of training, and I'd not once heard from Becky. Not a phone call, not a text. Shoot, I'd settle for a message in a bottle or some good old-fashioned smoke signals. Anything would be better than this blasted silence.

It'd been hard to concentrate all week. Each lesson in fluctuating weather patterns and changing topography only brought to mind the unpredictability of Becky's behavior. Each drill with the chainsaw a reminder of her sharp wit and cutting actions.

"Masterson, get your head in the game and your eyes on the line!"

Rightfully chastised, I shook the wayward thoughts from my head, wishing they were as easy to erase as the doodles I used to make on my Etch A Sketch as a child. Distractions, mental or otherwise, could be the difference between life and death at the scene of a fire. Although this was only a drill, it needed to be treated as serious as the real thing.

A few hours later, the training instructor's voice rang out. "That's a wrap, folks."

We all helped clean up the equipment and store it properly away in the trucks. Hot and sweaty, some of us more streaked with black soot than others, we were all ready to return to the training center and shower.

The drive back to the city was uneventful. Conversation buzzed around me, but I wasn't in the mood to contribute. I had kept to myself most of the week, and there wasn't much of a point in changing that pattern now that it was the last day and we'd all soon be heading back to our own stations.

"Masterson," the training director called as soon as I stepped out of the truck at the center. I walked over to the man who could have rivaled Arnold Schwarzenegger in size.

"Sir?"

"You've done good work this week, Masterson. I'm going to fax over your certificate of completion to your chief as soon as we're done here."

"Thank you, sir."

"Now go get cleaned up, pack your bags, and hightail it out of here."

I grinned. "Yes, sir!"

I strode toward the large bay doors but paused and turned when the director called my name again.

"One more thing," he said as he closed the gap between us. "You've been a bit distracted while you've been here."

He held up a hand to stop the protest forming on my lips.

"Now, I didn't say anything before because you were able to perform your duties and excel in your studies. I assume it's a personal matter, and it needs to stay just that, personal. Which means, don't let it bleed into your professional life. Work it out. Figure it out. Do something. But as soon as you put on that uniform, make sure your head is where it needs to be, focused on the job at hand. You understand me, son?" His gaze bore into mine.

"Yes, sir. I do."

"Then that will be all."

I turned and continued my path toward my bunk. I needed to get this situation with Becky sorted out. Stuffing what few personal belongings I brought into my bag, I slung the strap over my shoulder and left the center. My need to see my wife, talk with her, and resolve this issue overrode my desire for even a shower. Some things could wait, and others could not.

I cranked up my Jeep and rolled down all the windows. The weather was still hot, but not as stifling as it had been when I first came to California almost two months ago. Going seventy down the interstate created a rushing circulation of wind in the vehicle, the tumultuous noise of displaced air drowning out any other sound.

On a whim, I exited the highway and stopped at a Walmart. Flowers were always a good way to say you're sorry to a woman, weren't they? Granted, I didn't know what I was apologizing for, but it was obvious I had done something wrong to garner Becky's wrath. The gesture couldn't hurt anyway.

Standing in front of the open cooler, I wished I was in a flower shop with a knowledgeable florist. I was smart enough to know that certain flowers held specific meaning, but I was a man. And there wasn't a man alive I knew who could tell me the significance of the blooms in front of me.

I grabbed a dozen roses. Classic. I should be safe with a classic, shouldn't I? But what color? They all looked pretty to me. After inspecting the bouquet I held in my hand, I returned them to the cooler. The white ones were pretty, but they were beginning to turn brown around the edges.

Growing impatient, I grabbed the bunch closest to me. Twelve long-stemmed red roses were clutched in my hand. They were beautiful. Vibrant. Delicate. At least two of those qualities I could contribute to Becky. I didn't think I'd call the feisty independent creature delicate though. I shook my head. The flowers weren't meant to be a reflection of her attributes. They were a peace offering. Or at least something to buy me enough time not to get the door slammed in my face if Becky hadn't cooled off in the week I'd been gone.

I paid the cashier and continued home.

"Becky?" I stuck my head around the front door and called into the house.

No one answered.

Stepping more fully in to the room, I called again. "Becky? You here?"

Still no answer.

Her truck was parked in its usual spot, so I knew she was around somewhere. Time to check the barn and pastures. I traipsed to the barn with the flowers held behind my back.

Scraping noises came from the far end of the building. The handles of a wheelbarrow stuck out of a stall door.

I didn't call out this time as I moved closer, but watched as she thrust a pitchfork under a mound of manure and lifted. When she turned, she froze at the sight of me. She didn't lower the pitchfork but held it in front of her like the weapon of a militiaman from the Revolutionary War. Pointed as it was at my midsection, I began to feel like Benedict Arnold under her accusatory gaze.

Remembering the flowers clutched in my clammy hands behind my back, I pulled them forward and brandished them as my own weapon of defense.

Her eyes glanced down at my proffered gift and then darted back up to my face. Tilting the pitchfork over the wheelbarrow, the contents fell with a thud. Becky let the tines rest on the ground but didn't make any move to accept the roses. She stared, waiting for me to speak.

I swallowed and lowered the flowers. I guess the bouquet wouldn't work as an armistice after all. "Becky, we need to talk. I'm sorry for whatever I—"

"I want a divorce." Her voice was steel.

I was incredulous. "What?"

"Or an annulment. I don't want to stay married to you."

I made to step toward her, but she shifted her weight back

and gripped the pitchfork with both hands.

I held up both my hands.

"It has to be after Poppy"—she swallowed hard, then lifted her chin— "after Poppy dies. Then we don't have to pretend anymore."

"Pretend?" My voice rose. "Is that what you've been doing? Pretending? Was this all some sort of game to you?"

We glared at each other, her knuckles white as they gripped the pitchfork's handle. Her whispered "no" was barely audible, but I heard it. The one word doused the fire of my rising anger.

"Becky, talk to me. What is really going on? Before I left for Michigan, I thought things were going in the right direction."

Sparks shot out of Becky's eyes at the mention of my home state. She didn't voice a complaint, but at least now I knew the origin of the problem. The origin was all I knew, however. I still didn't see the problem. I had asked her, and she had said I should go. Should I have asked her to come with me? I had just assumed it would be too much trouble finding someone on such short notice to take care of Lady, Mittens, and all the horses. Maybe she felt like I had left her behind.

"Is that the problem?" I asked. "Did you feel abandoned that I left you here?"

"Ha! That's a laugh." Sarcasm twisted her features. "I'm an independent woman. I have my own house, my own business, and my own life. I would never feel abandoned"—she spat the word—"by some man."

A sucker punch to the solar plexus wouldn't have left me more breathless...or disoriented. I tried not to take offense at being referred to as *some man* but was losing the battle. I shook my head. *Stay focused.* "Okay. Sorry. Bad choice of words."

I still felt like I was missing something. It was obvious Becky's anger was masking a deeper hurt, but I had no idea what I had done to cause it. And it didn't look like she was going to tell me any time soon. My only option was to keep probing and hope I eventually stumbled upon the answer.

"If you were fine with me leaving, then something must have happened while I was in Michigan that made you so angry."

Her eyes flashed again before her shoulders slumped.

I would have preferred the fiery fighting Becky to the defeated one who now stood before me.

"Look," she said, her voice soft and resigned. "It doesn't matter what did or didn't happen, okay? All that matters is that after Poppy dies, you sign the divorce papers." She turned her back and continued scooping and dumping. Conversation closed. For now. I'd not had my last word.

Desperation found me walking the halls of Grandview. No firefighter entered a burning building without a man on his six, and I found myself in need of such support.

Rita had already waved me through, informing me Mr. Sawyer was in his room reading. I found him there, a copy of C. S Lewis's *Mere Christianity* in his hands. He put the book down on his nightstand and indicated I sit in the only chair in the room.

"To what do I owe the pleasure of your company? And don't give me any drivel about just dropping by to see how I'm doing." Mr. Sawyer gave me a pointed look.

I laughed. "How *are* you doing, Mr. Sawyer?"

"Would be doing better if you'd start calling me something other than Mr. Sawyer. If you don't want to call me Poppy, then at least call me by my first name, Larry. You are family now. No reason to be so formal."

"Well," I said awkwardly, not knowing exactly how to proceed. "That's just it. I'm not sure how much longer I'll be a part of this family."

If he'd been a healthier man, Larry Sawyer probably would've launched himself out of the bed. As it was, harmful intent darted from his eyes. "What do you mean?" Larry's voice was razor sharp.

"I'm not going to pretend you don't know the parameters in which your granddaughter and I were married. You voiced your suspicions before the wedding, and you were right. Even with the unusual circumstances and the fact Becky and I had just met, I thought we could make it work. That if we put the Lord in the middle of our relationship, something beautiful and lasting could develop. But things have...changed."

"What has changed? Tell it to me straight, son."

"Becky wants to keep pretending we are happily married until you...well...until...you know..."

"Until I die?" the older man supplied.

"Right. And then she said she wants a divorce." I said it as a matter of fact, trying to hide the truth that the mere thought made my stomach plummet to my toes.

"Impossible. Rebekah Anne doesn't believe in divorce."

"That may have been true at one point, but she's obviously changed her mind."

The lines around Larry's mouth deepened as his lips turned down. "Do you know what brought this about?"

I shook my head. "I have no idea, and she won't tell me."

Larry sighed. "She always was one to keep things bottled up inside."

I appreciated the man's empathy, but what I really needed was advice. "What do you suggest I do? I don't know how to fix something when I don't know where it is broken."

Larry leaned over and grabbed one of the books on his nightstand. He flipped through the pages before turning the book toward me and tapping a certain point on the page.

"'You can identify them by their fruit, that is, by the way they act.'" I read aloud. "'Can you pick grapes from thorn bushes, or figs from thistles?'"

Larry took the Bible back. "That's from the New Living Translation."

"That's all well and good, but how is it supposed to help me?"

"Don't be so thick skulled," he scolded. "Let your actions speak for you. Does she think you dishonest? Be above reproach. Does she think you untrustworthy? Be ever faithful. You get the idea."

I mulled over the suggestion. "Do you think it will work? I'm not ashamed to tell you, sir, I have fallen in love with your granddaughter, and I don't want to lose her."

Larry's face split into a wide smile. "The truth always comes out son, one way or another. I know you two didn't come together in the conventional way, but I think God can use even the most unusual conditions to bring about His plan."

Chapter Twenty-Nine

Rebekah

There was an old Disney movie I loved to watch when I was a kid called *Doctor Dolittle*. They've remade the movie since producing the original, but childhood nostalgia placed my loyalties with the 1967 version. I used to pretend I could talk to my animals just like Dr. Dolittle.

It might seem crazy, thinking about a film I hadn't seen in over a decade, but I felt I could relate to one of its notable characters—Pushmi-Pullyu, the white llama-looking creature with two heads on opposite ends of a shared body. Pushmi would want to go in one direction, and Pullyu would try to go in another. And that was me. My head was pulling me one way while my heart pushed me in another.

Luke wasn't making my internal struggle any easier either. He'd spent the last two weeks doing all sorts of things that would make a normal woman ooh and aah. I had gotten so many flowers I could have made my own float for the Rose Bowl parade. More than once I had awakened early only to find the stalls already mucked, the horses fed, and a delectable feast of French toast, an omelet, or crepes—depending on the day—awaiting me at the table.

I had also received little notes and verbal words of praise. I'd been told I looked beautiful numerous times and that I was smart, funny, and kind.

With each compliment and thoughtful deed, the voice of the woman on the phone giggling and reassuring me she had *rewarded* Luke faded until it became difficult to recall at all. At first, all I had to do was conjure up that shrill voice, and self-righteous indignation would protect me against Luke and his attentions. But no matter how long I waited, or how much I tried, I couldn't find any ulterior motives to Luke's behavior. He never once attempted to move things to the bedroom and hadn't even tried to hold my hand.

My head told me to remember the facts. Luke had left under false pretenses, had even used the guise of an injured boy, to rendezvous with another woman. Common sense told me to wear these evidences as an impenetrable armor. My heart, however, argued like a first-rate defense attorney, planting reasonable doubt among all my head's logical arguments.

The bed barely moved as four tiny paws landed on its surface. Mittens butted my head with her own and then flopped down to share my pillow, pinning my hair under her body and pulling at the roots. Her long, fluffy tail twitched across my face, tickling my nose and leaving hairs in my mouth.

I sputtered and rolled out of bed while Mittens contently purred, happy to have my pillow all to herself. Who needs an alarm clock when you have animals roaming the house?

Grabbing my cell from the nightstand, I scrolled to the settings and turned off the Do Not Disturb feature. Seconds later, my phone dinged, alerting me to several missed calls. I rubbed the remaining sleep from my eyes as I punched the green icon on the lower right-hand corner of the screen.

This is Dr. Henshaw at Grandview Retirement Facility. I'm very sorry to have to tell you this Mrs. Masterson, but your grandfather has suffered a stroke and has been taken to Samaritan Hospital to receive proper medical treatment. If you have any questions, please don't hesitate to call.

The phone clicked in my ear, and the message was over. If not for my startled reaction, my hand reflexively tightening, to the front door banging open and Luke's frantic shouts of my name, I was sure the phone would have slipped through my fingers. This was the end. There would be no recovery. I was losing more than just my grandfather. It felt like I was losing a piece of myself as well.

For the first time, Luke barged through my bedroom door unannounced and uninvited. I managed to look in his direction but couldn't focus my vision. I felt like I was drowning. All I saw was blurred. Everything I heard, garbled. I tried to draw a breath, but my lungs refused to inhale any life-giving oxygen.

Luke stepped toward me and wrapped me up in his strong arms. I clung to him as I would to the reins of a runaway horse. My lungs finally cooperated, and I gasped in shuddering breaths.

"Shhh. It's okay. I've got you," Luke crooned in my ear as he rocked me back and forth.

After I didn't know how long, I finally managed to pull myself together somewhat. My nose was running, and I had the hiccups, but I felt I could stand on my own without Luke's assistance. I sniffed and gently pushed away from him. His navy blue T-shirt wet and crumpled from where I'd held on so tightly. The crisp yellow emblem over his heart not in its usual pristine condition.

Luke refused to leave me with no support. He cupped my

elbow and leaned down until our eyes were level.

"Get dressed, and I'll take you to the hospital. Or do you need some help changing clothes?" One side of his mouth quirked up in a devilish grin.

I saw through his thinly veiled attempt to make me laugh, to try and take my mind off the ominous truth. But I couldn't force an obliging chuckle past tightly compressed lips. I was doing all I could to keep it all in. One sigh, one escape of any kind, and I would fall apart into more pieces than Humpty Dumpty.

I moved to the dresser and opened a drawer, giving Luke a pointed look. Taking the hint, he left the room and closed the door behind him.

Poppy lay motionless on the bed in the hospital room, the white sheet and blanket pulled up to his chest. His arms were slack at his sides, with tubes taped and protruding from them. I slipped my hand under one of his, wincing at the paper-thin quality of his skin and the purple blotches dotting his limbs.

"Poppy, can you hear me?" My voice sounded small in my ears.

No response. Eyes closed, Poppy's chest barely rose and fell with each breath, as if he struggled against the weight of the blanket resting there.

A nurse in bright-yellow scrubs entered the room, the embodiment of sunshine herself. I resented the cheerful color, my mood more in line with a foreboding gray.

"I take it you must be Mr. Sawyer's family?" she asked with a smile, her perfectly white teeth framed by full lips that had been applied with just the right amount of lipstick.

I flicked her a glance and answered "Granddaughter" before returning my attention to Poppy.

She didn't seem put off by my shortness but continued checking monitors. I didn't pay her any attention until she tried to start up another conversation.

"In uniform, I see."

I looked down at myself. Since when were jeans and a T-shirt considered a uniform?

Luke's masculine voice answered from somewhere over my shoulder. "I was on duty when I received the call that Larry was in the hospital."

He had left work to come and get me? Another chink in my armor.

Out of the corner of my eye, I could see the nurse sidle up close to Luke. She lifted her hand and traced the insignia on his chest, flipping her jet-black hair and peering up at him through long lashes. Her voice lowered, and I couldn't make out the words she was saying to him.

Armor restored and cavalry called. I rolled my eyes. How shameless could one man be? Accepting the advances of a woman with your wife mere feet away, and in the hospital room of her dying relative.

Luke's hand came up and enveloped the nurses. Hot tears stung my eyes as I looked away.

"No, I'm sorry," his voice rang out. "Coffee later would be impossible." A warm hand cupped my shoulder. "I'll be here with my wife."

I peeked at the nurse, her eyes darting between Luke and myself. Her cheeks turned red as she stammered, "You're...she's...I'm..." She darted out of the room faster than Lady after a squirrel.

"Sorry about that," Luke murmured, my shoulder feeling bereft of his touch as he dropped his hand.

I wanted to blame him, to justify my previous denouncement of his character. But I couldn't. He hadn't done anything to encourage the woman's attention.

"Does that happen often?" I asked.

"More than you'd think," he muttered. Most guys would sound pleased or proud of the fact. Luke sounded almost disgusted.

I didn't know how to answer, so I went back to watching over Poppy. Nothing had changed, and any thread of hope I might have harbored began to fray.

A soft knock sounded at the door, and an older, spectacled doctor with a gray mustache entered. "Brittany told me family members had arrived." The doctor extended his hand, and Luke and I shook it in turn. "I'm Dr. Turner."

"How's he doing, Doctor?" I asked, my eyes resting on Poppy.

Dr. Turner approached my grandfather. "As you know, leukemia is a cancer that affects the white blood cell count in the blood. Your grandfather has more white blood cells than a healthy person. Along with these defective cells, Mr. Sawyer is also experiencing an increase in platelets, which, in some cases, can lead to clogging of the blood vessels, which in turn can lead to a stroke. This is what has happened to your grandfather."

I choked on my tears. Hearing the prognosis in medical terms did nothing to comfort me. Even so, I needed all the information I could get. "Did the stroke put him in a coma? He hasn't responded or opened his eyes since I've been here."

"Unfortunately, yes."

"Will he"—I swallowed hard—"will he wake up?"

"That's hard to say, ma'am."

My vision blurred as moisture filled my eyes.

Dr. Turner's voice became less businesslike and more compassionate as he spoke again. "No one in the medical field knows how much a comatose patient hears and understands when a loved one speaks, so go ahead and talk to him. Maybe even say your good-byes. Just in case."

I cradled Poppy's hand in mine, stroking his long fingers. I'd shooed Luke out of the room, needing some time alone with the man who'd raised me. The one man who loved me unconditionally and who I could trust without question. I was sure he was still hovering around somewhere close by, however.

I looked at Poppy's limp hand, unresponsive to my touch just as the rest of him was unresponsive to my voice. I could curse leukemia. Curse all cancer, for that matter. How could something as tiny as cells in your body cause a strong and healthy man to become weaker than a newborn baby? To end the life of one person and completely change the course of another?

I lifted Poppy's hand and pressed a kiss to the back of it. This hand that had held on to the seat of my bike, running beside me, holding me upright as I pedaled my little legs. Finally, with a push, he released his hold, and I flew down the sidewalk, a huge grin spread across my face as I mastered the two-wheeled contraption. Somehow, Poppy always knew when I needed support and when I needed to soar.

Uncurling Poppy's fingers, I held his palm to my cheek. Whenever I used to get discouraged, if I fell off a horse, or got a bad grade in school, or I caught the boy I liked kissing Amy Carmichael behind the slide on the playground, Poppy would place both hands on either side of my face and look me straight in the eye. He'd tell me how much he loved me and how special I was. He'd say, "Rebekah Anne, sometimes in life we fall down, and sometimes life pushes us down. Either way, we've got to pick ourselves back up and brush ourselves off. No matter how you feel or what someone else might tell you, you're a child of the King. And that makes you God's princess.

And you're my princess too." Then he'd kiss my forehead, swat me on the behind, and send me on my way.

Reverently, I placed Poppy's hand back onto the cot. Scooting my chair closer to his head, I softly pushed the white wispy hair off his brow with my fingertips.

"What am I going to do without you?" I whispered.

Poppy had believed in me when no one else had, when I wasn't even sure I believed in myself. He was the one who had cosigned the loan that had allowed me to buy the ranch and follow my dreams. He never told me I needed to get a conventional nine-to-five job or the security of a weekly paycheck. He never seemed worried that I wouldn't succeed. He only ever said how proud he was of me.

I laid my head against Poppy's shoulder.

"I don't know how you did it all those years. You were mother, father, and grandfather to me. I hope you know how much I appreciate everything you did. How much I love you."

We stayed like that for a long while—Poppy seemingly unaware of me in his comatose state. No flutter of his eyelids, no jerk of his body, no movement of any kind. If it weren't for the hum and beep of the monitors I would have thought he'd already breathed his last breath.

My heart was breaking, but my eyes were dry. I needed to be strong for my grandfather.

"It's okay, Poppy," I reassured him, even though I wasn't sure if he heard me or if I was just talking to myself. "I know I've been telling you to hold on, to fight. But you've fought a good fight, run a good race. The finish line is in front of you. You don't have to hold on for me anymore. I'm going to be fine." I swallowed the lump in my throat. In time I was sure that would be true.

Lifting my head, I kissed his saggy cheek. "Good-bye, Poppy."

Three days later, Poppy was gone. I thought my world would have come crashing down like the walls of Jericho, but instead I didn't feel a thing. I was completely numb. It was as if I had been shot with a thousand doses of Novocain all over my body. I could have been run over by a bus, and I doubted I would have felt the impact. I shouldn't have reacted that way, I knew. I was prepared. I had said good-bye. But I couldn't help feeling bereft. The sense of loss was keen.

I was unaware of everyday occurrences, such as the passage of time. If it was time to eat, I would find food in front of me. If it was time to sleep, I would be tucked into bed.

In the back of my mind, I knew there were things that needed to get done. I needed to find a funeral home and make the necessary arrangements. Pastor Dunbar needed to be informed of Poppy's passing so he could prepare a eulogy. I should have been thankful my list wasn't longer. When my parents had died, Poppy purchased several plots so the family could all be buried together. He didn't have a lot of material possessions, so I wouldn't have to worry about dealing with money-grubbing relatives. I grunted. Who was I kidding? Poppy had been the last member of my family. Now I was all alone. I would have taken any relatives, even the money-hungry type.

Pushing myself off the bed, I ran my hand through my hair. Or at least I tried to. My fingers snagged on several tangles, causing me to wince with pain. The numbness seemed to be wearing off, and I was feeling something again.

Lifting my eyes, I looked at myself in the mirror above the dresser. Dark bags sagged under bloodshot eyes. My hair went out in all directions around my head, testament to the night I'd spent tossing and turning. My mouth was dry, and I worked my tongue over the roof to build up saliva. A lick across my teeth had me running to the bathroom and my toothbrush. No one should have a film that thick covering her teeth.

Dissolving myself of morning breath, I jumped in the shower, making sure to use plenty of conditioner to get all the knots out of my hair.

When I finally emerged, Luke was sitting at the table, a cup of coffee in his hand.

"Welcome back," he said with a small smile. My mind supplied his inferred *to the land of the living.*

"Don't you have a job you need to get to?" I groused.

His smile slipped, and I immediately regretted my surliness.

"Actually, I took a few personal days off."

I slumped into the seat opposite him, reached across the table, and stole the steaming cup of joe, sipping it with appreciation. It would have been a completely natural act on my part. That is, if I wasn't determined he was an adulterer I was soon to divorce. However, that fact seemed to have slipped my mind in lieu of Poppy's passing.

"I'm sorry, Luke," I apologized. "I didn't mean to be so snarky. But you don't have to take time off on account of me. I'm used to taking care of myself. I'll be fine." The falsehood of the last three words left a foul taste in my mouth. I wasn't fine. I wasn't sure when I'd be fine again. But I needed to convince Luke otherwise.

"Are you saying you don't want me here with you?" His voice was quiet, his eyes sad.

The internal battle I had been struggling with raged within me. Which would win, head or heart? If I were honest with myself, the answer to his question was an easy one. I did want him here with me. I didn't want him to leave. Not today, not ever. I opened my mouth to tell him just that, when the door burst open.

"Lisa!" I cried. "What are you doing here?"

Lisa rushed in and flung her arms around me, nearly squishing me in her hug.

"Luke called me," she said, her words echoing in my ear.

I closed my eyes and returned my friend's exuberant embrace. When I opened them, Luke was slipping through the door. His unanswered question hung heavy in the air around me, the response dead on my lips.

Rebekah

"Oh, Becky," Lisa crooned. "I came as soon as Luke called."

My head still spun with the fact Lisa was sitting with me, that Luke had called her in the first place, and that I had let him walk out of the house without telling him I wanted him to stay. With the way I'd treated him, I wouldn't be surprised if he went to get the divorce papers himself.

I pulled my focus back to the conversation at hand. "I'm so glad you're here," I said, still a bit distracted.

"I'm glad to see you're more yourself now. Luke told me how out of it you'd been. Said he practically had to spoon-feed you. He was really worried. He cares for you a lot, you know."

How had I not realized it had been Luke all along who'd been the one looking out for me? Why had he done it? I surely hadn't deserved it. I could no longer fool myself that his kind actions had ulterior motives. I'd already decided to go with my heart. As much as I tried to hold on to my hurt as a shield, I'd slowly been stripped of that armor until I was utterly defenseless. I was in love with my husband. I admit it. There was nothing left to do but forgive him of any indiscretion.

But maybe there was a scenario that had occurred in Michigan other than the one that *woman*—my Christian charity restrained me from calling her something more colorful—had portrayed. Was there a way to silence the doubts lingering in my mind?

She squeezed my shoulder. "I have to tell you, even though I agreed to find you a husband and we prayed about it, I was still skeptical that everything would turn out all right. It was just too crazy to conceive. But look at the two of you now. You guys are obviously in love. The whole thing is so romantic."

Lisa's incessant prattle registered through my introspection.

Lisa! She'd been there. Maybe she would know the truth.

"Hey," I interrupted, "you saw Luke during his trip back east, right?"

"Yeah. I had dinner with him and his family one night."

"Was that before or after he supposedly saw Marty in the hospital?"

"After. Wait, what do you mean supposedly?" Lisa scratched the side of her head.

"I called Luke when he was in Michigan. Only he didn't answer. A woman did. She told me Luke had gone there to see her and that she had *rewarded*"—my mouth twisted as I spat the foul word—"him for his effort."

Lisa's jaw hung open. "I don't believe it. Becky, he told us he loved you that night. Why would he say that if he'd been with another woman?"

If only all the pieces would line up. "He said he loved me?" My voice was small, unbelieving, as my heart raced.

Lisa nodded. "Did you talk to Luke about it? What did he say?"

"I know I probably should have confronted him, but what

if he just denied it? Could I trust him to tell me the truth? In my experience, cheating men are also liars."

"I'm going to get to the bottom of this." Lisa retrieved her purse from where she'd dumped it by the door. Rummaging through her Vera Bradley bag, she withdrew her phone.

Lisa gave me one confident nod of her head with an accompanying wink. I returned the gesture with a reticent smile. I was starting to have second thoughts. Maybe not knowing for certain wasn't so bad.

"Hey, honey, I'm here with Becky, and she just told me something very interesting. We need your insight on the matter." Lisa relayed all I had told her.

I followed along with the discussion as best as I could, being privy only to Lisa's responses. "Mhmm…Oh really?…Isn't that interesting…Yes, he should have told her." The conversation turned decidedly more personal when Lisa's voice grew intimate. "I miss you too, but we'll see each other in a few days. I love you." Pause. "Bye."

I pounced as soon as she ended the call. "He should have told me what?"

"Apparently, Marty's mom has made advances toward Luke in the past. He turned her down one too many times, and she fired him from being Marty's tutor. Sam thought Luke should have told you about her, but since Luke didn't date her or have any interest in her whatsoever, he thought it was a nonissue. He said you had too many other things you were worrying about."

My breath left me in a whoosh, and I felt like I had been punched in the stomach. "So, what? She made it all up?"

Lisa squeezed my hand. "Looks that way."

I shook my head. I was completely dumbfounded. Why would anyone say something so malicious, so vengeful? And I had believed every foul word like it was the absolute truth, never questioning the word of a stranger over that of my own husband.

A groan strangled in my throat as I remembered the horrible way I'd treated Luke since he'd come back. He'd presented me with a beautiful and thoughtful gift, an exquisite music box, and I'd called it stupid. Stupid! If only I could go back and tell him how much I really loved it. How much the gesture meant to me. How much he meant to me.

I bolted off the couch faster than if someone had poked me in the behind with a knitting needle. "I've got to go find Luke."

I needed to talk to him, and it couldn't wait another minute. I never once thought that a proper grieving granddaughter would go gallivanting off to declare her undying love in the wake of her grandfather's death. Okay, maybe that was a bit dramatic. But if I *had* thought of it, I knew Poppy would have approved. He did, after all, want to see me happily married before his passing. I arranged the married part. Thankfully, God provided the *happily* portion. Now to go find that husband of mine and assure I *stayed* happily married.

Lisa chuckled as I dashed out the door.

A few feet from the house, I paused, looking right and left. Which way to search first?

Lady barked from the barn. It wasn't one of her happy I-found-a-squirrel-to-chase yaps either. No, this one was low, laced with a warning growl. I sighed. I wasn't in the mood for a detour, but I needed to make sure nothing was threatening the horses. Coyotes were known to roam the area, and I didn't relish the idea of doctoring bite marks, or worse, losing an animal.

Lady's next bark ended in a pain-filled yelp, and I sprinted the rest of the way to the stables. Searching through the stalls, I found her lying in a heap on a bed of hay.

"Lady!" I rushed to her side.

Only I never made it.

Once over the threshold of the stall, I was grabbed from behind in a vice grip, the biting point of knife pressed to my neck. I inhaled sharply, and my punishment was immediate and twofold. The jerky movement of my involuntary gasp caused my neck to rasp against the edge of the blade. The small puncture stung, but it could have been, and still might become, much worse. I needed to stay as still as possible. I gagged. And breathed as little as possible. The stench of the unwashed body that held me turned my stomach.

The man's chest rumbled against my back in his mirth. "My day keeps getting better and better."

My mouth filled with saliva, but I didn't want to swallow. I wasn't keen on my skin moving against that blade again. With small movements, I asked, "Who are you? What do you want?"

"Who am I?" The man snorted. "With all the horses you've stolen from me, little lady, you'd think you'd know who I was." Then he leaned his head down till his mouth was next to my ear. A wiry beard scratched my face. Bile burned my throat.

"But don't you worry none. We've time to get better acquainted." The knife that had been pressed to my throat now traced a line down my cheek as my assailant caressed me with the blade. "Maybe you can pay me back for all your thieving ways." The hand that didn't hold the knife slid down and cupped my breast.

My heart pounded in my chest, and my head raced to find a way out of the situation. I had been scared before but thought I might be able to talk some sense into the guy. But he had just doubled the stakes, and I wasn't the betting kind. Desperation clawed at my every nerve.

My only saving grace was the fact I wasn't entirely alone. Yards away, Lisa sat in the house. If I could somehow get her attention, she could call for help.

A car door closed in the distance. The man and I both froze. Hope began to rise until the turn of an engine squished it like a tiny ant. The crunch of tires driving away was a death knell.

"Looks like it's just you and me."

My breathing came in heavy gasps, and I swallowed a whimper. I willed Lady to get up. She was my only help, but my hero still lay motionless on the ground. What had the guy done to her? A quick kick wouldn't have rendered her so pathetically immobile.

"You don't have to do this," I pleaded.

His evil chuckle curdled my blood. The flat of his blade lay vertically on my cheek at a slight angle, the tip pushing into my skin. The vile beast increased the pressure. I could either move my head or feel my blood run down my face.

Turning my head, I met cold black eyes. Eyes I'd seen just days before. Mr. Bronson. He leered at my recognition, crooked teeth flashing behind his grimy facial hair. He crushed his mouth hard against mine. My teeth cut into my lip, the metallic taste of blood dancing across my tongue.

Mr. Bronson pulled me out of the stall toward the entry. Where were we going? He stopped near the trash can that held yards of cut orange bailing twine. He bent down to withdraw a piece of rope, and I saw an opportunity for escape. The door to the barn was wide open and only a few feet in front of me.

I dashed forward.

An anvil-sized fist to my temple dropped me to my knees. Bright spots swam in my vision, and my ears rang. My head jerked back as one of his massive paws pulled my hair. Tears stung my eyes, and my scalp throbbed.

I whimpered as he replaced the knife at the base of my neck, right above my collarbone. Hot, rancid breath tickled my ear as Mr. Bronson whispered in an all-too-calm tone of voice, "Try that again, and you're dead."

I closed my eyes tight, and twin tears streaked down, wobbled on my chin, and fell to the floor.

A yank on my hair and I was scrambling as fast as I could sideways on my hands and knees. I held my head and neck at an odd angle, trying to alleviate some of the shooting pain from being half dragged.

We entered another empty stall. If only I'd kept some of the horses in today. Mr. Bronson shoved me in the hip with a booted foot, and I sprawled onto the sawdust-covered ground.

"Hands behind your back," he barked.

I scrambled to my feet and obediently turned my back to him, placing my hands together. The coarse bailing twine cut into my wrists as he tied them together. With a push to the shoulder, I landed once more on the unforgiving floor. A sharp pain in my lower back made me suck my teeth.

I looked up and watched in horror as Mr. Bronson began unbuckling his belt, his knife still present in one of his hands. I had to do something, and I had to do it now.

Lifting my leg, I kicked with all my might. My foot landed square in his groin. The man doubled over, dropping the knife. I clambered toward the weapon, shoving it under a thick layer of sawdust behind me.

"Why you little—"

His hand crossed his shoulder and came down hard on the side of my head.

My body shot backward with the force of the blow. Darkness enclosed around me in slow motion. Then all went black.

Chapter Thirty-One

Luke

Larry Sawyer had been wrong. The old adage "actions speak louder than words" was wrong. And the Bible, at least in this respect, was also wrong. Either that, or Becky was blind and didn't see my "fruits."

I had done everything I could possibly think of to show her that I was trustworthy, honest, and hard working. That I loved her. But she didn't want me to stay. I'd given her the opportunity to stop me from leaving, and she hadn't said a word. Her silence spoke volumes

Kicking at a small rock in my path, I chuckled derisively. God had said if I loved her, she would love me in return. Where was the fruition of that promise now? I'll tell you where. In the rectangular form of divorce papers.

I mentally checked over everything I had ever done and said in my relationship with Becky. Coming to the end of the tally, I stopped dead in my tracks.

My forehead smarted from the impact of the palm of my hand. How could I have been such an idiot? I had gone to such pains to *show* Becky that I loved her, but I had forgotten to *tell* her.

No time like the present. I turned around, imagining walking up to Becky, taking her hands in mine, looking deep into her eyes, and saying—

My nose twitched. I inhaled, and a faint but familiar smell swirled in my nostrils. "Is that smoke?"

I squinted, peering through the trees. A jolt of adrenaline shot through me at the orange glow in the distance. Pumping my arms and stretching my legs, I raced through the underbrush and dodged saplings, making a beeline toward the fire.

Too many questions assailed me as I neared the burning building.

Becky's barn.

My heart pounded with adrenaline. I needed to clear my mind. Keep it professional. Good thing Becky was safe in the house with Lisa. One less thing to worry about.

Quickly assessing the situation, I scrambled for my phone.

"Nine one one dispatch. What's your emergency?"

"I'm at 8920 West Laurelbrooke Avenue in Meadowlark. The barn is on fire. Please send the fire department." I pushed the End button and dropped the phone. I knew the woman with the no-nonsense voice would've told me to stay on the line, but there was no way that was going to happen. I needed to call Becky.

The ringing was loud in my ear as it came through the speakers of my phone, but…was that…?

My blood ran cold. Becky's phone was ringing in the barn.

Stripping out of my shirt, I plunged it into the water trough and held it up to my face as I dashed through the open door of the barn. A wall of heat hit me with staggering force. What I wouldn't have given for a Nomex jacket and a SCBA mask.

I needed to search the area fast. There was way too much fuel, what with the wooden structure, the hay, and the sawdust littering the floor, to think this fire wouldn't spread in record time. Already the hairs on my arm felt singed from the sheer temperature surrounding me.

Crouching low, I removed my shirt from my mouth and shouted, "Becky!"

A terrified whinny, along with the crackling of fire, was all the answer I received.

Continuing down the aisle, I searched. Smoke made my eyes water, and my lungs ached from lack of oxygen. One of Becky's precious linemen might as well have been sitting on my chest.

A hacking cough sounded ahead of me and to the right. A stall door burst open, and Becky's bent frame emerged, silhouetted in front of the orange flames just beyond. Without a glance in my direction, she turned right and limped away from me and toward the center of the angry inferno.

She stumbled and reached a hand against the wall to support herself, her shoulders shaking as her lungs attempted to empty themselves of carbon dioxide and fill with oxygen. Still she shuffled forward. Was she disoriented? I needed to get to her before she became charbroiled.

Ignoring everything I knew about staying as low to the ground as possible, I sprinted to her side and swung her around by her arm. She screamed and clawed at me. I tried to pin her arms, but she continued to fight and push against me. One of her eyes was swollen shut, and the other was filled with intense fear. Blood oozed from a cut on her lip.

"Becky! Becky! Calm down. It's me," I shouted, trying to get through the hysteria that clutched her.

I had to get her to stop fighting me so we could both live

to see another day.

Images of Lopez slapping sense into the autistic boy surfaced. I ground my teeth. The situation might be dire, but there was no way I was going to strike a woman, much less the woman I loved.

Releasing Becky's arms, I put both hands to the sides of her face in a grip only slightly gentler than a vice. Licking my chapped lips, I tilted her head up until our mouths met. I could taste her blood, feel the swollenness of her precious skin.

She redoubled her efforts to fight against me. The vibration of a strangled scream slapped my lips. Real tears, not those produced by the fire's smoke, burned my eyes. Yet I did not relent. We were running out of time.

I deepened the kiss, my mouth moving over hers gently yet insistently. Loosening my grip with one hand, I caressed her cheek with my thumb. Slowly she began to soften against me. The crazed look in her one good eye dissipated, recognition flashing in its place. Her lips began to respond beneath mine, and I pulled away. As much as I wanted to continue the kiss, the hiss of the fire moving toward us took precedence.

Snatching Becky's wrist, I pulled her toward the entrance. "We've got to get out of here."

A quick twist and tug, and my hand grasped nothing but air. I turned toward Becky's retreating back.

"I've got to get Lady and Artie," she yelled over her shoulder.

Stubborn woman. We were all going to burn alive like Dark Age martyrs.

I swung her back around and jammed my finger in the direction of the door. "Get out, now. I'll get the animals," I growled.

She hesitated a moment and then limped away. I sighed in

relief. At least she would soon be safe. Turning toward the ever-growing flames, I doubted I would have the same fate.

The shriek of a horse's cry and the loud thud of hooves against wood directed me toward Artie's stall. The metal pin holding the door closed seared my skin at first touch. Gritting my teeth against the pain, I flung open the door and watched as the large animal darted out, eyes wide and nostrils flaring.

One down, one to go.

The thick smoke brought me to my hands and knees. I only had time to look in one more stall. Every second I stayed in the burning building reduced my chances of making it out alive. I crawled to the door, the palm of my burned hand throbbing.

It was hard to see through the dense haze, my watery eyes, and the spasms of coughing that racked my body every few seconds, but there appeared to be a dark mound in the corner of the enclosure.

My strength was leaving me as my body was depleting of life-giving oxygen. I pulled myself toward the mass. Lady's body lay motionless. Wrapping an arm around her body, I shifted the dog's weight onto my lap. With one arm around her chest and the other under her tail, I hefted the animal up, staggering under her weight. Why couldn't that woman own a Chihuahua?

My steps were slow and excruciating. My skin burned from the heat at my back and the clothes that had absorbed the fire's intensity. The fabric scourged me with every forward movement. I stumbled and clutched the dog closer to my chest.

In the distance, the sound of siren wails combated with the noise of the blaze's destruction. The men and women in uniform wouldn't be able to save Becky's barn, but they would be able to keep the fire contained to the one building. Her home, at least, would be safe.

Blessed sunlight beckoned to me from the small opening of the doorway. Stepping over the threshold, strong hands gripped my arms, supporting and leading me to safety.

Becky jerked off the oxygen mask covering her nose and mouth and limped toward me, leaving a protesting fireman in her wake. Her eyes darted up and down, yo-yoing between my face and the still form of her beloved dog in my arms.

Her gaze at last rested solely on me while a sooty hand absently stroked Lady's head. "Are you okay?" she croaked. Her voice sounded like gravel from the smoke she'd inhaled.

My eyes roamed her body, taking inventory of the bruised and swollen eye, cut lip, and ripped jeans that revealed a nasty gash on her left calf. Her face and arms were smudged with dark ash. Sawdust and hay clung to her hair.

"I'll be fine." I managed a hoarse whisper—my own voice had taken a beating by the fire. "But how did you—"

"Mrs. Masterson, we really need to see to your injuries." A uniformed fireman cupped Becky's elbow and drew her back toward the oxygen tank.

So many unanswered questions shot through my mind. Was someone responsible for Becky's bruised and bloodied body, or was it just some kind of horrible accident? The weight in my arms tipped the scales to more than an accident. The logical conclusion would be that whoever harmed Lady also hurt Becky and started the fire.

Was this linked to the threatening note I'd found in Becky's jacket pocket? She'd been so sure it was just an innocent prank from some mischievous teenagers. Well, arson and attempted murder were anything but innocent.

More sirens filled the air as an ambulance approached the foray of first responders. Two men exited the vehicle, snapping on latex gloves over their hands. One moved toward Becky. He squatted down to her level. After speaking to her for a few moments, he began probing, first her face, then her leg.

"Sir?"

It's amazing how much a person's mind can tune out. I'd been intently focused on Becky, but now, with only one word, that focus shattered, and the sights and sounds surrounding me flooded my senses. The spray from the large water hoses roared. The fire hissed. Falling timber thudded to the ground as the barn collapsed one beam at a time. Uniformed personnel scurried in their efforts to abate the flames. Flashing lights flitted from surface to surface in a twirling rotation.

"Sir?"

A young paramedic gained my attention through all the chaos.

"Sir, I need to check you over."

I allowed the man to lead me toward the back of his ambulance. An oxygen mask settled in front of my nose and mouth as the elastic band slid over my head. He reached for the dog, and I allowed him to take her. The paramedic's palm warmed the back of my hand, rotating until my own palm was face up. A salve was applied to the burn that puckered the sensitive skin.

An overwhelming need to be with Becky almost strangled me.

I removed the mask and stood. The forced oxygen made it less difficult to breathe, but being with Becky was more important than making my lungs' job easier.

A restraining hand grasped my arm. "Sir, I need you to sit."

"And I need to see my wife." My voice was anything but intimidating the way it barely came out above a whisper.

The paramedic seemed to have compassion on me anyway and nodded. "I'll have Jeff bring her over."

A few minutes later, Becky hobbled across the expanse,

one arm slung around the second paramedic's neck, his own wrapped around the second paramedic's neck, his own wrapped around her waist for support. I shook my head but couldn't help the grin that tugged at the corner of my mouth. The stubborn woman must have refused a stretcher.

"There, you two are together. Will you both cooperate now?" Exasperation laced Jeff's voice.

Reaching over, I slid my hand into Becky's, interlaced our fingers, and squeezed. If the blasted plastic masks weren't over our faces, I would have finished the kiss I'd started back in the barn. Becky leaned her head against my shoulder, her eyes focused on the ground.

The paramedics were just doing their jobs in their desire that we keep the masks on, but there was something I had to say, and it couldn't wait. I still needed to tell Becky how much I loved her.

Becky pushed her own mask to the side before I had the chance. "Can you check my dog, please?"

Jeff quirked a brow, and Becky dutifully re-covered the lower portion of her face.

Bending down, the man knelt by the dog. He placed the end pieces of a stethoscope in his ears and pressed the circular part to Lady's ribs. Frowning, he cupped a hand around Lady's nose.

He sighed as he stood, shaking his head. "I'm sorry, but your dog is dead."

Chapter Thirty-Two

Rebekah

Everyone had a breaking point. Even the best dam-building beavers, when faced with a flash flood, watch as their world literally gets swept away in a torrent. My own dam had been taking a beating, the pressure building. Little fissures had developed, but this was too much. This was my breaking point.

My chest constricted, making it increasingly difficult to breathe. Which, with the forced oxygen entering my nose and mouth through the mask secured to my face, one would think was impossible. It was as if Mr. Bronson was right there, but instead of his horrible knife to my throat, it was his huge, rough, calloused hands squeezing, tightening, cutting off my air supply.

I stared at the lifeless form just a few feet away from me. Lady had been more than just a dog, just a pet. She had been my protector against unseen enemies, my companion on lonely nights, my partner on the ranch. She had been a part of my family. And now she was gone.

I flipped the mask over my head and slid off the back of

the ambulance onto the ground. I wrapped my arms around Lady and buried my face in her soft, downy fur. I squeezed my eyes shut, but I would never be able to hold back the grief that weighed down my heart like an anvil.

Streams of tears flowed freely down my face, my shoulders convulsing with the deep loss I was drowning in. The sound of whimpering reached my ear. Was the paramedic wrong? Did Lady still live?

I lifted my head, but my faithful canine still didn't move. Her chest didn't rise and fall. Only then I realized the whimpering had escaped my own lips.

Strong hands grasped my upper arms and lifted me to my feet. Turning, I buried my face in a powerful chest, the hard muscles offering a wall of protection. Warm arms wrapped around me, supporting me when I thought my own strength wouldn't hold me up a second longer.

In a fluid motion, Luke slipped an arm under my knees and hefted me in the air, cradling me against his rock-hard body like a newborn baby. A few steps and I sat on his lap, his arms around my shoulders, my face still hidden in his chest. He rocked me back and forth, pressing kisses to the top of my head. A scratchy blue blanket was placed over my frame, and I snuggled deeper into Luke's embrace.

The initial deluge of grief began to abate, and the sobs that had racked my body turned into sniffles and hiccups. I refused to release the death grip I had on Luke's shirt or lift my head from its safe position, however. I couldn't bear to look upon the evidence of all I had lost. I needed to soak in the essence of Luke's strength a little longer.

"Mr. and Mrs. Masterson?"

My time was up. Ready or not, I had to come out of my safe hiding spot. Lifting my head, my gaze collided with a shiny silver badge pinned above the heart of the police officer who stood before us. He stood with his feet slightly apart, his black uniform crisply pressed. The man was so tall I had to tilt my head back to look into his thin face. His Adam's apple protruded from his throat in sharp angles.

I tried to push against Luke's chest and slide off his lap, not wanting to show weakness in front of a stranger and man of the law. The actions, however, were counterintuitive, for in response, Luke merely tucked me in closer and held me a little tighter.

"What can we do for you, officer?" Luke asked as he slowly trailed a single finger first down and then up my arm.

"I'm sorry." The officer's Adam's apple bobbed as he spoke. "I know this probably doesn't seem like a good time, but I'd like to ask you a few questions while the details of today's events are still fresh in your mind."

I took a long swig from the water bottle one of the paramedic's had given me. "I don't think I'll ever forget what happened today."

The officer inclined his head, and Luke pressed a kiss to my temple.

"Would you mind telling me what happened? For the record and with as much detail as possible, please."

"Well," I began but stopped to take another drink. It might have been the smoke or the effects of my sobfest, but my throat was scratchy. "I stepped outside my house and heard Lady barking and growling from the direction of the barn."

"Lady is your dog?" Officer Adam's Apple interrupted.

I nodded, my eyes flooding once more with tears.

"So you went to investigate?" probed the tall man in uniform.

I nodded again. "Yes. I wanted to make sure nothing was disturbing the horses."

"Then what happened?"

"I entered one of the stalls, and Mr. Bronson grabbed me from behind and held a knife to my throat."

Luke's body stiffened at my words.

"Mr. Bronson? Does this Mr. Bronson have a first name?"

I forced a shrug. "I'm sure he does, but I don't know what it is. I've only ever heard him referred to by his last name. You can ask animal control though. They have his name on file."

The officer wrote in his notepad. "I'll be sure to do that."

"Anyway," I continued, wanting to get it done and over with. "Mr. Bronson seemed really happy to see me. He thought I could pay him back in a...special...way for the horses he said I stole from him."

"You stole horses from him?"

"What do you mean *special* way?"

The two questions came at me simultaneously. One was asked with curiosity and a little accusation, the other with thinly veiled anger.

I sighed and rolled my eyes. "No, I didn't steal his horses. Animal control confiscated them, and I rehabilitated them."

Turning my head, my gaze bore into Luke's. "The man grabbed my breast. How do you think he wanted me to repay him?" I threw the words at him. I knew I shouldn't be taking my frustration out on him, but my nerves were raw and my patience thin.

Placing his hands on either side of my face, he peered into my eyes, searching my very soul for the answers to unasked questions. He sighed and rested his forehead against my own. I closed my eyes, relishing the closeness of the moment.

A throat cleared, and I raised my head. A single tear formed a stripe on Luke's sooty cheek. Lifting my hand, I brushed the little rivulet of water away with my thumb and offered a small smile. It felt good to reassure him for a change.

"What happened next, Mrs. Masterson?"

"I tried to escape, and he clubbed me in the head with his massive fists. Then he tied my hands behind my back with bailing twine. When he was distracted trying to undo his belt, I kicked him in the groin, and he dropped his knife. I was able to hide it in the sawdust before he came after me and knocked me out cold."

Luke sat rigid behind me. It was a good thing Mr. Bronson wasn't there at that moment, or the officer would have had to arrest two people.

"When I came to, the barn was on fire. I managed to find the knife under all the sawdust and cut my hands free." I turned to Luke. "That's when you came in."

Luke nodded and turned his attention to the officer. He picked up the story where I had left off.

"Becky was limping out of the stall when I got there. She headed toward the fire, and it wasn't until I assured her I'd find Lady and let the horse out of the stall that she finally left. I let Artie out of his stall and found Lady. By that time the fire department was here."

The officer nodded, his pencil moving across paper as he jotted down our statements. "Okay, I think I have everything I need at this point." He looked at Luke first and then me. "Rest assured, serious charges will be filed against Mr. Bronson."

Luke squeezed my shoulder.

Officer Adam's Apple nodded and marched back to his vehicle.

Luke's thumb and forefinger gently grasped my chin, drawing my attention to himself. I still sat on his lap, my legs draped over the side of his and my back resting in the crook of his arm. I would have imagined his legs were close to numb by then because of my weight, but he showed no discomfort.

His gray eyes regarded me with intent. I could have stared into them for the rest of my life. Except for the wretched crick in my neck that was developing because of the odd angle. I tried to ignore the pain, not wanting to interrupt the moment.

Before I knew what was happening, he hoisted me into the air like a child and set on my feet. I barely stood on my own strength before being lifted yet again. This time I found myself straddling Luke, our faces merely inches apart. What do you call a piggy-back ride when the person being carried was on the front instead of the back? Whatever it was called, that was how I was being held. That is, until he sat back down, bringing me to sit on his lap for a second time—face to face.

"Becky, I need to tell you something." His eyes searched mine, and the seriousness of his tone caused my stomach to flip.

Was this something I wanted to hear? Maybe all my efforts of rejecting his kindness and my stubbornness of insisting on divorce had worn down his resolve to stay with me. Was he going to tell me he was leaving?

I held my breath, steeling myself for the words that would cut me deeper than Mr. Bronson's knife ever could have.

Looking down, I avoided his eyes. I couldn't bear to look into them. My fingers fidgeted with the edge of my shirt.

"Becky," Luke's warm breath caressed my cheek. "Can you look at me please?"

My nose began to tickle, my mouth flooded with moisture, and I had to blink my eyes against the heat building behind them. All sure signs the waterworks were about to start again. I shook my head at Luke's request.

Luke again rested his forehead against the top of mine. His hand came up to hold the back of my neck.

"Becky, sweetheart." His voice sounded strangled, the pleading quality tore at my resolve. "Please."

Slowly I raised my head to meet his gaze. Against my best efforts, a tear welled in the corner of my eye. I ignored it, focusing instead on fortifying myself for whatever Luke was about to say.

Luke's face inched closer to mine, and my breath hitched as his lips softly kissed away the offending rivulet of water.

"Why are you crying?"

I sniffed and shrugged.

Luke sighed, and I thought I detected a slump in his posture. "Are there always going to be secrets between us?" he asked.

Keeping my thoughts and feelings tucked inside had always been a way to protect myself. It was a way to avoid conflict. To escape the critical looks of those who might think I was weak if I showed my struggles. Sometimes, I felt if I ignored my emotions long enough the problem would go away.

But look at what keeping things bottled up had gotten me. If I had just confronted Luke about the woman in Michigan, it would have saved me weeks of pain and heartache. We could have used that time to get to know each other better and build our relationship. Instead, I might have completely destroyed it.

It was scary, and it was hard, but Luke deserved to know what I was feeling. I swallowed against the lump that had formed in my throat.

"I...I'm scared." I forced the admission past my lips.

Luke's thumb stroked my cheek. His eyes never wavered from my own. "What are you afraid of, sweetheart?"

It was hard to open myself up, to become vulnerable, especially when I was caught in the directness of his gaze.

I knew it was cowardly, but I looked down, severing the unspoken connection. I bit my lip before answering. "I'm afraid of what you're going to say."

"And what do you think I am going to say?"

I couldn't take much more. The pressure of the unknown

had been building inside me, and I felt as if I were about to explode. I flung my arms around Luke's waist and buried my head in his neck. Pretending to be strong hadn't served me well in the past. I might as well confess my needs and desires, the desperation I felt at the thought of his leaving.

"Please don't leave me," I cried, my voice muffled. My body shuddered as he held me close. "I...I don't want a divorce."

His strong arms felt good about me. It felt right. Like it was where I belonged. When they fell away, I felt myself sinking. I tightened my own hold about him, frantic to regain what I was losing. His hands grasped my upper arms and tugged. He was pushing me away.

Our bodies separated and I hung my head. I had opened up. I had let him in. And now I was being thrust aside.

Served me right. I deserved it.

Luke's finger nudged my chin up. A small smile played across his lips.

"Becky, I wasn't going to tell you I was leaving," he said.

"You weren't?" Was there still hope? Did my black cloud have a silver lining after all?

"No." He chuckled, a sound that rumbled deep in his chest. His smile widened until it consumed his entire face. "I was going to say I love you."

"You...you love me?" I might have sounded like a blabbering idiot, but it was a complete paradigm shift and my mind was scrambling to catch up, to understand the implications, to take it all in.

His smile faded, and his expression turned serious. He held my face with both of his hands. His gaze locked with mine, and his eyes...well...let's just say I knew what romance novels meant when they said the hero gave the heroine a smoldering look.

"Becky," he said. "I"—his lips descended upon mine in a featherlight kiss—"love"—his warm breath fanned my mouth before our lips touched softly once more—"you." This time his kiss lingered. The stubble on his chin scratched my cheek, and the smell of lingering smoke burned my nose. And I loved it. Loved it all. Because I loved him.

I had uncorked my feelings and given them a voice, and the result couldn't have been more glorious. The walls I erected to protect myself from hurt had only served to imprison me. I could see now that Luke had been trying to tell me all along that he loved me through all the little things he had been doing. Could I do the same thing?

Luke began to lift his head, ending a kiss he had kept sweet. I was eager to show him that I returned his feelings, that I loved him too. That I could put love into words and actions just as he had done.

Flinging my arms around his neck, I brought his head back down toward mine. My exuberance, however, should have been tempered. His mouth smashed into mine in a crushing blow, our teeth clanking, causing my jaw to rattle.

I released my hold on the nape of his neck and opened my eyes. Luke pulled back only slightly and offered a wink before closing his eyes and angling his head. He took the lead, his mouth giving and receiving. His sturdy hands came around, one to my lower back, the other into my hair. He gathered me closer until our bodies were pressed together. A passion burned inside me ten times hotter than the fire Mr. Bronson had set in the barn.

When my lungs screamed for air and I felt like all my insides had been melted, Luke unlocked our lips. He must have had better lung capacity than I, because he continued to rain down little kisses. My eyes, my nose, my cheek, my chin—nothing was neglected.

I didn't know if it was only a memory or if God put it there, but unbidden, Genesis 24:67, a verse in the Bible at the tail end of the Isaac and Rebekah story, popped into my head. I was the only person I knew who would think of a Bible verse right after such a display of passion.

"You're grinning as if you have a secret. Care to share?" Luke asked.

"Isaac brought her into the tent of his mother Sarah, and he married Rebekah. So she became his wife, and he loved her; and Isaac was comforted after his mother's death," I quoted.

Luke quirked a brow, which caused me to giggle.

"Isn't it amazing how much alike our story is to theirs? Well, except I'm Isaac and you're Rebekah. But you came halfway across the country and became my husband. I fell in love with you, and even though Poppy has passed, you have been a comfort to me." I stopped talking long enough to taste his lips once more. "I don't know what I would have done without you."

Later that night I snuggled deep into Luke's side. His chest rose and fell in an even rhythm, his breathing heavy in slumber. I sighed. I didn't know it was possible to feel such utter contentment.

The Bible was full of stories where God had used bad or unusual circumstances to work out something beautiful and good. Me and my insane plan to grant Poppy's last wish were proof that God still had his hand in people's everyday lives.

Rolling slightly on my back but keeping my body pressed against my husband's, I stretched my arm out as far as possible, grasping for my phone on the bedside table. My fingers grazed the device, and I extended my reach even further. Painstakingly, I managed to maneuver the phone into my hand.

Nuzzling myself more securely into my husband's side, I hid the phone under the blanket. I didn't want the brightness from the screen to wake Luke up.

My thumbs flew over the small keyboard illuminated on the display.

The Isaac Project was a success! Thank you, my Eliezer.

I smiled as I punched Send.

Luke's arm curled around my shoulder as he slumbered on. Pushing with my toes against the mattress, I stretched up and kissed him lightly against his stubbly cheek. His eyes fluttered open, and he regarded me with a drowsy expression.

"Hey, beautiful." Sleep had given his voice a husky tone.

"Hey." I gave him a shy smile.

The tiredness of his gaze melted away, replaced with desire that came from a man in love. My own affection and yearning rose within me. Our lips and bodies met, each giving fully of ourselves to the other.

Epilogue

One Year Later

Rebekah

The stadium was filling with fans of all kinds. There were the more "normal" people who showed support of their team by wearing jerseys or team colors. And then there were the more extreme. Those who painted their faces or even stripped off their shirts and painted their bodies to show team spirit and synchronicity. These were the loud, boisterous fans. The ones the Jumbotron loved to display on its gigantic screen above the field.

The players filed onto the field, the clock ticking down the remaining seconds before kickoff.

I swiveled my head from left to right, peering behind me in both directions to try and get a glimpse of my husband. Where was he? The line at the concession stand must have been longer than we thought. If he didn't hurry, he would miss the first play of the game.

"Excuse me."

I smiled as the deep timbre of his voice reached my ears. Leaning forward, I watched as he shuffled sideways, sidestepping legs that were squished to make room for his passage down the narrow row to his assigned seat beside mine.

"Did you get it?" I asked as I licked my lips.

"One soft pretzel, as my lady requested." He extended the food and bowed over it in a dramatic show of courtly gesture.

I grabbed the hot, doughy treat, eyeing the spheres of salt dotting its surface. "Mustard?"

He extended his other hand, revealing five yellow packs of the tangy condiment.

My mouth watered. Leaning over, I gave him a kiss. "Thanks."

"I don't know how you can eat that with mustard." His mouth twisted in disgust as he settled into the hard red stadium seat.

I grinned around a mouthful of pretzel. "We'll just blame it on weird pregnancy cravings, shall we?" I placed a hand on what used to be a flat stomach only a few months before, now curved in the gentle roundness of expectant motherhood.

The game started and consumed the attention of thousands of fans, although the arena was anything but quiet. Then again, since when was a football game quiet? Shouts and jeers erupted around us as the ball switched possession between the teams. I might or might not have made a few loud comments myself when the referee missed an obvious call.

The game stopped for a commercial break, and the cameras positioned around the field scanned the crowd for interesting characters. It was always fun to watch people on the big screen.

The camera swept slowly along a row. As people realized they were on the screen, they waved or jumped up or did something silly. It was very entertaining. The camera stopped on a young couple holding hands, he in a Rams jersey and she in a 49ers. Heat rose to my cheeks as I realized it was Luke and I displayed on the screen for all to see.

I knew what they wanted. It was what they always wanted when they stopped on a couple. They wanted to see a kiss. Well, I was more than happy to oblige.

Luke and I rose to our feet at the same time. We smiled into each other's eyes as his head came down and his lips claimed mine. The response around us was varied. A few booed, obviously displeased that a Rams fan and a 49ers fan could toss aside team rivalry and fall in love. Others cheered, celebrating true love's victory over any obstacle. Luke bent down and kissed my protruding belly. Even the naysayers couldn't deny the sweetness of the act.

The commercial break ended, and the game resumed.

Luke leaned over and spoke in my ear. "I got something else at the concession stand while I was there."

I turned to him, my curiosity piqued. I hadn't seen anything else in his hands when he had come back.

He held out two small bags, one in each hand. "Pick a hand."

I tapped his left.

He opened the bag and pulled out the cutest little onesie I had yet to see. It was red with gold letters saying "Football first: Nap Later!" and had the Niners logo of San Francisco's initials inside an oval.

"Luke, it's perfect!"

He beamed with pleasure. My gaze snagged on the other bag.

"What's in that one?" I asked as I tried to peek inside.

He withdrew another equally adorable onesie. This one was gray with the St. Louis butting ram on front and said "Tiny Fan."

I loved this man so much. He was already proving how great a father he was going to be.

Luke shrugged, looking a little sheepish at his purchase. "I thought the baby could decide which team to cheer for."

Leaning over, I took the two articles of baby clothing and draped them both over my growing tummy. "They're perfect."

The crowd erupted around us as people launched to their feet, arms raised in victory. Others slumped in defeat in their chairs.

We had missed a vital play in the game, the Niners scoring a much-needed touchdown. The only disadvantage to being at the field and experiencing the game live was no instant replay with commentator walk-through.

And yet I didn't feel any sense of loss or disappointment. I loved the game and I loved my team, but in the grand scheme of things, it was still only a game.

The flutter of life danced across my belly, ending in a hard kick to the ribs. I splayed my hand over my stomach, caressing the little one yet to be born.

I had experienced much loss in the last year. Both Poppy and Lady had died, leaving me a complete orphan, devoid of any blood relations or family. But God was true to His word. Not only did He never leave me, but he sent Luke into my life as a comfort in a time of great grief. Luke became my husband, my companion and partner, and ultimately my new family. And now that new little family was growing.

Luke

I marveled at the woman beside me. Her indelible spirit was inspiring. When I looked back on our short time together, I had to shake my head. I would never have known how true my uncle's words were going to be. Everyone knows there will be hard times in every relationship, but it's when we decide that saying "I do" means forever, no matter what, that true love shines.

"Go, go, go, go!" Becky was on her feet, pumping her arm in the air to punctuate each word she shouted to the player sprinting down the field toward the end zone.

Becky and I were now a team, much like the players on the field below us. We had to work together for our relationship to succeed. And we needed to follow our coach, God, and his playbook, the Bible. That didn't mean we wouldn't be tackled by life's hardships. Even the best players, the best team, had plays that were thwarted. But through it all they stuck together.

I grinned at the victorious smile my wife flashed me as the 'Niners added even more points to the scoreboard. She wore red and gold, and I wore blue and gold, but where it counted we were on the same team—team Masterson. Now and forever.

Made in the USA
Lexington, KY
25 February 2019